ALMOST REDEMPTION

ALMOST
REDEMPTION

Inspired Stories Based on
Actual Supreme Court Rulings

VICKY WALL

NEW YORK

NASHVILLE MELBOURNE

ALMOST **REDEMPTION**
Inspired Stories Based on Actual Supreme Court Rulings

Published in New York, New York, by Morgan James Publishing. Morgan James and The Entrepreneurial Publisher are trademarks of Morgan James, LLC. www.MorganJamesPublishing.com

The Morgan James Speakers Group can bring authors to your live event. For more information or to book an event visit The Morgan James Speakers Group at www.TheMorganJamesSpeakersGroup.com.

Shelfie

A **free** eBook edition is available with the purchase of this print book.

CLEARLY PRINT YOUR NAME ABOVE IN UPPER CASE

Instructions to claim your free eBook edition:
1. Download the Shelfie app for Android or iOS
2. Write your name in **UPPER CASE** above
3. Use the Shelfie app to submit a photo
4. Download your eBook to any device

ISBN 978-1-68350-170-1 paperback
ISBN 978-1-68350-171-8 eBook
ISBN 978-1-68350-172-5 hardcover
Library of Congress Control Number:
2016912357

Cover Design by:
Rachel Lopez
www.r2cdesign.com

Interior Design by:
Bonnie Bushman
The Whole Caboodle Graphic Design

In an effort to support local communities, raise awareness and funds, Morgan James Publishing donates a percentage of all book sales for the life of each book to Habitat for Humanity Peninsula and Greater Williamsburg.

Get involved today! Visit
www.MorganJamesBuilds.com

To Charly Yarnoff with gratitude

CONTENTS

FOREWORD

Well crafted, developed, and portrayed. Vicky Wall's strong character development and story telling abilities show her many years of teaching English, training in the law, and studying the application and intersection of life, law, and human behavior. In her stories, Vicky uses her well-applied humor, her well-placed logic, and delivers well-honed messages of life readers can carry forward into their lives. The stories demonstrate Vicky's deep insight into process where legislator's craft poor laws leaving judges to rule more like legislators leaving a trail of questions about where we as a society are headed. Rulings seem to create new liberty rights like erotic dancing, pornography, and late term abortion. While prayer has been removed from school, football games, and graduations, conversations revolve around genitalia and which bathroom to use.

I was lucky enough to have been Vicky's law professor in numerous fundamental classes. Over the years, Vicky visited my District and then my Circuit Courtrooms to faithfully observe and take notes of cases before me after which we would discuss interesting legal issues and have stimulating debates. Who else but a teacher and legal scholar could write so poignantly about Courts at all levels upholding the rights of people in a dignified society that ultimately may be the very destruction of the people it serves? I am honored to call Vicky Wall my friend.

Vicky has written a must read book because questioning, such as hers, is what keeps our society moving forward.

Rosemarie Aquilina
30th Circuit Court Judge
Professor of Law
Author

ACKNOWLEDGMENTS

Many people contributed to these short stories. I would like to thank just a few for their knowledge, experience, suggestions, and encouragement.

My sister, Jennifer Iturraldi, thank you for listening to me read several first drafts and for suggesting ways to make the stories better. You did this without a hard copy while on the phone in a number of settings—even while walking your dogs and taking a bath.

My brother, Tom Wall, thank you for your encouragement.

My friend, Peggy Monahan, thank you for the title "Story Changes Everything."

My friend, Judge Rosemarie Aquilina, thank you for your encouragement and for always taking the time to answer all of my many questions.

My friend, Lania Melvin, thank you for the name of the secretary, Mrs. Gunther.

My friend Rosalea Huizenga, thank you for sharing your story about a mission trip to the Dominican Republic.

My friend Connie McAleer, thank you for sharing your knowledge of French.

My Monday morning Bible study at The Peoples Church in East Lansing, Michigan, thank you for your support and love.

My friend Pastor Ken Bieber, at River Terrace Church in East Lansing, Michigan, thank you for sharing how you would give pastoral care to a Christian whose faith was challenged.

My Sunday night group from River Terrace Church, thank you for your suggestions for improving a story.

My friends Tom and Bobbie Frankovich, from Mount Hope Church in Lansing, Michigan, thank you for your prayers and support.

My friend Doug Henderson and his daughter, Aliyah, from Mount Hope Church, thank you for listening to me read one of the stories, helping me with the current lingo and responding positively to my writing.

My friend Nancy Reynolds, thank you for the story about your niece who decorated you when your energy was low and you wouldn't light up—at least until she made certain adjustments.

My friend Dr. Norma Sutcliffe, thank you for listening to me read two stories and untangling the confusing action in "While Some May, Others May Not."

My next door neighbor, Nadia Barth, thank you for reminding me of what little girls are like.

Photographer Charles Weaver Cushman, thank you for your amazing photographs of New York City in 1941-1942.

Any mistakes in the law appearing in these stories are my own.

ANYTHING BUT JESUS

Amos 5:19

You will be like a man who runs from a lion—only to meet a bear.

S he sat in Professor Schuler's office. He had surprised her with an invitation, but before he could explain his office phone beeped. He took the call and stood up to face the window. As she waited to receive the details, she gazed at the series of framed pictures covering the back wall of his office. The pictures portrayed the history of vacuum coffeepots beginning with glass pots in 1830s Germany. Space devoid of matter, she thought, soon filled with rising steam and, later, steaming water to initiate the vacuum phase. An empty space inviting transformation. Sometimes the result pleased, sometimes not. In the vacuum in which she now sat, wondering if she would be pleased or leery, she filled the empty time by gazing at the coffeepots and the dog hair clinging to her coat like moss to a rock.

Professor Shuler continued with his phone call, so she perused the long narrow table pushed against the wall opposite his desk. On its dusty surface, the professor displayed his collection of antique vacuum pots and a newer Asian model made by Toshiba. The first time they met to discuss her scholarly paper, he explained that a microchip controlled the new vacuum brewer. Like Rudolfo, Professor Shuler poured out his heart as he described the workings of vacuum pots and their history. She listened to the music filling the office and tried not to yawn. Unlike Puccini's male lead, the professor's rangy long curls were white, not black. After his solo, he offered her a cup of the fragrant beverage made for those who appreciated fine coffee; she declined. Young law students could live on caffeine, but she was no longer young. One cup a day or she couldn't sleep at night. Besides, her favorite cup was made at McDonald's.

She crossed her corduroy-covered legs and studied the professor's face. She agreed with his students who considered him hot and had smiled when she saw red chili peppers next to his name on ratemyprofessor.com. She watched his perfectly formed but small frame glide into his desk chair and observed how his wrinkled shirt ballooned over the belt in his pants. Had he lost weight since the term started? Continuing his conversation, he swiveled in his chair and faced the window. His passion for the law made him a popular professor. He was not arrogant or stuffy. No, his appeal was in the easy way he wore his intelligence, like a soft summer shirt, the kind you wanted to touch.

She wasn't the only student who found him engaging. During class breaks, the younger students hurried to talk to him. The kids smiled, and so did he. Before class began, the auditorium always filled up quickly. No one walked in late. Before the start of term, she overheard one student say that he read the entire syllabus over Christmas break. Simply put, Professor Shuler made a discussion of individual rights, free expression, and equal protection exciting. He wasn't so engaging with coffeepots.

She knew, however, that this professor and constitutional law were not universally loved. Her law school friend, Brenda, was bored.

"Carrie," Brenda said, "I don't care about the laws governing my genitals and what gay men can do with theirs. Besides, the Constitution is a living document that needs to change with the times. Get with it, girl."

Carrie disagreed. She believed new law should adhere to the original document and that this document did not need updating. She feared that progressive interpretation of the Constitution added new liberty rights not on the minds or in the hearts of the Founding Fathers. Her directed study examined freedom of speech for high school valedictorians, a topic of no concern to Brenda, who had sat through the high school graduations of her own two kids and those of numerous relatives. She was emphatic. "No one listens to those speeches, Carrie. No one cares."

But Carrie did care, at least most of the time. The Court did not protect a valedictorian's speech rights to make expressions of faith, but it did support political speech. And while Professor Shuler reminded her that high school students did not receive full free speech protection, she found this decision arbitrary and capricious, a favorite law school phrase both she and Brenda loved. They tried to use it often, especially in restaurants away from school where strangers might believe they were lawyers. However, after several years of going to school part-time, a stockpile of "legal speak" burdened their heads, and they tired of showing off.

Carrie was changing. She questioned if she was turning into someone better or worse. Was she turning into a new Toshiba model or resisting change to stay in the past? After retiring from teaching, she filled the void in her life with law school. While she still felt passionately about kids and their speech rights, she had transformed from being an optimistic believer in all children into one who accepted reality. Some of her former students were headed to jail. She felt depressed watching young men and women stand before a judge during motion hearings at the circuit court, and she did not join the chorus of those who believed the defendant didn't know what he was getting into or simply made a poor decision. Too many of those decisions were as permanent as the ink on their skin. Didn't they know that no matter how hard they stretched their shirts, the judge could still see the tattoos on their necks?

Professor Shuler stood and looked at her. She wondered if he had said something to her she hadn't heard. She raked her fingers through her short hair and moved forward in her chair. Lowering her glasses, she looked over their gold frames at his eyes, which were blue.

Carrie wanted to write a paper arguing that student valedictorians should have the right to invoke the name of Jesus in graduation speeches. In fact, censored speech in public schools had motivated her to apply to law school. Prior to making a final decision about her future, she heard a news reporter detail what happened to a valedictorian who thanked Jesus after being told she couldn't mention His name in her speech. School officials pulled the plug on her microphone. That news report had been the tipping point. She studied for the LSAT, applied to law school, and put her house on the market. She moved to a state she had never visited and where she knew no one. She had to understand what had happened to free speech in a nation founded upon religious freedom by Christians.

Before Professor Shuler finished his phone call, a young student walked into his office. Short and trim, she shook her wavy brown hair behind one shoulder of her black pinstriped suit and took a seat next to Carrie. After crossing her legs—legs covered in fishnet stockings, her feet held hostage in four-inch heels—she leaned over and introduced herself. When Carrie leaned in to hear her, she noticed an imperfection in the fishnet. Carrie wondered if this future attorney was headed to Rhode Island to prosecute criminal activity at the waterfront.

"Hi, I'm Lyn Loveless," the young woman whispered as her intense floral perfume assaulted Carrie's olfactory glands and their preference for sweeter, softer fragrances. Lyn extended her hand for the obligatory handshake. "Professor Shuler suggested I stop by to meet you. We're both writing a scholarly paper on free speech issues."

"I'm Carrie Westfield," Carrie replied, assessing the likelihood that she and Miss Fishnet had much in common other than a directed study project with the same professor. "Are you writing about free speech for high school students?" Carrie asked. Lyn nodded, so Carrie continued. "I'm focusing on their right to speak about their faith in valedictory speeches."

Lyn shook her head as she looked up from her red fingernails. "No, I don't think the schools are the appropriate venue for religious speech." She smiled at the professor. "Faith talk always makes nonbelievers feel like second-class citizens."

Carrie clenched her jaw muscles. Her opponent studied her phone. As Carrie wondered what the professor had in mind, inviting both of them in at the same time, she watched Lyn help herself to the coffee steeping in the Toshiba coffeemaker. Lyn turned to offer a cup to Carrie like a hostess at a political event assessing the financial standing of a new donor. Carrie shook her head.

Professor Shuler finished his conversation, smiled at both students in front of him, and rubbed his hands together. "I see you've become acquainted. It would be helpful for you to understand the opposition as you lay out the arguments in your papers." He lowered his head and glanced over the rim of his glasses, first at Lyn, then at Carrie. "What better way than to understand the arguments held by the other side." He ended his speech with a flourish of his hand like a conductor directing a Mozart symphony. Then he took on a different character in this mini drama. "So, Lyn," he said like a gameshow host, "what is the basis of your opinion?"

"First, Professor," Lyn began, planting her feet squarely in front of her, "I base my objections to religion in public schools on the separation of church and state. The Establishment Clause states that the government shall not create religion, and the Free Exercise Clause provides that government shall not interfere with the practice of religion." Carrie watched as Lyn, without missing a beat, removed her weapons from their arsenal. Lyn continued. "Public schools are funded by all taxpayers, but not all those taxpayers believe in a religion."

Lyn paused but continued to address her comments to Professor Shuler. Carrie wondered if Lyn had forgotten she was in the room. "Second, high school students do not have the same speech rights as adults. Echoing the *Tinker* standard, the courts do not uphold speech that would materially disrupt a legitimate curriculum function, and that includes graduation ceremonies." Carrie's opponent turned briefly in her direction and continued. "Third, student speech cannot impinge upon the rights of other students." Lyn smiled again at Professor Shuler, then lifted her coffee cup. "This is so much better than the coffee in the vending machines downstairs."

Carrie could feel her engine rev up as she lifted her eyes from the multicolored floor covering and turned toward Lyn. "Why do you assume that religious speech disrupts a classroom? Do you have any evidence of that?" Carrie observed that Lyn and the professor exchanged knowing looks, but she continued. "During the sixties, students wore anti-war T-shirts, and Justice Fortas determined that symbolic political speech did not disrupt classroom lessons. Any teacher would tell you otherwise. Everything disrupts the attention of teenagers. But since the Court determined that political speech was not disruptive, what evidence is there that religious speech is disruptive? Why not treat both types of speech equally?"

Lyn shook her head patiently. "You've probably not been in a high school classroom for some time, Carrie," she began slowly. "Students are engaged when they express their political beliefs. You know, political speech is the most protected speech by the courts. Students don't want to share personal religious beliefs, but we stray from the important arguments."

"Excuse me," Carrie interrupted, "but I have been in classrooms recently. I taught in them for thirty years."

"I don't think you understand the role of a teacher," Lyn corrected. "The role of a teacher is to challenge students with new ideas. A teacher needs to stimulate students to feel confident in expressing untraditional ideas so they don't become choked by the past."

Like a toreador, Lyn had flashed the red cape.

"But the Court does use anecdotal evidence to support its arguments," Carrie asserted. "The Court has referred to the personal experiences of students in their opinions. Justice Fortas stated that some students felt excluded from the larger group when their classmates prayed at graduation ceremonies and before football games." She paused, gathered momentum, and charged ahead. "The Court ensconced a few disgruntled students in a protected class to prevent them from feeling outside the norm and then took away the rights of the majority." She looked down at the button hanging from her coat and wondered if her argument was hanging from a thread as well.

"Carrie, let's get back to the wall of separation between church and state," interjected the professor as he noticed Lyn shifting in her chair. "I believe you did some research on that."

"Yes, let's get back to the metaphor that a wall exists between church and state. Jefferson wrote this metaphor in a letter to the Danbury Baptist Association, not in the Constitution. He wrote the letter because he knew it would offend New England Federalists whom he believed exploited religion."

"Carrie!" Lyn stated with indignation, like a nun disciplining a student who questioned the virgin birth. "Separation of church and state is one of the mightiest monuments of constitutional principle!"

Carrie bit her lip as Lyn looked up at the clock behind the professor's desk and stood. "I've got class in fifteen minutes across the street, Professor. You know I like to be on time."

"Lyn, before you leave . . ." Professor Shuler hesitated as he checked his phone for messages. "I want to know if you and Carrie can attend a consultation with me at a local middle school." As Lyn listened to their professor, Carrie thought how well this twentysomething student fit into the progressive mindset, and she pulled at her slacks that didn't fit anymore. She had lost ten pounds her first term at school and never gained it back. She noticed Lyn's foot tapping.

Professor Shuler spoke quickly. "The principal called me for legal advice about a speech issue. You may not agree with my advice, but you'll understand as the various outcomes are discussed."

Carrie watched Lyn's eyebrows rise. Would Lyn deem such a trip worthy of her attendance?

"When is the meeting?" Lyn asked.

"Next Tuesday at 8 a.m. I can pick you up here in front of the school at 7:30."

"You know I work out Tuesday mornings," she reminded him. "Okay. I could meet you at the school. Email me the address," Lyn said and left the office.

The professor turned to Carrie, raised his eyebrows, and waited for her to respond. "Yes, I'd like to attend the meeting," she said. "Why does the school need legal advice?"

"The faculty voted to begin the school day with a one-minute moment of silence. The students can sit quietly, plan their day, meditate, or pray. Now one of the parents is threatening to sue."

"Yes, I do want to hear your advice," Carrie said. "I'll wait for you outside on the corner." As she put her notebook and pen away, she remembered the decision in *Wallace v. Jaffree*. "You're going to advise them to stand firm against the ACLU, right?" she asked facetiously.

"Not unless the district has extra cash they don't know what to do with," said Professor Shuler.

"I'll have to buy a lawyer suit," she said.

"I found my first court attire at Goodwill. I probably still have that suit. My wife thinks I've become a hoarder."

Carrie smiled but wondered why Professor Shuler knew when Lyn exercised. She didn't ask.

Professor Shuler stood up behind his desk. "I'd better go because now is the time when my students start freaking out about the final exam. I have to hold a lot of hands," he said smiling. He slipped into his suit jacket, grabbed his book, and gallantly held the office door open for her. He walked briskly out of his office and down the hall. Carrie followed, but not in his footsteps.

Part Two

Hurrying to the elevator, Carrie wondered if Brenda was already in class. She walked quickly down the hall. Yes, Brenda was there, sitting in the first row. "What are you smiling about?" Brenda asked as Carrie sat down next to her.

"Professor Shuler just asked me to go to a meeting with him at a local middle school. I'm so happy that I won't be able to concentrate on what Professor Charter talks about tonight." She pushed her hand through her short hair. "I need a haircut and a highlight. And a suit."

Brenda stood up and pulled on her coat—they still had ten minutes before start of class. "Your hair looks okay. You're just going to a consultation. Nobody will notice your gray roots or your suit."

While Brenda went outside to smoke, Carrie arranged her coat on the back of the chair and unzipped a pocket in her backpack on wheels, a contraption rarely used by the younger students. Even Brenda, a decade younger than Carrie, put her books in a backpack she slung on her back. While Brenda complained a lot about school, she had always wanted to be an attorney. When Brenda's brother offered her a job at his firm after she passed the Bar, she decided she had nothing to lose.

Brenda returned, reeking of cigarette smoke. "Why did he ask you to go to this meeting?" She took out her laptop. "I mean, you know enough to go; I didn't mean you don't know anything, but why did he ask you?"

Carrie folded her hands on the desk in front of her and turned to look at Brenda. "He's my advisor for my directed study project. Remember, I'm writing a scholarly paper."

"So?"

"The paper I'm writing is about free speech issues in public high schools," Carrie explained as she removed her glasses and rubbed her eyes. Before she put them back on, she looked at the only friend she had in law school. Brenda filled the vacuum created when Carrie pulled up roots and left everyone she had known for thirty years. But her encouragement was rare. If a dog had to live on it, he'd starve. "He also invited a young woman named Lyn Loveless who's writing a paper on the same topic."

"Lyn Loveless has already published in the school law journal. You have a lot of competition and may not get an A," said Brenda.

Carrie suddenly felt cold. She looked around the room for open windows but then remembered the windows didn't open. Gathering her coat over her shoulders, she listened as the clicking on computer keys intensified. "You don't sound too happy for me," she said.

"I've just never heard of a professor inviting a student to a meeting off campus. I wonder if there are school rules against it."

"Surely you jest. This will be a great experience. Don't you think he's a great professor?"

"He's okay. I'm just not blown away by him like you seem to be."

Carrie watched as Brenda fired up her laptop. To prevent her from starting in again with one of her lectures about how easily impressed Carrie was by professors, Carrie said, "I'm spending the day in the library tomorrow. What are you doing?"

"I have a job. Remember? I'm not a lady of leisure."

"Yes, you have a part-time job," Carrie reminded her. "Did you see Professor Charter when you came back into the building?"

Brenda shook her head. "You know she's always late, and she always lets us out early too. Students in other sections of Advanced Legal Writing tell me their profs keep them the full three hours. We might not be prepared for the final."

Carrie heard laughter in the hall as Professor Charter swung into the classroom dressed in the same black suit, the only one she wore. The texture of her short brown hair reminded Carrie of a Brillo pad. The young professor's hair never moved. Regardless, her eyes sparkled as she sized up her students like prospective jurors. If Carrie had been on that jury, Professor Charter would probably win her over on the strength of her smile alone. After greeting the class, she told them about the case she had just won.

"My client nearly lost custody of his children because of the filthy conditions in his home. I argued that he needed help from the county to teach him how to clean a house. The county will provide him with cleaning help, so he gets to keep his kids," she said as she removed handouts from her briefcase and placed them on the table beside the podium.

Carrie sat back in the chair and hoped her face didn't register the shock she felt. The county had money for cleaning help? And they would give it to a man who claimed he didn't know what to do with dirt? She grabbed her water bottle and drank while remembering the houses she had cleaned for professors as an undergraduate student. Maybe this was one case where her professor wouldn't win her over. She wondered if Professor Charter was proud of herself for coming up with a solution to her client's problem or proud of the fact that she bamboozled a judge and jury. Then again, Carrie thought, living with their father was better for the kids than living with multiple foster families. She knew the judge ruled according to what was in the best interest of the children.

"I will be arguing before the state supreme court next week. I'm defending the medical marijuana law for my client, and you are welcome to come and watch."

The benign drug of choice, Carrie thought, but didn't shake her head as she copied the address of the supreme court into her notebook. Maybe she didn't share all of Professor Charter's ideas.

She listened as the professor discussed their next writing assignment and outlined the facts of the case.

"I don't care which side you want to argue in your brief," Professor Charter said, "but make it convincing. Either the police violated Cesare Greer's due process rights by not videotaping the interview with him, or the police satisfied his rights under the Constitution, and he is guilty of sexually assaulting a minor and should be charged with first-degree sexual assault." When the professor told them to get into groups to discuss defenses, Carrie joined the smaller group at the back of the class. Brenda followed her.

Before class ended, Professor Charter flashed a picture of an historical home on the overhead. "My partner and I recently bought this building for our office. If you can get there, I want to discuss your first drafts at my office. I can also meet you here to discuss your brief if that would be more convenient." Carrie gazed at the pictures of the building's interior. She felt her mouth open slightly as she viewed the wood-paneled foyer, staircase, and offices, and she smiled at the cardboard boxes crammed with files lining the perimeter of the office. An Oriental screen stood in the corner, and a stone fireplace swept across the wall behind the biggest desk Carrie had ever seen. Like her professor, the desk dominated the room.

After class, Carrie stood in line to ask Professor Charter a question about writing the brief. When her turn came, the professor put down the papers in her hand and looked at her. Carrie felt her eye twitch.

"How can I help you, Carrie?"

"In pre-law class," Carrie began, "we wrote briefs using a sample provided to us." She hesitated as she tried to write out the question in her mind before asking it. "The brief was written in a dry, matter-of-fact style. Are we supposed to defend our clients passionately in a brief or present the client objectively?"

"If you don't defend your client passionately, who will?" her professor stated. "The purpose of a brief is to convince the judge that your client's rights need protecting. Flat, objective writing doesn't convince anyone."

That was exactly the answer Carrie wanted to hear, and she grinned like a kid as Professor Charter drank from a coffee cup she had brought to class over two hours ago. "Which side will you argue?" she asked.

"His due process rights were satisfied, and he is guilty of having sex with a minor," Carrie stated.

"Okay, passionately argue your client's side. Your job is to place the Detroit police department in the best possible light in front of the judge. I noticed most of your classmates will argue that Cesare Greer's rights were violated, but either side is good. Do you plan to litigate when you graduate?"

Carry fought with the corners of her mouth. "I'll decide that after I graduate," she responded and stepped aside so the next student could move forward. Although Carrie didn't have an answer, she liked the question.

She saw Brenda standing by the door. Brenda rarely spoke to professors. "Which side will you argue?" Carrie asked.

"His rights weren't violated," said Brenda.

"I don't think so either," agreed Carrie. "I plan to lay out the arguments to convict this son-of-a-bitch. He was a family friend who took advantage of the family's trust to have sex with a fourteen-year-old girl. Her older brothers treated him like a brother, and their mother had treated him like a son."

"Did you read the court transcript?" Brenda asked. "The victim's mother had taken him shopping for his prom tuxedo. The little shit."

Carrie shrugged into her coat, and they walked into the hall. "Of course I read the transcript," said Carrie as she handed Brenda her gloves. "You forgot these again." She wondered who took care of Brenda when she wasn't around.

As she listened to Brenda complain about the writing assignment, Professor Charter, her husband, kids, and the weather, Carrie imagined herself in her Cessna 172 ready to take off. She remembered how she soared above the runway in Kenosha, Wisconsin. In contrast to her activities at the small airport, she didn't do much flying or soaring in law school. While flying encompassed science, adventure, beauty, and freedom, as Wilber Wright had said, law school was different. A deluge of memorization, followed by a storm of pressure before, during, and after exams.

"Two papers in one term," Carrie said when Brenda wrapped up her arguments against Professor Charter. "Now my GPA will go up." She observed a frown on her friend's face. Carrie's desire for encouragement flew off into the horizon.

They stood quietly in the empty elevator. It didn't move. Carrie thought about the case and wondered if things would have been different for the victim if her father had lived in the home. Could a twenty-year-old have sex with a young girl in her bedroom if her father was present in the home? Her father's absence created a vacuum in the young teen's life, one Cesare Greer easily filled with attention and sex for a love-starved girl barely out of puberty.

"Did you press the button?" Brenda finally asked.

"No. Do we have to press a button?" asked Carrie.

"You think?"

Carrie pushed the button, and the elevator descended to the main lobby. Carrie looked at Brenda and they laughed at themselves, their late enrollment in law school, and Charter's idiot client who didn't know how to clean his house. They exited the elevator laughing.

"What were we thinking when we decided to start law school?" Brenda asked. "Do you remember?" Carrie shook her head and yawned. No, she couldn't remember, but she was grateful she hadn't flunked out.

Carrie turned when she heard an elevator ping. She watched Professor Charter step out of the second set of elevator doors and walk into the lobby. When Brenda headed to the ladies' room, Carrie didn't follow her but walked over to the professor instead. "The historical building is beautiful," Carrie said. "I bet you are thrilled to be there."

"Thank you," the professor replied. "We are thrilled. When you come for your conference, I'll give you a tour of the entire building. We already have plans to remodel the bathrooms downstairs and install a shower." As they stood talking, Carrie noticed that they huddled together. She liked this woman.

"Do you like to write, Carrie?" Professor Charter asked.

"Yes, I do. This term I'm writing a scholarly paper with Professor Shuler about the rights of valedictorians to invoke the name of Jesus and their faith in valedictory speeches."

"You're writing in favor of religious speech?" asked Professor Charter, pausing. "With Professor Shuler?"

Carrie nodded.

"I'm surprised to hear that," Professor Charter continued. "He has a reputation for being deeply anti-religious."

Carry closed her mouth. "I thought he seemed to favor broader speech rights for high school students. Maybe I've misread him, but he has never indicated he disapproves of the topic or my position."

"I'm glad to hear it. Maybe he's mellowed as he's gotten older," Professor Charter said. "Or maybe he likes you and wants to be open to a position contrary to his own."

Carrie studied Professor Charter's face for signs of dissimulation but found none. Before she turned to leave, the professor said, "Since you enjoy writing, you'll have a good time writing this brief. I look forward to reading your first draft. See you next week."

When Benda returned, she hesitated when she saw the professor.

"Doesn't her office look beautiful?" Carrie asked, recalling the pictures Professor Charter had shown in the classroom.

Carrie felt Brenda's eyes on her. She turned to see her friend watching her. "Why are you so excited about an office?" Brenda asked. "It's just a house. Lots of people buy them."

Carrie looked at the only friend she had in law school. She knew Brenda had never purchased a house on her own; her husbands did that, both of them. Carrie thought that if Brenda could sing, she would be a prima donna in the opera.

"When they're in their thirties?" Carrie asked. "That's quite a house for two young attorneys to buy this early in their career. The house is registered historical property and three blocks from the capitol."

"If you say so," Brenda said as she zipped up her coat and headed out the back door. Over her shoulder she yelled, "I'll call you." Carrie knew she would because Brenda was a woman of her word. Carrie also knew that Brenda was warming up to lecture her again about being easily impressed. As she drove home to the suburb where she now lived, she remembered the first of Brenda's lectures about law professors. It took place shortly after they first met.

"They're pompous fools, Carrie," she had told her with authority after drinking several margaritas at a bar popular with law students and faculty. "All dressed up in a title. They sound good because they spout memorized sections of Court opinion. But they never come up with an original thought of their own." Brenda concluded her argument by pounding the table. "You better look out, Carrie. Now don't go anywhere. I'll be right back." Carrie watched Brenda stumble toward the door and decided she would have to drive her home. She noticed that their Contracts professor stood near the exit, blocking Brenda's escape. He opened his mouth, but before he could say hello, she heard Brenda. "What are you looking at?" she demanded as she pushed by him. Fortunately, student names did not appear on exams, only identification numbers. What a night that had been!

Carrie drove east and merged with traffic heading to a community of thirty thousand or so residents. Brenda lived a couple of miles away, and while they shared geography, Carrie realized she had never had a close friend who felt contempt for tradition and authority. Brenda did not have a career but a succession of part-time jobs that usually lasted a year or so. The same night Brenda told her she better watch out, she also told her that she had been terminated from her current part-time job. "My employer told me I didn't contribute to a positive work environment," she said. "Can you believe that?"

Brenda seemed to be stuck in adolescent defiance. But Carrie had little choice in friends given the age difference between herself and the traditional students like Lyn. By default, Brenda's friendship filled the social emptiness in her life.

Carrie appreciated having at least one law school buddy but regretted not being able to talk with her about the changes occurring in her own life and the world around her. While law school filled the void created when she retired, she wondered if she was drifting away from the person she used to be. She remembered a picture of innocent children standing around Jesus and wondered if that guileless child within her had been replaced by one who questioned everything and felt cynical about the changes around her. When she started law school, she stopped wearing her cross and never mentioned that she went to church every Sunday. Was there a place for Jesus in the legal community? Over the years, the law had stretched to accommodate a lot—everything it seemed but Jesus.

Recently, Brenda announced that she had stopped going to church because Christianity was just one religion out of many. "Carrie, we took our kids out of Catholic school," Brenda explained. "We want them to appreciate all religions. We want them to be free to become Muslim if that's what they believe." Carrie worried that her friend had become spiritually unmoored.

Carrie slowed and turned into her driveway. As she watched the garage door rise, she thought about the last conversation she had with her dad.

The progressive movement had flooded countries around the globe, and some of its flotsam had hit the shores of her dad's native country. Her dad told her, "Our relatives back in Sweden left their church because they believed Christianity made the new immigrants feel like outsiders. The government is tearing down churches or transforming them into social centers. In their place, mosques are being built."

Carrie had considered what her father said. "Dad, the Swedes are becoming a nation of sheep, and I fear the one we live in is following right behind."

If Brenda had heard this conversation, she would accuse Carrie of being politically incorrect. Maybe she was. What would the Court decide if a Muslim valedictorian invoked Allah in a graduation speech? Would the justices determine that religion could be invoked, but just not Christianity? Carrie hoped the Supreme Court would uphold all religious speech in the public domain.

Part Three

The following Tuesday, Carrie parked her car on a side street at 7:20, shoved quarters into the meter, and walked around the corner to the law school entrance. The sky was clearing, and the early spring temperatures had begun melting the snow. She stood outside the building, scanning the intersection, hoping he would arrive early or at least be on time.

Professor Shuler pulled up in a blue Prius at 7:25. Carrie wondered why the car was so dirty but refrained from teasing him. When she opened the passenger door of his car, she saw spilled coffee dripping down the console between the driver and passenger seats. The professor's pant leg also looked stained.

"I should have warned you, Carrie. I spill a lot of coffee. Here," he said, and handed her some paper napkins. Carrie accepted the napkins and saw that her professor's hand shook. She climbed into the car, fastened her seat belt, and thought about what the professor and her mother had in common.

When Carrie's mother divorced her father, because he was just too boring, she started drinking more than a single glass of wine at dinner. She explained her decision to divorce Carrie's dad by saying, "My God, Carrie, he's still a Republican! He doesn't have a progressive bone in his body!"

After the divorce, her mother started hanging out at the local bars. She found a job at a law firm where she worked as a legal secretary and slept with every attorney in the office. Carrie and her brother rarely saw her. Gone were the family evenings spent debating politics after dinner, the walks across town for ice cream, and the bike rides to the home where their dad's immigrant grandparents first lived when they came to the United States. Her mother didn't understand why her husband's parents were so proud to be Americans. "What's so exceptional about this country?" she asked. "All countries are exceptional."

Carrie looked over at Professor Shuler and wondered if he drank too much, was contemplating a divorce, or if he hated religion. But she forgot about his private life as she watched their progress down the icy streets. He darted around potholes and slow-moving vehicles. To relax, she imagined water sliding down an icicle when the sun touched it. She opened her eyes and saw city trucks throw salt over dangerous stretches of roadway. Nothing detained them as they drove north to their intended destination, a middle school in a university town. Carrie had worked in a similar community and wondered if the school administrators and staff in the school they were visiting today would be that much different from the ones where she had worked. Maybe they were all the same.

From the CD player, she heard Harry Connick Jr. sing like Frank Sinatra. "No one can replace Frank," she said.

"I've got Sinatra as well," Professor Shuler said, and then went back to his driving. Later he added, "I'm not much of a talker in the morning, at least not until the caffeine kicks in. On the weekends, no one in my house speaks before noon. I'm a good listener though."

Carrie wasn't much of a morning talker either so she looked outside. The sky was cerulean, the same solid blue color that graced the pages of the *Book of Hours*. Over the weekend she had attended a lecture and slideshow about the magnificent pictures in these books that had once been used to teach children how to read. They were passed down in families, one generation to the next, and although the pictures depicted Bible stories, they had been painted in secular workshops, not in monasteries. Her favorite portrayed floating stairs leading up from the manger to the top of the stable. Transfixed by the color and designs in these pictures, she had felt herself stepping into someone else's prayers.

"Did you see the exhibit of the *Book of Hours* over the weekend?" Carrie asked.

"No, I didn't, but my wife and I visited the Cloisters in Upper Manhattan when we were in New York a couple years ago. The books are beautiful."

"What a contrast to the books used to teach reading in schools today."

"My youngest daughter is reading out of a book called *Mary Has Two Mommies*, and my son is reading a novel by Robert Cormier that describes how the main character masturbates. My wife is upset. But I think the new curriculum will help kids learn to be more accepting of those who are different, as well as about their own bodily functions."

"Yes, a number of academics believe masturbation increases reading scores," Carrie said. She saw a smile begin to form on Professor Shuler's face and figured the caffeine had kicked in. "National test scores don't support this thesis, but the scores are probably incorrect."

"We're almost there," he said, slowing down to the speed limit. "Did I tell you that I went to this school when it was taught by nuns?"

Carrie looked askance at these revelations. "No, you didn't." Waiting for him to explain, she looked at the neighborhood. A brilliantly colored male cardinal perched in naked, gray branches waiting for spring to metamorphose them into leaves of black cherry, red oak, and American beech.

Professor Shuler presented the school's history with one hand while he maneuvered the steering wheel with the other. "Built at the beginning of World

War II, the school has stood for over seven decades," he lectured. "The architect went to Washington for permission to use war materials for its construction. Designed to accommodate two thousand students, enrollment dropped to less than half that because the neighborhood changed. The city sold the building to the Catholic Archdiocese. That's when I attended."

"But it's a public school now. What happened?" Carrie asked. "Another enrollment problem?"

"Exactly. The school now holds fewer than a thousand students because the neighborhood has changed again. Enrollment continued to drop, and the student body is now integrated with a near even split between white and black students."

This school, Carrie realized, was a mirror image of the one where she had taught for half her teaching career.

At an intersection, their progress was held up by a red light and several cars. Carrie watched plows shove the snow into huge piles. "The rising temperatures should melt it by the weekend," the professor said as he accelerated down the street. She watched pedestrians walking along the sidewalks, their brisk gait unimpeded by heavy boots. Some waited for buses. They wore light coats or jackets. Carrie had already forgotten her winter garments after stuffing them into the back of her closet. She dropped the window to get some fresh air and could hear birds sing. Life after law school, she decided, loomed large like a smile.

But as they drew closer to the school, the sky abruptly changed like the shutter in a box camera. Working behind the scene unobserved, Mother Nature leeched the monochromatic blue out of the sky and rapidly replaced it with the color of dirty snow and ice.

They turned left into the faculty parking lot, and a possible career in law seemed to bleed out like a crime victim on a dirty street. After teaching middle school students for over three decades, here she was again at another middle school. They pulled into a slot reserved for visitors. "Good, there's Lyn's car," Professor Shuler said. "She always likes to be first."

Carrie looked at her professor and wondered where else he met Lyn. She watched as he reached into the back seat, grabbed his briefcase, and opened the car door. Cautiously, she stepped out of the car.

As they walked to the school entrance, he said, "I attended this school just before it was sold. Then I transferred to St. Thomas on the other side of town for high school."

"Has it changed much?"

He nodded. "Unfortunately, the city doesn't have the funds to maintain it. Sooner or later it will be put up for sale. There's a rumor that the Muslim community is going to buy it, tear it down, and build a mosque." Carrie looked at him. "Until then, the school board will lose more money if they go to court over this new program voted on by the faculty."

She looked up at an eight-story clock tower that stood to the right of the entrance, dominating the building. Carrie wondered what some of the more precocious students did in the clock tower when they weren't supervised.

"When the scandal broke about President Clinton and Monica Lewinsky," Carrie said, "oral sex became very popular at the middle school where I taught. I wonder what sort of activity goes on in that empty tower."

"Carrie, this isn't an urban community like the one where you taught," said Professor Shuler. "I bet their extracurricular activities are pretty tame by comparison."

Carrie did not argue but observed that classroom windows appeared on three floors of the yellow brick structure. Exterior sculptured reliefs decorated the building's façade. Some of the reliefs were cracked; corners were broken off of others. A few were missing. The pavement to the left of the entrance had buckled as though the roots of a tree had pushed through the cement to expose the rot beneath the surface.

In front of the building, a large gray object commandeered the entrance to the school. It appeared to be made of papier-mache. Carrie assumed it was a prop for a theatrical production—perhaps a cave. But she wondered what it was doing outside of the building. Perhaps it wasn't a cave but a tomb. Did any plays exist featuring tombs that were appropriate for a public school?

To the left of the cave sat a young man whose Vandyke beard emphasized his narrow face. He was dressed in a black-and-red checked harlequin suit. A full-length black cape draped over his narrow shoulders, and a black skull cap covered his hair.

"This can't be the heavenly angel outside the tomb of Jesus," said Carrie, recalling the school's religious history. "He's not wearing a white robe."

"He's also on the wrong side of the entrance, and the stone should have been rolled away by now. It's after dawn."

"Don't be afraid to step forward," the young man said like an actor in a play, "and embrace the future. Step around the stone to the entrance on your left. Further directions await you inside."

"Are you practicing for a play?" Carrie asked.

"Life is not a play, madam," he said, leaving his listeners with smiles that quickly slid off their faces.

Carrie and her professor walked around the obstacle in front of the school.

As they entered the building, Carrie saw Lyn talking with a short man who appeared to be the principal. He stood eye-to-eye with Lyn but with his head down, as though he were looking for wisdom in the linoleum tiles under his feet. Curly brown hair tickled the edge of his starched white shirt and brown suit, and a bald spot the size of a yarmulke flashed at them like a traffic light. Carrie noticed his small feet comfortably ensconced in brown loafers as the man and Lyn walked across the hall and stopped in front of Professor Shuler. She also observed that a tight skirt and high-heeled boots did not impede Lyn's march across the floor.

"Professor," he said warmly as he extended his right hand to Professor Shuler. "I've already met Lyn, and this is . . ."

"I'm Carrie Westfield," Carrie said as she shook his hand.

"Carrie, I'm Mr. Wassermann, the principal. Before we meet with the faculty advisory board, I want you to observe some homerooms where the 'Minute of Silence' is in progress. One of our student assistants will show you around. I'll meet you back in the office."

A smiling, heavyset African American student walked toward them wearing baggy pants that dragged below his hips and a large, shiny sports shirt. "Welcome to the school," he said, shyly turning his head away. "I'm Charles." He directed them to the stairs and returned to the office.

Scuffed red linoleum tiles covered the stairs and floor, and at the top of the stairs Carrie saw light gray lockers flanking a drinking fountain. In front of the fountain, two boys, one white, the other black, exchanged small packets. Neither student seemed discomfited in the least by their presence. Above the fountain, Carrie could make out the faint outline of a cross, a remnant of the school's religious past.

"What is that shadow above the drinking fountain?" demanded Lyn. "Is that a cross? That should have been painted over by now. You would think the painters would update this building."

"Shrinking school budgets," said the professor.

They stood near the fountain and watched the marijuana sale conclude. The buyer and seller drifted down the hall.

"Marijuana laws need to be updated to the twenty-first century," Lyn said. "The courts and law enforcement waste so much time and resources on a drug that is basically non-addictive."

"I've heard it builds strong bones and teeth, just like milk," said Carrie. She saw a sneer forming on Lyn's face.

Some of the doors to the classrooms were open. Inside the first, Carrie watched a few students walking around the room talking to each other while others threw a foam football to kids in the back of the class. One girl painted her nails; another combed and sprayed her hair. The male teacher, dressed professionally in a shirt and tie, stood by his desk. Several female students moved around him. One of the girls standing next to him stroked his tie. Obviously, thought Carrie, this faculty member is not onboard with the "Minute of Silence" program.

"Now that's a relaxed classroom," said Lyn, "one where everyone can learn."

"What exactly are they learning, Lyn?" Carrie asked. Lyn didn't respond.

Inside a second classroom, the students sat quietly listening to announcements. When they ended, several students bowed their heads and folded their hands in prayer. A female student who sat near the back stretched her arms before her on her desk, held her hands palms-up, and pressed her thumbs to her middle fingers. Others sat quietly. One student watched the clock.

"I see illegal activity," Carrie said. Professor Shuler smiled, but Lyn pursed her lips.

They took the stairs back down to the first floor. Before they entered the office, two students jostled for position to enter the office first. The shorter one entered first while the taller boy held the door open for Carrie, Lyn, and Professor Shuler.

"She's hot!" said the taller boy, and his friend came back outside the office to gape at Lyn's saucy behind. "Sweet," he declared.

At eight o'clock, the bell rang and students charged into the hallway for their first-period classes.

In the main office, they waited and watched as tardy students lined up to sign in late. Two secretaries sat behind their desks. One talked on the phone while writing a note; the other stared at them. Her desk was larger and closer to the principal's office. On her desk stood a wooden nameplate that read "Mrs. Gunther." Having taken the measure of the three strangers, Mrs. Gunther rose and motioned them forward.

They entered a fairly large room next to the office where faculty members sat around a large oak table. Instead of relaxing in familiarity, Carrie felt acid creep up her throat until she remembered she was only an observer. She wondered if faculty meetings were the same everywhere regardless of locale.

Carrie saw teachers talking with each other and noticed they did not look up when she, Lyn, and Professor Shuler entered the principal's office. After grabbing a cup of coffee, the principal took a seat at the table. His staff turned to face him as he made introductions and extended offers of coffee, juice, and pastries. Once everyone resettled in a chair, the meeting got down to business, maybe not the business of law but other issues foremost in the minds of those seated around the table.

"The ACLU is threatening to sue the district," the principal began, trying to focus the teachers' attention, which Carrie knew would be like herding cats. He unbuttoned his suit jacket. Since greeting them in the hall, he had donned a pair of large black-framed glasses. Carrie assumed he wore glasses to enlarge his small, bearlike eyes. She concluded that the glasses failed to distinguish him from other men and to command their respect. Accustomed to being interrupted, he paused.

"Excuse me, Mr. Wassermann," interjected Miss Waxman, the art teacher, whose dark pink lipstick traveled above the natural outline of her mouth. White-framed glasses dangled from a pink rhinestone lanyard around her neck; she placed the glasses on her nose as if she wasn't sure she couldn't see and didn't know those she addressed.

"The problem is not the ACLU or the parents who contacted them." She lowered her voice and hissed like a Texas rattlesnake. "The real problem is Susan Phelps." To underscore the passion of her public censor of another faculty member, her eyes made a borehole into the top of her boss's downturned head. Carrie watched as the art teacher's colleagues nodded like bobble heads in agreement.

"In my opinion," echoed Miss Reed, the guidance counselor, "that woman is obsessed with religion." Carrie doubted Miss Reed weighed more than a hundred pounds. The delicate lady perched her glasses on top of her head and pulled at the collar of the white blouse that popped up like crocuses above her gray suit. She folded her hands.

"Speak up, Hilde!" ordered a stentorian voice from the front office. "You know I can never hear you when you whisper." Hilde did as she was told and repeated her concern that religion might break out like lice inside the school. "Okay," the voice dictated. "You can continue."

Carrie wondered who would talk next when Miss Waxman reasserted herself. "Now listen," said Miss Waxman as she sat up straighter. "Susan Phelps and her crowd have begun an assault on this school and its curriculum. She's starting small with a one-minute meditation, but what she really has her sights set on is religion. She wants to reintroduce prayer and religion into the curriculum." The art teacher spat out the last sentence as if she suddenly realized she had eaten kitty litter by mistake. While Carrie was enjoying this morality play, Lyn sat looking at her iPhone.

"I don't know what her plans are," said a man shaped like a barrel and dressed in a gray and red gym suit. The lanyard and whistle circling his neck dragged across the cream cheese in front of him. Ignoring the cheese, he grabbed a jelly doughnut, tore it apart, and stuffed half of it into his mouth. He swallowed and said, "But I've been here for three decades, and I've seen a lot!" To underscore his experience and knowledge, he poked his finger at those around the table. "And I never seen folks more divided at this school."

Carrie tamped down a smile when she saw a small dab of jelly adhere to the tip of his nose like a punctuation mark. He swallowed, popped the remaining doughnut into his wide mouth, and leaned back in his chair. Carrie thought she saw additional jelly turn the period into a question mark, but she was probably mistaken. He folded his thick, hairy arms across his chest and waited for someone to disagree with him. No one did.

"Are any of you telling the students to pray?" asked Mr. Wassermann. The faculty members shook their heads.

At the door to the office, the head secretary, Mrs. Gunther, a heavy woman in her forties, stood and assessed those sitting around the table. She wore a dark brown suit with a straight skirt. When she moved, the skirt stretched like an accordion to accommodate her weighty backside. A soft pink blouse completed her attire. As Carrie's eyes rode up and down its ruffles like an escalator, she felt slightly dizzy.

Mrs. Gunther's words reached the room before she did. "What the teachers are telling the students doesn't matter a hill of beans," she said, placing one hand on her hefty hip. "If the school provides time for meditation or prayer, it is endorsing these activities. You should hear what the parents tell me."

"What are they saying, Mrs. Gunther?" asked the principal. Carrie noticed Lyn sticking her phone in her pocket. Mrs. Gunther had her full attention.

"My lips are sealed, of course. I respect their privacy," the secretary said, turning toward Professor Shuler. She nodded at him. "I know about attorney-client privileges, Counselor. I'm just saying, that's all." The phone rang, but Mrs. Gunther remained at the door like a magistrate waiting to issue a warrant.

"I feel so sorry for the children who don't believe," Miss Reed lamented, "and for those youngsters whose parents don't take them to church. Or synagogue, Mr. Wassermann," she quickly added. Carrie thought Miss Reed's compassion burned as brightly as a nanowatt.

The barrel-shaped gym teacher asked, "Isn't there supposed to be a line in the sand between religion and government? I mean, I thought the government couldn't teach religion, and aren't schools part of government?"

Before the principal or the school's attorney could respond, Miss Reed said regretfully, "You know, the kids who don't believe in religion feel left out. They feel like outsiders. I can tell you that for sure."

Carrie looked at Lyn, who sat looking at Miss Reed. Her opponent's left leg bounced up and down rhythmically. Either she agrees with Miss Reed, thought Carrie, or she has to use the restroom.

"How many kids tell you that?" asked Mr. Wassermann.

"Well, I don't have a number," Miss Reed said, her face flushing. "I don't know how many children feel like outsiders, but even if only one child feels left out, that child will feel left out for his entire life. This program threatens the mental health of every youngster." All heads turned toward Miss Reed, who took a tissue from her suit pocket and dabbed her eyes. "If you only knew . . ."

"Zip it, Hilde!" Mrs. Gunther threatened.

"Back in the day," began the gym teacher, "a clergyman said prayers at graduation ceremonies. At the beginning of football games too. It was tradition. Why did the district change our traditions?" He looked around the room for an answer. Hearing none, he reached for another doughnut.

"Your question, Norbert," responded Mr. Wassermann, "is a perfect segue into a statement from the district's legal counsel. Attorney Shuler is here to discuss the legal ramifications of the new 'Minute of Silence' program voted on by the faculty."

Carrie listened as her professor laid out the legal issues. "The constitutionality of the 'Minute of Silence' program has been previously litigated," Professor Shuler informed the faculty. "The Supreme Court decided in 1985 that a program to meditate or pray violates the Establishment Clause because the school is endorsing religion." The faculty members seemed to consider the attorney's counsel, leaning forward in their chairs.

"The district spent a hundred thousand getting rid of that crazy music teacher at Raven," said Mrs. Waxman. "Yes, our union dues were spent protecting her rights because she didn't have sense enough to resign after they caught her in the backseat of her car with a—"

"Dirty laundry, Mrs. Waxman," bellowed Mrs. Gunther, who had stepped back into the front office.

Professor Shuler looked around the room before continuing. "If the school continues the program, the parents who object will sue and win their case against the school district. To litigate the issue in court will cost well over a hundred thousand dollars."

As Lyn nodded in agreement, Carrie wondered if Lyn understood the vacuum that progressive judges had created in the lives of young people. The Court had obliterated any trace of religious values and guidance in public schools. Would the bear that took the lion's place be better or worse?

"I would advise your school district to cancel this program," Professor Shuler said. "The Court determined that a 'One Minute of Silence' program sends a message to the nonbelievers that they are outsiders and, as such, are a class of people the Court needs to protect."

Carrie saw Lyn lift her nose and stare at the American flag. How long will flags be allowed to remain in school, she wondered.

"Norbert," said Mr. Wassermann, "I don't know what has happened to our traditions." Carrie thought he looked like Melville's Ishmael lost in the middle of the ocean.

"The majority of the teachers like the program," the principal explained further. "They said the students leave their homerooms quietly and—"

"That's what Susan Phelps claims," interrupted Mrs. Waxman. "She can't prove it."

"Now, I'm not taking sides," Norbert assured his colleagues, "but the kids do come into the gym more quietly after homeroom."

"That's because they're so tired from all their homework," fluttered Miss Reed. "The teachers give far too much homework. These students are still children developing their bodies and minds."

"You can say that again," said Mrs. Gunther, who stood in the doorway again. "They're developing themselves into teenage sex addicts."

"You know," said Miss Reed, "Andrea Cousins is pregnant. Poor child."

"Summing up," Mr. Wassermann stated, "we can continue the program, get sued, and lose in court."

Professor Shuler nodded.

Carrie willed her mouth closed and did not give in to her desire to shake her head or spit.

As the meeting broke up, a winded, red-faced teacher ran into the room, apologized to Mrs. Gunther, and said, "Mr. Wassermann, they're at it again. I just walked in on them in the tower!"

"Were they using a condom?" asked Mrs. Gunther.

The male teacher removed his glasses and rubbed his eyes. "Yes. The empty package was on the floor."

"Well, they're learning something!" said Mrs. Gunther as she piled several doughnuts onto a clean plate and left the room.

"Why wasn't that door locked?" asked the principal, but no one responded. No one seemed to hear his question. The teaching staff sat in their seats staring into space. Carrie looked at the dirty paper plates, napkins, and coffee cups that lay scattered across the table, the remnants of their discussion about the possibility that religion would take over their school. Instead of answering the principal or picking up the disposable utensils and china, the teaching staff had apparently settled into a temporary malaise. Carrie wondered if the faculty sat remembering their own youthful escapades. She noted that Lyn had returned to the mysteries of her iPhone.

"Get your minds out of the gutter and pick up the trash on that table!" huffed Mrs. Gunther. "Who do you think I am? Your personal maid?" Those around the table roused themselves, cleared the table, and walked out of the office exchanging theories for the recent upsurge in sexual activity inside the school building. Carrie heard Mrs. Waxman ask, "So who's the father of Andrea Cousins's baby?"

"I bet it's that handsome Tyrone Johnson," swooned Miss Reed. "He is so cute!"

Mr. Wassermann asked, "Norbert, will you handle Romeo and Juliet?" Norbert sniffed the air like he had discovered dog mess on his new white Nikes and left the office muttering.

The principal smiled at Professor Shuler. "Let me show you and your externs around the school, Paul."

On the first floor, Mr. Wassermann paused in front of an open door. "This is one of the life science labs. Students learn about practical applications of science rather than the abstract concepts." They looked inside the classroom where red-faced students stood in pairs beside lab stations.

"Now let your partner put the condom on the banana," directed the teacher.

"Do we have to eat the bananas when we're done?" asked one of the boys.

"Oooh yuck!" responded his peers.

"This is serious!" exclaimed the teacher. "Pay attention to what you are doing so you don't get someone pregnant. You don't want to bring an unwanted baby into the world, do you?"

Lyn sidled up to the principal and said, "Contraception is such an important subject for students to learn, Mr. Wassermann."

"Yes, it is, Lyn," said Mr. Wassermann, purring like a happy cat. "I'm glad you appreciate the progress we've made in sex education. Not everyone does." He looked at Carrie. She looked at him.

Mr. Wassermann directed them to another classroom down the hall.

"Mr. Wassermann," said Carrie, "does the curriculum include anything as outdated as math?"

"Come this way," said Mr. Wassermann.

The three members representing the legal community trailed the educator around the corner where they entered a third class and stood at the back of the room. The teacher discussed the students' next project. "I want you to experience what it feels like to have a gender or sexual preference different from your own."

"Does that mean . . ." began a boy at the back of the class. He started to laugh. "Do I have to dress up like a girl?" The students around him laughed too but stopped when the teacher pointed to the visitors standing at the back of the classroom.

"You can give your reports on your favorite president dressed as someone whose sexual orientation is different from your own."

"Hey! I'll be glad to talk about my man Obama, but I ain't dressin' like no girl, Miss Hardwick," said an African American student. "I'd get beat up in the hood, Miss. I ain't lyin' neither."

Before the principal could continue their tour, his pager buzzed. "I'll call you, Paul," he said, and hurried out the door.

Professor Shuler, Lyn, and Carrie continued their tour.

Outside a social studies classroom Carrie paused with her legal companions and observed a young female teacher discussing a project in world religions.

"I want you to choose any religion," said the teacher. "You may study Islam, Buddhism, Judaism, or Hinduism for your report."

"I'm Catholic," said a student in the front row. "Could I study Christianity?"

Carrie held her breath. "No," the teacher said. "Anything but Jesus. You already know about that." The teacher walked over to her desk where the arms of a beige sweater stretched across the back of the chair. "Mary," she said as she looked toward the back of the classroom, "could you close the door? I feel a chill in the room."

The girl looked at the floor as she closed the door.

"The school has an interior garden. Let's see it before we leave," suggested Professor Shuler. As they walked toward the office, Lyn summed up her estimation of the school curriculum.

"It's encouraging to think that our state is led by progressive-thinking people. This school is a paragon of good teaching methods and values," she said. Carrie decided it would be easier to argue with a ticking time bomb than to change Lyn's mind about anything, and so she said nothing.

Behind the main office, they entered a conservatory that was steamy, warm, and fragrant. Large plants, labeled in both English and Latin, rose toward the top of a glass roof, seeking the source of life. The young man with the Vandyke beard, whom they had seen at the school entrance, squatted on his haunches and planted small plants beneath a banana tree. He now wore gray work pants, boots, and a black T-shirt.

They crossed a small wooden bridge that spanned a narrow stream of water curling its way in and around the garden. Carrie could see black letters on several large stones covered with plaster that had been placed around the path leading to the exit. "Words of wisdom?" asked Lyn as she read the first stone aloud: "In Us We Trust." Further along the garden path, they saw a second stone.

"To Your Own Self Be True," Professor Shuler read.

The third stone lay about six feet away from the second. "This one says 'Do What You Think Is Right,'" Lyn said.

Near the exit, a fourth stone, the largest, appeared. Carrie said, "This one says 'Your Own Talent and Will Power Lead to Success.'"

"Sounds like a lesson in self-determination," said the professor as they left the garden. Lyn nodded in agreement. Carrie thought it sounded like a lesson in navel gazing. If she had the staff the Lord gave Moses, she would have used it to strike the floor and watch swarms of locusts descend upon the school. But having neither a staff nor bug repellant, she asked instead, "Do you really believe that adolescents have the ability to make wise choices?"

"Don't we all have an internal guide to knowing what is right and wrong?" asked Professor Shuler. "Most kids make good decisions."

"Yes," said Carrie. "Teenagers make decisions based on satisfying their desires. They have the capacity to come up with a reason to support anything they want to do."

"Carrie," said Lyn, "you don't appreciate how much knowledge young people have today. The Internet exposes them to so much."

"Yes, kids today have access to lots of facts, but that doesn't translate into wisdom and good choices," said Carrie. Sensing that the topic of conversation had been exhausted, she asked, "How long has the conservatory been in the building?"

"It was here when the building opened," Professor Shuler said as he looked around the large room. "The biology teacher used to maintain it. She chose her best students to help, and I was one of those students."

"Did she transfer to the Catholic high school you attended?" Carrie asked.

"Professor," said Lyn, her arms akimbo. "You didn't tell me you were a good Catholic boy."

"There are a lot of things I haven't told you, Lyn, but now you know," he said. Carrie noted that neither of her companions asked if the school where she last worked was similar to the one they were leaving.

On their way to the parking lot, Lyn said, "I'm hungry. Let's go for breakfast."

"That's a good idea," agreed Professor Shuler. "Let's go to the twenty-four-hour grill near the school." Carrie felt as if the professor and Lyn were reading from the same script while she stood without a copy.

"I'll meet you there," Lyn said, and charged toward her car.

Sure, Carrie thought, I'll come along—and at the restaurant Lyn could make her into a new politically correct woman. She couldn't wait!

"I'm sorry, Professor," she said, "but I can't go with you. I've got an afternoon class, and I have to take my dog to the park."

"I'll drop you at school, Carrie," he said and then yelled to Lyn, "I'll meet you in twenty minutes."

On the drive back to the law school, Carrie asked Professor Shuler what he thought of the progressive curriculum, but he skirted the issue. "Each year," he said, "the law school accepts more students who are better prepared than the group the previous year."

She decided not to bring up the results of international studies showing how the United States had dropped to seventeenth in math and twenty-third in reading compared to other developed countries, or mention how much the United States spent on education per pupil each year compared to every other country in the industrial world.

"Were you surprised that I advised the school to drop the 'One Minute of Silence' program?" he asked.

"No, your job was to protect the school district and its resources, and you did that," she answered. The law was simple, she thought. Wasn't it? You just undermined the vision of the Founding Fathers, and when the nation crumbled, you smoked some weed.

He nodded and shoved a Frank Sinatra disc into the CD player.

"You know what I don't like about progressives?" Carrie asked.

Professor Shuler glanced at her. "What?"

"I don't mind sharing the stage with them," she said, "but they insist on throwing everyone who disagrees with them into the audience."

Carrie's eyes were drawn to a carwash. She looked at her professor.

"I think I'll stop at this carwash and wash away the principles of the Founding Fathers," he said laughing. "You're a patriot, Carrie, just like your father's ancestors."

Yes, Carrie thought, and now my mother has switched to the other side.

Part Final

Carrie arose with the sunrise. She anticipated another great meeting with Professor Shuler, the last one this term. She had taken her exams and now would present her paper for his final judgment. He had already read the first draft; she hoped this one would knock his socks off and wondered if anyone still said that.

She found a perfect parking place close to the building and took the elevator to the sixth floor. Before entering the office, she checked her folder once again for her final draft. She flipped through all thirty-seven pages, admiring the proper legal footnoting at the bottom of each page. Seventy-five footnotes! She anticipated seeing a smile on Professor Shuler's face. Since the department secretary was on the phone, she walked past her and continued down the hall to find her professor.

But his office was dark and the door locked. When she looked through the narrow window beside the door, she saw an empty room, bereft of personal belongings. The coffeepots, pictures, and books were gone.

Retracing her steps to the assistant, she stood before her desk. When the woman hung up, Carrie said, "I'm here to see Professor Shuler. I have a one o'clock appointment."

The secretary swept her hand over her brow as if to clear her mind of facts and figures that didn't add up. "Didn't he email you?" When Carrie shook her head, she sat back in her chair. "Turns out he didn't contact a lot of his students. I just talked to another one on the phone. He's not here to see you; he left early."

"But his office is empty!" Carrie stated. "His coffeepots are gone. Did one of them explode and cause a fire?"

"Yes, the coffeepots are gone," the assistant lamented. "I'm going to miss those old pots." She snickered and looked up at Carrie. "No, there was no explosion."

"The coffeepots were unusual, weren't they?" said Carrie, choosing a nonjudgmental word instead of the one she was thinking.

"Yes, and the fancy blend of coffee he made every morning tasted like stain remover. Did you ever taste it?"

"Never," Carrie declared. "Do you know if he'll be back?"

"He isn't coming back," said the assistant. "He's got a new job at another law school out of state. In California, I think."

Carrie's mind left the sixth floor of the law school and submerged in the deep waters of the ocean. She felt like Jonah at the bottom of the sea, in the whale's belly. No one could hear her; no one could see her.

"Why didn't he tell anyone he was leaving?" Carrie asked.

"Well, he did tell one of his students, a young woman by the name of—"

"Lyn," Carrie blurted out. "I met her in his office."

"Yes, Lyn was the one."

"But is he selling his house? Is this a permanent relocation?"

"You mean, is his wife joining him? That is the $64,000 question. In fact, everyone in the department is placing bets on the outcome. What do you think will happen?"

"I don't know. I never met his wife."

The phone rang, and the assistant informed another student that Professor Shuler would not be able to keep his appointment. Professor Shuler, Carrie thought, must be the kind of man who would eat nails rather than expose his plans for the future.

"Professor Shuler was my advisor for a directed study, and I have my final paper," Carrie said as she showed the secretary her work, but not her disappointment. In what she hoped was a noncommittal tone of voice, she asked, "Will he be back in the office again before he leaves for California?"

"Oh, he's gone. I'll take your paper and forward it to him."

"Could I please have a receipt for the paper?"

"You know Professor Shuler well, don't you?" the woman stated as she pulled out a form, filled it in, and handed it to Carrie.

"Yes, I have encountered the Shuler type before," Carrie said. "How about you?"

The assistant hesitated. "Oh, sure. You know, I think I'm going to win the office pool."

Carrie hesitated. "The office pool?"

"Will he move out of state with his wife or . . ."

"Right," Carrie said. "When will you know if you've won?"

"When we find out whether his wife puts their house up for sale, and we see a for-sale sign in the yard," she said.

In the lobby, Carrie thought about the two women, tangled like two rosebushes. Would he plant both in his garden in California? At the entrance to the building, she paused and looked out the wall of windows and started counting the cars passing through the intersection. Performing mindless tasks always helped her think.

Approaching the building, walking against the red light, she saw one of the rosebushes wearing a sleek black suit, her skirt tight with pride. Next to her traversed a tall, muscular man with just enough gray at his temples to affect maturity and experience. His suit said money.

Carrie thrust open the door and walked in the direction of Lyn and her mysterious companion as the two strode toward the entrance to the law school. They met on the curb where Carrie stood at the nexus of tradition and progressive thinking.

"Carrie!" Lyn cried. "You have to meet the love of my life. Carrie, this is Philip Stanton. We just became engaged, and you are the first to hear of it."

Philip extended his large and forceful hand to her and they shook hands. The vigor of Philip's handshake surprised her. "Hey, congratulations," said Carrie. As they stood outside the law school entrance talking, she realized that to passersby the three of them must appear to be a tableau of friendship and goodwill.

Lyn lifted her left hand, and Carrie beheld a diamond as large as the frozen precipitation that broke her window during the last hailstorm. "Wow!" she exclaimed, and as Lyn and Phillip played at being lovers, she watched the traffic light turn colors. "So where are you headed?" Carrie asked. She could always be counted on to ask the obvious; they were headed to the entrance of the law school.

"I'm taking Philip to meet Professor Shuler," Lyn said. "I haven't been able to reach him for nearly a week, and we want to take him for breakfast before Philip has to fly back home. Was he upstairs in his office?"

"I haven't seen him, but make sure you bring Philip up to the department office. Everyone will be excited to meet him," Carrie said as she noticed Lyn staring at her coat and slacks.

"I don't have your address or cell number," Lyn said as she pulled out her phone. "I'd like to send you an invitation to our wedding."

Carrie recited the information, puzzled by this sudden flush of friendship. Was Lyn congratulating herself on throwing Carrie off guard, or was Carrie imagining they were opposing counsels in a courtroom. Lyn stuffed her phone back into her purse and looked up. She took Philip's hand and continued talking. When they turned and disappeared inside the building, Carrie tried to dispel the sense that she had just stepped out of a film shoot.

Carrie crossed the street and saw someone waving in her direction. She took a few more steps before she recognized it was Brenda, who suddenly tacked to the left and disappeared inside the local drugstore. Carrie followed.

Brenda, whose school sweatshirt nearly swallowed up her small frame, stood in front of the counter, smiling at the clerk. She dug into her purse and gave the woman some money. "Feeling lucky again today?" the clerk asked, handing Brenda some lottery tickets and a pack of menthol cigarettes.

"Estelle, you know I feel lucky every day," said Brenda. "And one of these days, it's going to pay off. I won't have to work another day in my life."

"So you're busting your behind in law school just for the sweatshirt?" asked Carrie.

Brenda slid the tickets into her billfold and opened the pack of Kools. As they walked out the door, Brenda yelled, "See you later, Estelle!" As they walked, Brenda turned away from the wind, cupped her hand, and lit the cigarette with a plastic Bic lighter. They stopped in front of a corner building whose windows revealed pictures of an apartment complex. In the three years Carrie had been attending law school, no renovations had begun. The future was on hold for students wanting to live closer to school.

"I thought you wanted to become an attorney, Brenda, not a lottery winner."

"I can do both," said Brenda. "Was that Lyn Loveless you were talking to?"

"The very same."

"Did she show you the rock on her hand and invite you to the wedding?"

Carrie hesitated. "Yes, she did. Did she invite you too?"

"Yes, and she invited everyone who was drinking at Flanigan's last night," said Brenda. "I guess she actually thinks we'll buy her an expensive gift, fly out to the Hamptons, and witness her marriage vows. No one really knows her!"

"Well, at least we know she's not running away with Professor Shuler," said Carrie

"Everyone knows that, Carrie. Where have you been?"

"But Professor Shuler's secretary just told me there's an office pool about his marital plans. It sounds like the staff is betting on whether his future plans include his wife or Lyn. He's moving to California."

Brenda stopped and faced Carrie. "I can't believe you spent the term working with him on a scholarly paper and just found out he's leaving."

"Yes, and the emphasis was on the paper," said Carrie. "How do you know all this?"

"Maybe because I go out sometimes after class with our classmates," said Brenda. "I actually talk with other students at Flanigan's, a place you refuse to enter."

"Oh, I know where it is," said Carrie. "I just don't go there very often. It smells like old air conditioners. Besides, you know I don't drink."

"Let's go now and have a drink for the road," Brenda said. "You can ask the bartender all about your Professor Shuler. She knows everything."

Before following Brenda, Carrie glanced at the stalled building project behind them, at the once colorful pictures of new apartments advertised since she started law school five years ago. The building had sat vacant due to a lack of interest in luxury living. She wondered what would eventually fill the empty building, but shook off speculation when Brenda pulled her into Flanigan's. The last sound she heard, besides the traffic flowing through a green light, was the first toll of church bells. Squaring her shoulders, she accepted the invitation, or was it a challenge?

"All right," she said. "After you."

Doppelganger: The Business of Sex Pandering

Proverbs 6:27

*Can a man scoop a flame into his lap
and not have his clothes catch on fire?*

S o how was your trip, Ben?" his secretary asked. "Did you see enough Renaissance art to last you a lifetime?"

"A lifetime and then some. Susan has always wanted to visit Italy and see Michelangelo's Sistine Chapel—in the chapel. I would have been satisfied with a picture in a book, but the chapel is awesome. He painted the ceiling while lying on his back and the place was unheated."

He picked up his messages, looked around, and poured himself some coffee.

"Your client from the adult bookstore called again," said the secretary, "and I scheduled him for 9 a.m."

"Good." Ben turned and walked down the hall to Nadine's office since Michael was usually in there as well. He opened the door and walked inside.

Both Nadine and Michael began peppering him with questions about his trip. He knew they would, but then would quickly get back to their trial preparation.

"Welcome back. How was the food?" Nadine asked. "How was the wine and the weather? Everyone who goes over there comes back with a smile on his face. You look pretty good."

"The food was magnificent," confirmed Ben. "Smaller portions though. You never felt stuffed. The wine was great too. The weather was cool but dry. We got there at the right time, before the heavy tourist season begins. We even had time to visit the Zwinger Palace in Dresden."

Michael joined in, "Yeah, and you and Susan had great sex. Right? Nothing like a vacation far from home to spice things up."

Ben smiled. "The Alameda Adult Book Store owner will be here at nine."

"What's he like?" asked Nadine.

"Like any other client who's worried he's going to lose his business," said Ben.

"Yes, but he won't really lose anything. He'll just have to separate his businesses," said Michael. "Of course, he'll eat the cost, right?"

Ben nodded.

"He'll probably lose. Do you think he'll appeal?" asked Nadine.

"I think that's what he'll want to discuss today," Ben said. "It's good to be back."

"Glad you and Susan enjoyed Italy," said Nadine. "Bernie and I loved it."

"Susan wants you and your significant others to come for dinner this Saturday, prepared by none other than yours truly and my lovely assistant, Susan," said Ben. "We will wine and dine you with authentic Italian cuisine. You know we took a cooking class outside of Rome near Siena in Tuscany. Caterina and Nonna Cianne taught cooking classes to guests from all over the world. Susan will tell you all about it on Saturday."

"The usual time?" Nadine asked and Ben nodded. "But don't bring any wine. We'll be drinking a Castello delle Quarttro Torra Chianti and a Vernaccio di San Gimignano."

"Your accent is impressive, Ben," said Nadine.

"So is my new ability to drink," said Ben.

"Your trip was a chick's fantasy, Ben," Michael teased. "I can see you wearing an apron and stirring up tiramisu. Yes, Janice and I will be glad to eat your fancy cuisine, and we'll check you after dinner to make sure you made it home with your balls intact."

"Someone tell Sam," said Ben. "Where is he?"

"At the court," said Michael. "He thinks the other side is ready to talk. I'll tell him when he gets back."

The meeting with his client went well, and he did want to appeal if the verdict upheld the city ordinance. After going over his brief, talking with clients, and doing some research on Westlaw, Ben decided to take off early. This case had piqued his interest; he wanted to see the store. As he walked out of the office, his legal secretary stopped him.

"Where did you say you were going?" she asked.

"I didn't," Ben replied.

"How long will you . . ." she began.

"No more questions. I'll see you tomorrow morning," Ben called over his shoulder.

It had cooled off some. As he walked toward his car, he could feel the breeze off the ocean. Perfect, he thought. The ocean had always calmed and relaxed him unlike the unrest he always felt on the land, especially inside his law office. While he had relaxed on his vacation, the stress hit the minute he walked back into his office. Litigation was like that, but he enjoyed the fight as well as the money. But the week of trial? Forget his home life; he charged double for that week in the courtroom.

He knew it all came with a price, though. He had seen the statistics: lawyers had the fourth highest rate of suicide. Pharmacists, dentists, and doctors were higher. Why pharmacists, he wondered. He knew a lot of lawyers who drank too much. Fortunately, he and Susan weren't a statistic.

He unlocked his black BMW 735 and stretched out his legs before starting the car. He lowered his windows, inserted the disc, and turned up the volume on Guns N' Roses *Use Your Illusion I*. Before applying the gas pedal, he turned around to make sure his symmetric statuettes of male sheep remained firmly attached to the shelf below the back window. A gift from his law school buddies as a joke, the rams aggressively announced to the world his desire to batter, crush, and force his opponent to submit. In duplicate, they kept watch on the world outside the back window of his car. He proceeded to the corner and turned left.

He had found the directions to Alameda Adult Book Store easily enough on the Internet, so he didn't have to ask anyone in the office for help. They would have laughed if he told them he was doing his fieldwork for the next case which appeared on the court docket in two weeks. He had the feeling he was being watched but hadn't seen anyone in the courthouse parking lot or in his rearview or side mirrors, so no one was following him. He continued down the street to the entry ramp where he'd drive west of the city and catch the expressway to the adult bookstore being sued by the City of Los Angeles.

The city had ordered adult bookstores to be dispersed throughout the city and prohibited owners from establishing two or more adult stores in the same building. Ben's wife, Susan, a federal administrative law judge, thought it was reasonable to allow only one porn shop in a building. But he didn't understand the necessity of the law promulgated by the City of Los Angeles restricting the number of adult bookstores to just one in the same establishment. He had argued with his wife.

"What difference does it make whether a building has one or two adult bookstores? City residents will understand quickly that where there's a little smoke, there is usually a fire."

"That's precisely the point. While one business will attract a certain number of customers, two stores will attract customers from a wider area. Then the entire neighborhood is blighted and not just one building," Susan had argued. "Besides, the secondary effects of property devaluation, prostitution . . ."

"Yes, I know," Ben had asserted and completed the list. "An increase in crime, sexual assaults. Come here, counselor. Let me kiss those sensual lips." Sometimes he wondered why he had married a woman who knew as much as he did and who could argue just as well. Next time, he decided, I'll marry someone without a law degree. At the conclusion of their arguments, he usually took her in his arms. He wasn't stupid. Their sex life was great, at least most of the time, and she was usually always ready, but not after a serious argument. After their debates, he made a point of pulling her slim body close to his and kissing her.

Privately, however, he considered Susan's argument without merit. He felt a man's natural interest and curiosity about sex should not be restricted by government. Besides, a man always knew when to back off and not get out of control.

Although he and Susan usually told each other everything, he hadn't told her where he was going after work, just that he might be late. Good, he thought, pulling onto the expressway; traffic is light, and I'll be there in ten minutes.

Thirty minutes later, he pulled up in front of a one-story building with a huge billboard over its entrance of a man and woman kissing, the kind of picture he had seen on paperback romance novels sold in drugstores. He found a parking space near the corner, and although it was not 6 p.m. he forgot to put change in the meter.

He stood near the back of his car and looked more carefully at the sign. Beneath the romanticized couple, the words "Explore the Passions" appeared in large purple letters. The color purple was repeated in the woman's eyes and in the silk scarf that fluttered in an imaginary breeze. Beneath the huge sign, a wide open passageway led to the store, which he entered without thinking twice.

No protective roof or ceiling covered the long passageway. Customers were exposed to the elements. Dark twelve-by-eight windows in huge panels flanked the walkway. He tapped one to make sure they were made of glass, but discovered they were made of thick plastic. It looked like the plastic had been covered with cardboard. No one could look inside and no one could look out. "Storage rooms," he said aloud. No one heard him, but he looked around him anyway and wondered who he might encounter inside the store. He hoped it was no one he knew.

On either side of the entrance into the store, two identical black chandeliers with yellow bulbs glowed without emitting much light. He hesitated then climbed two stairs into a large open entryway. To his left, he saw a window display filled with Valentine's Day decorations. At the bottom of the window he saw two smiling cherubim, their eyes gazing at the action above them. They looked like the cherubs he had seen in pictures by Raphael. But instead of gazing at the Madonna and child, they stared at the genitals of a well-endowed man and a woman with big breasts.

"Does anyone actually buy a Valentine's gift here for someone they love?" he whispered. To the left of the display stood the entrance to the store. He gripped the door handle just as a customer emerged from the store. The man looked just like him—dark pants, a starched white shirt open at the collar, and polished black shoes. He had started to lose his hair, but instead of hiding the effect of aging by combing the remaining strands of graying hair over his balding head, his stylist had cut the rest of his hair very short. Except for his mustache and beard, the outbound man could have passed for Ben's brother. As they passed each other, they both dropped their eyes and hurried in opposite directions. He exhaled and realized he had been holding his breath.

The interior of the store was bright, but he squeezed his eyes to adjust to the glare that bounced off the white walls. Fluorescent ceiling lights buzzed. In front of him, he saw a large stand with multiple metal arms from which dildos in various sizes asserted themselves aggressively, all pointing upwards. He smiled. "They look like members of a marching band," he said to himself. The rubber penises were covered in plastic and firmly attached to cardboard cases. He tried to imagine inserting some of the larger dildos into Susan, but couldn't. They hadn't gotten into sex toys and had never been to an adult store together, not even when they were in school together. Of course, there hadn't been time to do much exploring in those days, not even in the summer because of externships at different law firms.

Next to this display glistened shiny bottles of lubricants in black and bright colors of purple, blue, and scarlet. Each one contained a different fragrance. One of the fragrances must have been sprayed in the room because he could smell jasmine. To the right of the shiny bottles and tubes, he saw another room filled with sheer lacy garments in red, white, and black. He saw panties and thongs on shelves beneath the nighties. A buxom female mannequin greeted him at the door. Beneath a black lace nightie, she appeared nude, her large nipples hard and the areolas dark and full. She looked so real that he felt himself blush.

Opposite him, he saw a woman standing behind a counter. She smiled and looked at him coyly, like she was going to ask him something but already knew the answer. When he walked closer to where she was standing, the floral fragrance of her perfume welcomed him.

"Can I get you something?" she asked as she bent over the counter. Her blouse was so low he could see that her nipples were hard. When she stood up, he shoved his hands in his pants, the way teenage boys did to cover their embarrassment. Her sheer black blouse encouraged him to stare and enjoy her ripeness. She wasn't embarrassed when he looked at her. She arched her back and nearly handed him her treasures on a silver platter. He took his hands out of his pants and pushed his erection forward, matching her confidence and hoping she would stare. She noted the bulge in his pants and licked her lips. "Honey, you look like you're happy to see me." He just smiled. Where is she headed, he asked himself, and for one crazy moment he hoped she would beg him to unzip his pants.

Instead, he said, "How long have you worked here?"

"Long enough to know you one of the finest customers I ever seen."

"I'm going to check out the rest of the store. I'll stop back before I leave."

"I'll be here, sugar."

He turned to find the door, but saw no exit. "It's over here," she said, and he touched her arm when he walked by, letting his hand graze the side of her breast. The bulge in his pants was so uncomfortable now that he knew he needed to get back to his car. In a room beyond this one, he saw shelves displaying DVDs with titles like *Big Tit Cheerleaders*, *Ass for Days*, and *Betty Cockers*. He smiled. Beyond this room he could see stands holding scores of magazines displaying colorful pictures of attractive young women with beckoning eyes and parted lips who had enormous breasts and behinds. Pictures of young men pushing their hips forward displayed their hard penises.

He looked around him before taking a magazine from the rack and opening it up to a picture of a nude woman with full lips, her tongue lifted to the side of her mouth. A satin sheet snaked in and around her legs, exposing only part of her voluptuous body. Shaping the magazine into a roll, he looked around for a cash register. When he walked back through the store, he found the room with the mannequin, but the voluptuous clerk was gone. Had he imagined her?

He had to walk to the front of the store before he saw a cash register. A young overweight girl stood behind the register. She was dressed in a T-shirt with a picture of a dildo on the front and the name of the store above the head of the artificial penis. She stood looking out the door and drinking from a plastic bottle of Coke. The store clerk rang up his purchase without looking at him. He paid in cash and left, walking quickly back to his car. Under the windshield wiper, a ticket fluttered in the breeze. "Damn!" he said aloud, but the young man who approached him, his face a riot of acne, passed by looking straight ahead.

As Ben unlocked his car, he noticed a dark worm crawling up the driver's window. Before he could brush it aside, it flew off into the night. He unlocked his car door but did not immediately climb into his car. Instead, he scanned the streets for passersby and police cars. Once inside the black leather interior, he tore away the thin paper bag covering his magazine. He found the excited model waiting for him in the middle of the magazine and flipped through the pages. She looked like the woman behind the counter. Her long brown hair, sensual face, and full breasts appeared on several pages. On the last page he viewed her shaven pubis, her legs open and inviting him in. He took off his suit jacket, laid it over his lap, and unzipped his pants.

It didn't take long. He was surprised by the intensity of his ejaculation. He shuddered and breathed through his mouth. His entire body felt electrically charged by the model's pouty lips and direct brown eyes. He felt he knew her. Although he had just had an explosive release, he wanted more, something a little dangerous.

Down the street two men dressed in open shirts, white chinos, and sandals approached. They looked at him. He quickly started the car, pulled out of the parking space, and threw off his suit jacket. At a stop sign he adjusted his pants and decided to drive through a fast-food restaurant for coffee and a hamburger. When he threw out the paper bag and coffee cup, he would shove the pornographic magazine into the trash.

The sun was setting when he pulled into the driveway. He saw the lights were on in the kitchen, but the rest of the house was dark. His shoulders relaxed when he didn't see Susan's car in the driveway. As he opened the kitchen door, he noticed a worm crawling out of one of the roses in the rosebush beside the door. Half-eaten petals drooped from the stems and covered the ground. "Worms," he muttered and entered his home.

As he stood at the kitchen sink washing his hands, Susan opened the door and walked into the kitchen. "You're home. Have you had something to eat?"

"I grabbed a burger at In and Out."

"Where have you been?"

"Questioning my whereabouts, are you, counselor?"

"No, just curious. You usually tell me where you're going."

"I'm not going anywhere right now."

"Is everything all right?"

"Why?"

"You just seem a little . . . I don't know, agitated."

"I'm fine, and you look great. Is that a new outfit?"

"No, are you sure you're okay?"

"I'm sure. Come on, let's go for a walk." He reached for her hand and she stepped into his space.

"You smell like onions and scented candles."

He smiled and opened the door for her. "They're providing scented candles now with their burgers."

On their walk they discussed the menu for Saturday's dinner party with Ben's partners and their guests. Marriages had come and gone, new relationships established. Ben agreed with Susan that it was a challenge to remember all the new names. Compared to recalling the names of new lovers and wives, deciding on the menu wasn't difficult. "Let's just prepare what we made in Tuscany," Susan suggested. "We can begin with gnocchi and eggplant sauce . . ."

"I'd prefer pesto sauce," Ben interrupted. "Or we could make both."

"Okay," Susan agreed. "We'll make both. Then we'll make spinach and ricotto ravioli, chicken fillet in Vin Santo, tomatoes au gratin, with tiramisu for dessert."

"How about tagliatelle with sausage, zucchini, and saffron? There will be eight of us."

Susan looked at him, hesitated, but as they walked up the step into the kitchen, she agreed. "I'm going to ask Maria to come over. We'll need help cooking, setting the table, serving the wine and food. She can clean up as well. I'll call Vivaldi's and order the wine and the florist for the flowers." Ben grabbed his gym bag and headed to the door. "Irises and lilies would be pretty," Susan said as the kitchen door closed.

Part Two

"How was your field trip yesterday?" Ben's secretary asked smiling.

"Susan had made plans so I didn't go. Why do you ask?" he inquired as he went through the messages on her desk.

"Just curious. I've never been to an adult bookstore myself, but . . . just curious, I guess," she said. "I want to sit in on the trial next week."

"Okay. Hold my calls. Where's Nadine? Is she in her office?"

"She and Sam are both in her office."

He walked down the hall, but instead of stopping to chat with his partners, he went into his office where he washed his hands before sitting down to review his brief.

He was in court all day filing motions. In the morning criminal cases filled the judges' dockets; in the afternoon they heard civil cases. At the end of the day, as he walked through the straight halls behind the courtroom, he affirmed his decision not to return to Alameda Adult Book Store and not to cancel his weekly racquetball game with his law school buddy, a successful criminal defense attorney for miscreants in the entertainment field. He drove to his gym, parked, and called to Ben, who was getting his gym bag out of the trunk of his Porsche. After smashing the hell out of a small yellow ball, he and Ben chatted at the juice bar. In the parking lot, they confirmed their game for the following week and drove off.

But the following week as the lawyers squared off in the courtroom, one defending Alameda Adult Book Store, the other the City of Los Angeles, he called Nathan and canceled their game. As if someone else spoke into the phone, he found himself making up an excuse to a guy he considered part of his family. "Look, Nathan, I can't make it. The prosecutor withheld some of the evidence, so I'm going to have to stay late and work. See you next week." He felt guilty because Nathan had so readily accepted his lie.

He hesitated as he approached the store that sold aids for sex. Surprisingly, his steps weren't as resolute as they had been the week before. Instead of turning left inside the building, he decided to turn right where he entered a doorway leading down a flight of steps to the adult video arcade. Down a long hallway, he observed a half dozen or so small private viewing areas. Black curtains surrounded each compartment. From one of the boxlike rooms, he heard the sounds of mounting passion. Moments later, he heard a loud sigh of release. The anonymous sounds aroused him and he headed for the booth at the end. As he pulled aside the protective curtain, he stopped abruptly.

Inside the booth, a nondescript man stood facing a video screen displaying a fully dressed couple touching each other. The sound was off, and the man who stood before him looked dispassionately at the screen. He was dressed in a silver long-sleeved shirt and silver pants that hung low on his frame. He wore silver glasses. Two identical yellow light bulbs cast little light on the silent man, causing him to look like a ghost.

"Excuse me," said Ben, not backing away. "I didn't realize anyone was in this booth."

The man looked like he had visited Ben's dreams. His clothing glistened, and as he mutely faced him, Ben thought he appeared to have emerged from the ocean, his watery blue eyes languid and sleepy. He didn't smell of fish but of lavender and spices, and except for his clothing, he was Ben's double. They were the same height and weight, and both had an athletic build.

"Join me," said the man, his voice strong and resolute. Before entering, Ben scanned the hallway. It was empty, and he stepped inside.

"My name is Tag," said the man. "I doubt that you want to reveal your name. I have no problem with that. I will call you Mr. Secret."

Ben watched as Tag placed his hands in the pockets of his pants. He exuded masculinity. Immersed in the screen, he said again, "Join me. We'll have fun."

This stranger knew exactly what to do. When their desire was satisfied, Ben tried to clear his mind. He felt satisfied but confused, like he had been with his wife while at the same time had enjoyed sex with a man he had never met. He was one man in two places simultaneously.

After they had each reassembled their attire, Tag withdrew a card from his pocket. He placed it with great courtesy and confidence in Ben's warm hand. "Call me," he said, and left the booth.

As he stood in the dimly lit booth, Ben considered what part he would play in the drama ahead. It was a matter of conscience. He could not tell his wife, but he could not walk away from Tag and anonymous sex with someone stronger than he.

He drew aside the curtain that had hidden his secret activities and walked back down the hallway where he ascended the flight of stairs that brought him into the vestibule of the building, but not into the light. Two doorways opened before him; he hesitated, then walked to the one on his left. As he walked through the long hallway separating the entrance from the exit, he felt like a man without one definite home, a stranger to himself and to everything he had known. He turned right at the building's exit, but after walking for some time and not seeing his car, he turned and walked in the opposite direction.

Finally, he found his car parked beneath an aromatic eucalyptus tree. Raindrops dripped softly through its branches. He stood beside his car and swept off the beads of water that had left spots on the roof and hood. He didn't like water spots on the car's shiny black surface. As he opened the car door to retrieve a chamois, he caught his reflection in the driver's window. Who was this man, he wondered, who had just discovered the duplicity in his own soul?

That night as he sat on the side of the bed, he swept his hand over the clean smooth sheets printed with soft pink roses. In the pattern of the sheets he saw a dark worm crawling up the stem of one of the roses, heading for the fully opened rose. Startled, he turned to grab a tissue from the bedside table, but when he turned back to the roses in his bed, the worm lifted from the sheets and flew away, becoming invisible in the shadows of his bedroom.

"What's the matter?" asked Susan when he turned away from her small hand on his chest. "You were so quiet at dinner."

"I'm just tense. You know how I am during the week of trial. I'll be back to normal in the morning."

But when the alarm sounded, Ben jumped up from his wife's nocturnal embrace and quickly walked to the bathroom, locked the door, and turned on the shower. Beneath the warm water, he thought of the mysterious man from the night before. He thought he'd wait a few days to call him. If he could wait that long.

Part Three

The following Saturday, Ben stood in his kitchen at the granite island kneading dough and wearing a chef's apron when their guests started to arrive. "What the hell are you wearing, Ben?" demanded Michael as he ushered in yet another new woman. Ben wondered where he met all of his beautiful dates.

"Are you making gnocchi?" the woman asked. "I bet we went to the same cooking class in Tuscany, the one near Siena. By the way, I'm Nadia."

"Yes, Susan and I just got back. I'm Ben, your host tonight. Excuse me for not extending my hand."

The woman rushed to the sink, washed her hands, and extended her hand. "I love the feel of dough and floured hands," she said with a grin. "Want some help?"

Ben blushed and nodded his head. "When were you there?"

"Before I met Michael. A girlfriend and I went over, toured the country, gained five pounds, and took cooking lessons before we came home. Don't you just love Italian food? Michael, come over here and learn how to do something with food besides eat it."

"No, I'm a man. I do not enter a kitchen to do anything other than grab the orange juice and drink out of the carton."

"He's such a Neanderthal, Ben. He doesn't know that men are the best chefs and—"

"For the best sex life, men and women have to be different, not some politically correct amalgam of the two," said Michael.

"Sex, sex, sex. That's all you think about, Michael," complained Nadia with a smile on her face. Michael came up behind her and grabbed her breasts. She squealed and pretended to thwart his further assaults on her slender body. As she dropped the dough, Ben noticed she was built like a Barbie doll. He continued to watch her long smooth legs as she ran after Michael, who led the chase across the stone patio and out into the half acre of land surrounding the house.

"Where does he keep meeting these beautiful women?" asked Susan, who stirred the sausage and zucchini. "We've met, how many different girlfriends in the past decade?"

Susan rested her spoon on the stove and handed Janice a glass of red wine. "Several," said Janice. "He's got great taste in women, but why doesn't he ever want to marry any of them?"

"Marriage obviously isn't one of his goals," said Sam.

Sam's fiancé, Lucy, asked, "Janice, are you and Frank heading out to Montana again this May?"

"We are. We're going back to the Covered Wagon to do some more riding in Yellowstone National Park. Our dude ranch friends from New Jersey said they'd like to meet us there again. He practices labor law and she's a psychologist. We met them . . ." she paused.

"Three years ago in Wyoming at a dude ranch outside of Jasper," said Frank, completing her sentence.

"We've been riding here a couple of times each month to stay in shape," continued Janice. "We are almost ready for daylong rides which end at a local saloon. Riders secure their horses outside the bar by tying them up at a wooden post outside. I love feeling like a cowgirl for a week. And I love cowboy boots!"

Susan smiled. "How about you, Sam? Where are you and Lucy going this summer?"

"We usually don't decide until a month in advance," replied Sam.

"I'd like to spend some time in Alaska fishing and hiking," said Michael, who had returned from chasing Nadia around the yard.

"I want to swim with the turtles in Galapagos Island," said Nadia. "No roughing it outdoors in the cold for me. Michael can go with the guys like he did last year."

"Dinner is served," called Susan. "Fresh wineglasses are on the table. Let's enjoy a night in Tuscany." She motioned Maria to begin serving.

As he drove into the office the following Monday, Ben wondered if Michael had been right in describing his recent trip to Italy as a chick's dream vacation. His date had found his cooking sensual and had quickly responded to him as he shaped the potato dough into little dumplings. But Michael had returned from Alaska looking hearty and fit. Michael walked around the office for the next week standing taller, and his chest looked bigger. Ben, on the other hand, had returned from Italy five pounds heavier, and the waistband of his pants felt tight and unyielding.

Sitting in traffic, he wondered why he had agreed to a vacation in Italy. He could have encouraged Susan to travel with her sister or their neighbor, the one she went with to museum exhibits. He had enjoyed getting away, but he didn't get home feeling strong and emboldened, not the way he felt with Tag. Maybe the ancient Greeks were right; the strongest bonds existed between men, not between a man and a woman. And what about the bond between David and King Saul's son, Jonathan? David had said their love was deeper than his love for women. But then, David and Jonathan hadn't met in an adult bookstore.

On Thursday, the attorneys made their final arguments before a jury made up of the defendant's peers, community residents who lived in the county. Ben wondered how many of them, if any, had been to Alameda Adult Book Store and if any of them had seen him there. They deliberated for several hours and decided to uphold the city statute. Afterwards, when the judge and two attorneys talked with them, one male juror said, "It's reasonable to restrict the number of these adult stores to only one per building and to spread 'em around the community. But I'll be damned if I want one in my neighborhood."

His fellow jurors agreed. A woman spoke up and said, "I think they should be banned altogether! They cripple the morals of good men. My sister lost her husband to pornography; it broke up their family."

The judge thanked them for doing their civic duty and said the law didn't always mirror the opinions of individual citizens. He left the jury room with the champions of the law. In the parking lot, Ben called Tag.

Part Three

As he walked to the adult bookstore, after parking his car, Ben noticed a boarded-up building across from the store; it had previously been a restaurant. He figured few people who had just been to the adult store across the street would want to walk into a brightly lit family restaurant and examine the purchases made in the bookstore. The following month, the adult video arcade in the Alameda adult bookstore was scheduled to close. Ben wondered where he and Tag would meet after the arcade was shut down. He had never experienced such intense sexual pleasure before and didn't want to stop seeing his lover.

On the last night before the arcade closed, Ben's pleasure had been incredibly intense. He and Tag had hooked up with the voluptuous woman he had flirted with in the lingerie department. He hadn't had two orgasms in the same night since college. They had snorted some coke and he felt like he could go all night. Although he and Tag didn't talk about where they would meet next, he assumed Tag had the same feelings for him that he had for this man of mystery. Plus, he still had his phone number.

Driving home, Ben decided he would continue seeing Tag until Susan gave him an ultimatum. But even with that prospect looming, he didn't think he could curtail his desire. The man constantly remained at his side. Wherever Ben went, Tag followed, a secret presence inside his mind, reminding him of a dark passion he had never before experienced. During the day, he upheld the laws of the city and state, but after work he devoted himself to illicit pleasure. He could defend the rights of his clients but could not defend the vows he had taken twenty years ago; he felt they confined him and limited his free expression of sexual pleasure.

But where could they meet? He didn't know where his double lived or what he did for a living. He had not asked.

He realized that nothing separated him from those who had been caught breaking laws and came to his office willing to pay a sizable amount of money for his help. Every time he saw Tag, he was reminded of his own capacity for evil. He had read Joseph Conrad in college, a novelist who believed that a man had to know evil before he was capable of doing good. But he disagreed. Once a man has slept with the devil, he now realized, he is a man without a soul whose desire for more knows no bounds. Ben believed he was powerless to do anything about his need to explore the darkened hallways and serpentine passageways of his soul. As he parked his car in the garage, he had to admit he was as addicted as any junkie.

He opened the door and saw Susan sitting at the kitchen table. She had not turned on any lights, but sat there drinking a glass of wine. A nearly empty bottle stood open near her reach. "Nathan called," she said. "He wanted to know if you were all right since you didn't call or show up at the club for racquetball."

He froze. "You know my trial started this week. I've been busy."

"Ben, you said that last month."

"Susan, I'm in court with a new trial about once a month. I litigate; that's what I do. You know that."

"No, your new case isn't in trial this week or next," she said and stood up to face him. "I spoke with your secretary."

"I'm going to bed," he asserted, "in the guest bedroom. We need to talk when I'm not so tired and you haven't been drinking." He left the room, hoping he had been able to make her feel guilty.

That night he dreamed he lived in a desert area near a mountain. A large group of people dressed in white robes stood around him. They mumbled and complained that they had no leader, no one to guide them. Several approached the second in command and demanded that he make a god for them to praise and worship. They said they needed a god to lead them. They removed their gold earrings, rings, and necklaces, stepped over to a deep cauldron, and threw them in. The fire melted the gold. Craftsmen shaped the liquid.

The people watched and sang, but he could not understand what they were singing. Some danced and circled the pot of liquefied gold. Soon a shape emerged in the liquid gold, rising higher and higher into the night sky. Ben saw a huge phallus emerge from the cauldron; its enormous head rose above the tents surrounding the fire. The group chanted and bowed before the statue. Men grabbed the women near them, and no one resisted. They tore off their garments and kicked off their sandals. They lay in groups on the ground where they groped and fondled each other. Ben watched their naked bodies glisten in the light from the fire. He smelled the sweat from their aroused bodies but felt nothing. He heard the grunts and groans of men and women coupling like animals. Fiercely and without love.

The scene changed. It was daylight. He stood up and watched a man with a radiant face walk down from the mountain toward the people. In his hands he carried two stone tablets. Ben wondered what the marks on them said. The man looked around him and saw the sleeping naked bodies entwined and lying on the ground. At the center of his people, he saw a huge golden phallus, shining in the hot desert sun. He raised the tablets above his head and threw them onto the ground where they broke upon the rocks.

Ben awoke; his bedding lay twisted in a pile on the floor. The bottom sheet was damp beneath him. He felt hot and feverish. He sat up and tried to get out of bed, but leaned back into the mattress for support. When he collapsed, he fell onto the nightstand, hitting his head and knocking the lamp onto the wooden floor.

When he awoke, he saw Susan kneeling beside him. "Don't move. I've called an ambulance." He smelled the metallic odor of blood and reached for his head. Susan grabbed his hand. "Don't touch your face or head. Help is coming, and they'll be here shortly."

He looked at her pinched brow and her lips squeezed into a thin line. They waited, but he couldn't remember what they were waiting for. "Ben, the Supreme Court can't help you now," she said, and he looked at her quizzically. She held both of his hands until the paramedics arrived.

"Am I that busted up?" he asked, not understanding what the Court had to do with his condition.

"Your body will be fine, Ben. It's your soul I'm worried about."

When the paramedics took over, Susan stood up and answered their questions. "I'm not sure what happened. He said he thought he was coming down with something, so we slept apart. He must have tried to get up and then passed out. I heard the lamp hit the floor from our bedroom and ran in."

"We'll take him to City Hospital. You can follow in your car and park in the emergency lot." That was the last he could remember.

Part Last

Ben awoke in a private room at the local hospital, a place he had not been since Susan had her second miscarriage. He looked around the empty room and wondered if she had just stepped out for a cup of coffee.

He looked at his arm. White tape held an IV in place. He was hooked up to a bag that dripped saline into his veins. Had they taken a sample of his blood? He wondered if the drugs he had snorted the night before were still in his system.

Outside his window, the darkness lifted but the clouds looked heavy. He heard no birds and wondered how many floors up his room was. A light rain started to fall, and he heard the slap of water against the pavement from the traffic below. He felt very tired and his thoughts drifted without ever focusing on anything in particular. He saw no one in the hall, no porter pushing a rack of breakfast trays, no nurses walking in and out of rooms checking for vital signs. But he smelled cigarette smoke; maybe the staff was taking a break. He wondered why Susan had called an ambulance and when someone would tell him what had happened. What were they going to do to him?

It was difficult to think clearly. From what he could remember, Susan was talking to him about the Supreme Court and his soul, but he couldn't understand their connection. Did he have a new client? What had she meant when she said she was worried about his soul?

He felt confused like he did once when he drove home from a large city and made a wrong turn. After hours of driving in the snow and fog, he discovered he was headed in the opposite direction of where he wanted to go, and he couldn't figure out how he had ended up going in the wrong direction. He was nearly at the other side of the state. But how had he gotten there? He had decided that if there was a hell, that's what it would be like: driving in the wrong direction without knowing how you got there or where you were going. Just driving and driving and not knowing how to turn things around. His surroundings told him nothing. He saw billboards he didn't recognize and farms he had never seen.

At the time he had yelled and banged on the steering wheel. He had opened his window and cursed at the cars driving in the direction he knew he should be going. And he had cursed God for not being present when he made a wrong turn. Then he had pulled into a gas station, but didn't stop. He didn't want to admit he was lost to a gas station attendant who would conclude he was just some smart-ass college kid who didn't know his ass from a hole in the ground. He couldn't admit he had made a mistake then; maybe he still couldn't.

Where was she? He pounded the mattress and looked at the clock over the door. It was nearly 8 a.m.

He grabbed the phone beside his bed and punched the numbers he had memorized over the past several weeks. He wanted his new lover to know where he was, not so he could visit, but so he could imagine him in a setting outside the adult bookstore. A recording told him the number had been disconnected.

He must have dozed. When he awoke, the wind had picked up. He heard it whistle as trashcans banged against the pavement outside. He heard sand tick off the window and scrape against the side of the building. The hospital lights flickered then went out. He couldn't see out into the hallway because someone had pushed the door nearly shut. He thought he heard gritty shoes crunching on the tile floor and the sound of metal clanging as if the person were dragging shackles behind him down the hall to his door. Then he heard nothing. It was silent. He thought the storm had ended.

The door to his room stood ajar. It opened slowly, uncertainly. Finally! Someone would tell him where he was and why. He blinked and squeezed his eyes to focus on the wraithlike figure sliding into the room. A shadowy figure approached his bed, its face hidden behind clouds of smoke. He heard the man inhaling and exhaling as he stepped forward. Then the figure stopped. Ben looked straight ahead into an unconfirmed, undefined future, a future where he knelt beneath a golden phallus. The man took Ben's hands and held them in his own cold fingers. Ben turned and watched as the smoke retreated. A face, that could have been his double, appeared. In a low scratchy voice the man said, "I am you."

Delayed Reaction

Luke 17:1

There will always be temptations to sin,
but what sorrow awaits the person who does the tempting.

A security guard brought her into the courtroom, her hands cuffed behind her back. Young externs sat watching her, their laptops closed, their hands resting lightly on the arms of the chairs. Instead of reading court documents or writing them, they waited like hunters at a deer stand. They knew the charges against her, and they knew where she'd been. The young men had her in their sights.

The older law extern struggled to imagine the prisoner on a stage, dressed as she was in a baggy orange jumpsuit, with no makeup on. As she sat watching with her classmates, she heard no jokes about the prisoner's appearance or the charges brought against her by the state. As the guard unfastened the chain that circled the prisoner's waist and bound her hands, she wondered what images might be lighting up his mind.

The prisoner sat down at the defense table next to her attorney and rubbed her wrists. The two did not immediately make eye contact, and the older law student wondered when they would. The young and handsome attorney reviewed his client's file while his client surveyed the courtroom, assessing it like a prospective homebuyer searching the place for cockroaches.

The law extern looked at the empty space behind the judge's dais. Despite Judge Acker's attempts to make her feel comfortable, she didn't enjoy her externship at the circuit court. Her spirit dragged after witnessing the march of lawbreakers down the aisle and their unsuccessful attempts to hide gang tattoos, the identity stamps they chose to explain who they were. Listening to them tell the judge how they had gotten involved in a life of crime was like listening to busy woodpeckers knocking their heads against a tree.

Drugs, an older girlfriend, and dropping out of school were a common tale. Law enforcement dogged their movements because invariably they ended up selling the drugs they used in these relationships. She heard the jokes the young externs told on motions day when the young felons stood beside their attorneys, but she couldn't find the humor in confessions made in a court of law before a stranger in a black robe. It was hard to sit and watch young defendants who had short-circuited their lives by committing crime. What was funny about that? If she passed the Bar, would she become one of many attorneys who swept in and out of the courtroom, like brooms seeking dust?

Before going through security that morning, the older extern had paused outside the courthouse to gaze at the rose garden. Pastel-colored roses bloomed abundantly, and before entering the building she had inhaled their morning fragrance like the balm of Gilead. Waiting for the judge to address the next motion, she recalled a novel she had read multiple times in school. The story began with a rosebush. In the novel, Hester Prynne observed the wild rosebush outside the prison when she opened the heavy oak door to walk to a platform where she would stand before the men and women in her Boston community. Hester Prynne had noticed the rosebush growing wild outside the prison because its uncontrollable nature mirrored her own passions, which had refused to conform to the standards of those around her. But the prisoner sitting at the defense table—was her nature controlled by unbridled passion or tinged with something else?

The extern knew that both women stood before their communities because of their moral transgressions, that neither would ever be accepted by moral women, and that both lived in isolation despite the number of people who surrounded them. But had these women been victims of the evil in society, or had they perpetrated it themselves through their actions?

The faces of the young male externs revealed their fantasies. They imagined that passion and a wild sex drive drove this prisoner to perform. She noticed that Steve, the young man on her left, sat forward in his seat. His mouth was slightly open, his breathing slow but steady.

Unlike Hester Prynne, this prisoner in orange did not wear the scarlet letter "A" on the front of her jumpsuit. Hawthorne's character, the seventeenth-century woman who gave birth to an illegitimate child, had refused to identify the father. Did this prisoner remember the man whose child she carried nearly five years ago?

The law clerk entered the court, held the door for the judge, and called "All rise." The prisoner and her public defender, along with everyone else in the court, stood. They sat after the judge took her seat behind the bench and told them to be seated. Having served as a circuit court judge for over a decade, the judge was not unaware of evil and its debilitating influence on young and old, men and women.

"Danielle, is this the one Nina was talking about this morning?" whispered her friend Chantal, a young African American student from Georgia. Danielle nodded.

In contrast to the prisoner, Chantal's dark hair was perfectly groomed. She carried her five-foot-nine-inch frame with dignity and grace and hid the extra pounds her frame supported with layered clothing. In their first class together, they sat next to each other, but Chantal was distant and uncommunicative until the middle of the term. After three classes together, they became friends.

The air in the courtroom was dry. The prisoner wrinkled her nose and flipped her long wavy black hair out of her eyes. Chantal observed, hiding her mouth with her hand, "Her hair looks like she cut it herself, blindfolded."

Danielle whispered back, "It reminds me of shark teeth, jagged and dangerous."

The prisoner asked her attorney for a cup of water, and he asked the law clerk, who poured from a pitcher into a plastic cup and then brought both to the defense table. Action in a courtroom moved slowly.

It was difficult not to watch the prisoner; while those around her stood and waited, she never sat still. Her attorney studied her file, but his client shifted in her seat to have a second look at the courtroom behind her.

"Now she looks hopeful," Danielle said, "like a child waiting for a birthday cake." Danielle watched the prisoner's vibrant brown eyes scan her surroundings a second time, reading the faces of attorneys and their clients like a bookie scanning the figures on a betting sheet. Danielle figured the prisoner observed the police officer in the back near the door and saw the gun at his side. The young prisoner turned again to the left, glanced at the young people behind her dressed in suits, but swiveled her chair back to the front.

"She didn't spend much time looking at us, did she?" Chantal said. Danielle watched as the young woman dropped her head, but when her attorney turned to face her, she looked up into his eyes.

Danielle heard the defendant ask, "When does this thing start?"

The attorney smiled, holding her gaze. "Soon. Getting restless already?"

"I just want to watch you work. I want to see what you do to pay for such a nice suit," the defendant replied. "You smell good."

The attorney cleared his throat, and Danielle saw him look at the judge and pour himself a cup of water from the pitcher left on the table by the law clerk. "It's dry in here," he said. She smiled at him as she flipped her hair behind her shoulders.

"Do you think she's trying to turn him on?" Chantal asked.

"I think she's showing him that she has power too," Danielle said.

Danielle watched the prisoner press in closer to her young public defender. When he looked up, she pulled away. He watched her lift the back of her hair, revealing her bare neck, then returned to his documents.

The young prisoner, Danielle reflected, was not entirely similar to Hester Prynne, whose glossy hair had thrown off sunlight as she stood before the men and women of the Puritan town of Boston. The author had described its full radiance gathered around her shoulders, and her ladylike manner. While the defendant's hair was full and fell to her shoulders like Hester Prynne's, it lacked gloss the way an older model car no longer reflects the sun but absorbs it.

"Do you think this is her first court appearance?" asked Danielle.

Chantal shook her head. "This isn't even her second or third."

Danielle nodded in agreement and continued comparing the woman in front of her to the one she knew from a book. She decided that her comparison was becoming a study in contrasts. While Hester Prynne's life revolved around her illegitimate daughter, Pearl, this hearing was not about the prisoner's daughter or who her father was. Nina, the extern who had worked on her court file, told them that the State of California removed the prisoner's daughter from her custody four years ago, and the state now paid a foster family to care for her. No family members had stepped forward to take the little girl into their home. Today, however, the hearing was not about the child but about her mother's recent activities. Danielle wondered if the prisoner ever thought about the pearl she gave birth to but lost.

"If she doesn't stop spinning that chair," Chantal whispered, "I'm going to smack her."

"I'll hold the chair," said Danielle.

"Look at the guys. They're squirming in their seats," said Chantal. "No one is making jokes this morning."

"Even Dennis is riveted, and he has the attention span of a puppy," said Danielle.

Chantal added, "They're all imagining slipping between the sheets with her."

Danielle nodded.

"She looks like a hooker," Chantal stated and went back to the court document she was typing.

The prisoner's skin was firm and her shape sturdy but compliant. Danielle saw no bump in the back of her jumpsuit. What happened to her bra?

Danielle realized her own reactions exemplified a universal pattern. When a beautiful woman becomes an object of attention and controversy, other women become critical and suspicious. Danielle was doing the same without knowing the full story. "I don't understand exhibitionists," she admitted to Chantal. Chantal shrugged.

Like the women of 1642 Boston, Danielle thought, I want the prisoner punished. Those women felt the men in their small village were too merciful to Hester Prynne. They wanted the woman, who had given birth to a child without being married, to be ostracized as well.

"Did you ever read *The Scarlet Letter*?" Danielle asked.

When Chantal nodded yes, Danielle asked, "Do you think this defendant should be branded with a letter A on her forehead?"

"No, not unless she refuses to get her hair cut."

In the novel, the village women called Hester a "naughty baggage." The words were straight from Shakespeare. But when one of the village women said she ought to die, Hawthorne stepped into his novel in the next sentence to defend his heroine by saying that the accuser was the ugliest woman in the village. Hawthorne had fallen in love, Danielle realized, with the sinful character he had created. She wondered if she would do the same with the prisoner in front of her, but quickly dismissed the possibility.

While the attorneys waited for the judge to glance through the file before her, Danielle considered the fate of the prisoner. Would this woman recall the faces of her mother and father when she stood before the judge like Hester had? When she was released from jail, would this young prisoner provide for herself by sewing for the wealthy in her community and helping the poor? Danielle exhaled sharply and smiled.

"What's so funny?" asked Chantal. Danielle shook her head.

"You know," Danielle said, "we don't know anything about the men responsible for this prisoner's actions or Hester Prynne's defiance. They live in a shadowy world unknown to those who pass judgment."

Danielle knew that this young woman, like Hester before her, was in conflict with her community. She and Hester both defied the strict code of ethics around them and transgressed the rules of polite society. But was this young prisoner in front of her to blame? Were her actions a conscious choice like the actions of Hester, who decided to become intimate with the community's spiritual leader without being married to him? Or were the prisoner's actions today a delayed reaction to what had happened to her when she was too young to say no?

Judge Acker called the first name on her docket. "Counselor, bring your client to the podium." The young attorney stood and stepped forward with his client.

"Say and spell your name for the record, please," said the judge. The attorney nodded to his client, who spoke softly.

"Ma'am," said the judge, "the court reporter must enter your name in the record. To do that she must be able to hear you as you speak. Say again."

"Amanda Martinez," the prisoner said and spelled her name loudly enough for the reporter to hear.

"Thank you. It says here you were picked up for soliciting sex on May 2, 2013. Is that correct?" questioned the judge.

"Yes," the prisoner said. Her attorney whispered in her ear. She repeated, "Yes, Your Honor."

"It also says here that you are an exotic dancer at the Esquire Tap."

"Yes, Your Honor."

"It states that on the night of May 2, you danced nude without the required pasties and G-string. Is that correct?"

"Yes, Your Honor," said the defendant, "but I didn't know I needed them things. No one told me. Not my boss neither."

Danielle looked around. Even the young female externs, the ones who wore low-cut blouses and bent over in front of watching male eyes, listened. The other attorneys in the courtroom also watched and did not leave the room to call clients or talk with them in the hall.

"How old are you?" asked the judge.

"Nineteen," Amanda said as she squared her shoulders like the judge in front of her.

"For someone so young, you have a long police record." The judge reviewed the documents before her. "You were picked up for prostitution in Arizona when you were fifteen. Where are your parents?"

"I don't know where my dad is. He left when I was young. My mom is in jail."

"In what state?" asked Judge Acker.

"California," replied Amanda.

"When was the last time you saw her?"

"Before she went to jail."

"Counselor," ordered the judge, "step forward to the bench with your client, please."

The public defender took his client's arm and directed her to stand in front of the judge, who turned off her microphone and leaned forward.

"What do you think, Chantal?" Danielle asked.

"Her dad probably left because her mom caught him messing with her," Chantal said. "That's when my daddy left. My grandparents took me in so my mother could get herself together, but she never did." Chantal paused to take a breath. "So what do I think of this woman? I think she's a slut."

Danielle knew Chantal had been raised by her grandparents. One Saturday after their Defending Battered Women class, a class taught by Judge Acker, Chantal told her that she was flying to Georgia for Thanksgiving to see them. She was so happy she hugged Danielle. At the time Danielle did not ask for details, and today she wouldn't ask any personal questions either.

"I'm sorry you had a rough start, Chantal," Danielle said, but remained silent about the sordid details of her own life. She had stopped sharing those details years ago after ending therapy and group sessions. She had decided not to make a second career of her abuse.

"So what do you think of this girl?" Chantal asked.

"I am struck by her playful and seductive behavior with her attorney. She's tuned into him, but disconnected from what's happening to her. I wonder if he has any idea what he is dealing with."

"He only looks a few years older than our classmates," said Chantal.

"To them she just stepped out of an erotic movie," Danielle said. "They don't understand the abuse that probably led her into a life of strip clubs and prostitution."

Both women stood up. Danielle looked up at Chantal. "You know, when I wore heels, I was almost as tall as you. Of course, I haven't worn heels since my foot surgery, so now I'm shorter than nearly everyone. Older and shorter."

"And wiser," said Chantal.

Danielle smiled. "If I can remember what I've learned."

They walked down the hall to the jury room where they wrote court documents when trial was not in session.

"What do you think her chances are of getting out of this business?" asked Danielle.

"Zero," Chantal said as they stood under the camera, waiting to be buzzed into the rooms behind the court.

"I disagree," said Danielle. "I don't believe she's stuck in a life of stripping and lap dances."

"You're a dreamer, Danielle."

"No, I'm not. I'm a believer in redemption."

They grabbed their lunches from the refrigerator and joined several students who sat eating at the long table. Danielle pulled her chair up to the solid oak table, admiring its substantial character, and removed her lunch from a plastic grocery bag.

"Didn't we read a case about pasties and G-strings in Con Law?" asked Nina.

"Yeah, *Erie v. PAP'S A.M.*," said Roger, a trim young man whose colorful vests were a topic of conversation. "I got an A in Con Law."

"Everyone gets an A in Con Law, Roger," said Nina. "I booked it."

Danielle had become inured to the bolstering of her classmates. On a regular basis, they enhanced their reputations with new evidence supporting their cases before a jury of their peers. Danielle used to believe everything they said.

"Nude dancing is an inherently expressive condition, according to the Court," recited Steve, who had sat next to Danielle in the courtroom, ogling the stripper defendant. "The state cannot interfere with the expression of the erotic message. Laws have to be content neutral."

"What erotic message are these dancers expressing?" asked Danielle. "Do they express the dancer's desire for money to feed her cocaine habit or her alcohol addiction?"

"That's a stereotype, that exotic dancers are addicted to drugs," objected Nina.

"No, it's not," argued Chantal. "My cousin dated a woman who danced in a club. She did cocaine while she was a dancer, but after they started dating, she quit and went back to school."

Roger put on his glasses to Google exotic dancers. "Yes," he said, "a high percentage of dancers have drug or alcohol problems—70 percent."

"That's just one study," stated Nina. "Free expression is guaranteed by the Supreme Court. Women have a right to express themselves sexually. They just have to wear those pasties and G-strings."

Dennis, whose short attention span was engaged by the topic, asked, "How do those pasties stay on?"

"Must be a glue," said Nina. "Ouch! I bet it hurts when you take them off!"

"Is that why you decided to be a lawyer, Nina?" asked Steve, who peered over his glasses at the attractive woman seated across the table.

"F-ck you," she retorted.

"It says here," said Danielle as she read from her Con Law book, "that nude dancing falls in the outer ambit of the First Amendment's protection."

"What exactly is an ambit?" asked Dennis.

"A pasty that won't come off," blurted Steve. Danielle laughed with her classmates.

"One of the justices said any ban on nudity suppresses the erotic message," said Roger as he ran his fingers through his hair.

"To think," said Danielle, "that Justice Sandra Day O'Connor agreed with the opinion. She helped create the delusion that exotic dancing is freedom and not what it really is: exploitation of young women."

Feeling betrayed by the Court's ruling and the only woman on the Court at the time, Danielle threw the remnants of her lunch into the garbage can and walked to the door. "See you later," she said. As she opened the door, she heard Nina say, "She's so out of it!" The door closed, and Danielle headed toward the judge's chambers, wondering if young women today ever questioned what they read. On the other hand, maybe Nina was right.

Danielle asked Paul, Judge Acker's law clerk, if the judge was with someone, and when he said no, she knocked on the door to her chamber. The judge answered the door while eating from a Tupperware container. "Danielle, come in. I have more. Do you want some? It's tuna casserole I brought from home."

"No, thanks," Danielle said as she sat down in front of the judge's huge desk. Judge Acker continued her phone conversation and nearly disappeared behind the pile of folders, law books, and pictures of her five children. Danielle looked at the pictures of roses on the burgundy walls of the judge's chamber, pictures painted by domestic abuse victims who lived in shelters set up to protect them. Judge Acker had told her she purchased the artwork at fundraisers for the shelters.

"What's on your mind?" asked Judge Acker, standing over her. "The young woman with the long rap sheet?"

"Yes," Danielle said, looking up at the judge. "What's her story?"

"She's typical of the young women who dance in clubs and then start seeing customers their bosses set them up with," explained the judge, and she once again assumed the role of professor. Danielle wondered if Judge Acker expected her to take notes. "She said her mother's boyfriends abused her, so she left. She quit school to assert her independence but fell into the biggest trap there is for poor women with pretty faces and no education. They dream of empowering themselves by making a lot of money dancing in clubs."

"So what can you do for her?" asked Danielle.

"I want to keep her in jail as long as I can and off the streets. I hope I can eventually send her to the battered women's shelter. I have to check first to see if any beds are available." Women's groups would approve of everything Judge Acker said. But Danielle felt something was missing every time they talked. "Are you sure you're not hungry?" the judge asked again, playing the role of polite hostess very well.

Danielle shook her head. "But can't she leave a women's shelter whenever she wants? Do you think she'll stay?"

"I imagine she'll hook up with her boyfriend as soon as he calls. But I have to do something," said Judge Acker as she leaned over and grabbed two bottles of water from a small refrigerator. She handed one to Danielle.

"Thank you," said Danielle. She opened the water bottle, but before she drank she looked at the judge and asked, hoping to see some sign of emotion, "Doesn't this ever get to you?"

"Not really. When I put on the robe, the robe takes over. When I wear the robe, you wouldn't believe what people tell me," Judge Acker said. "It's all in the robe."

As both women drank water from their plastic bottles, Danielle decided the answer sounded rehearsed, like dialogue in a play about personal safety.

"You don't look too happy," observed Judge Adkins, pushing aside papers for a place to put the bottle.

"No," Danielle admitted. "I find it sad to observe these cases, especially the young people with no lives and no possibilities. The walls of a courthouse are built in futility. It's amazing that you don't feel it."

"Yes, it is sad," agreed the judge, "especially for someone of your age and experience. The younger externs haven't lived much life. What they observe isn't real to them." Judge Acker put the remaining casserole into the small refrigerator. "Didn't you say you taught in the inner city?"

"Yes, I did, but it wasn't sad," explained Danielle. "In teaching, there is still so much hope."

"Yes, I understand." Judge Acker nodded. "You taught them when their lives were filled with possibilities whereas I meet them after they make wrong choices, lots of them."

"In the jury room we were talking about the G-strings and pasties case," said Danielle. "What kind of protection is a string and two nipple covers? That decision exploits the very women it claims to liberate."

"It doesn't protect any of them," agreed the judge, "but the law does make it possible for the porn industry to make a lot of money. But that's not what's on your mind, Danielle. I see that look on your face. You want to help her, don't you?"

Danielle thought about that. It frustrated her that Judge Acker knew her so well while she could not begin to penetrate the judge's professional veneer.

"She's not beyond redemption; no one is," said Judge Acker. "But maybe I'm an optimist."

Paul knocked and opened the door. "It's time."

Judge Acker rose. From its hanger, she removed her black robe with the white lace collar. She slipped into it, squared her shoulders, and left her chambers for the courtroom where more lawyers and their clients waited. Danielle would wait as well.

Part Two

Danielle decided to see for herself where Amanda Martinez worked and what she had to do to please her boss. She asked Chantal to go with her.

"Sure, I'll go with you," Chantal said. "Since I want to become a public defender, this will be a good experience."

Later in the week, they drove to the other side of town. A river separated the commercial center of town from the section that had lost its economic promise. Before crossing the bridge, Danielle slowed down to look for a parking spot. She found one under a street light at the bottom of the bridge. The river flowed quietly beneath steel girders unaware of the activity around it.

After locking the car, they walked a block to the Esquire Tap. At the top of the bridge, Danielle had a better view of the surrounding neighborhood.

"Do you remember the River Styx in mythology?" Danielle asked.

"Kind of," Chantal said. "Didn't someone ferry the dead across the river to the other world?"

"Yes, maybe that's where we're going tonight, to the other side."

"Just pretend that we're doing investigative journalism," said Chantal.

Danielle pulled her coat closed. "It's chilly tonight. Thanks for coming with me."

"Not to worry," Chantal said as she looked around her. "This isn't a very good section of town, is it? Abandoned buildings and empty lots."

"Yes, the secondary effects caused by adult bookstores and strip clubs," Danielle said, remembering the line from her textbook. "I wonder which came first."

"Looks like an abandoned factory across the street," said Chantal. "The first floor windows are boarded up. There must be gangs in the neighborhood."

Danielle looked across the street and then at the empty lots surrounding the Esquire. "Do you see all the broken furniture outside in the lot? Maybe they're setting up for a yard sale."

"We should come back. I'd like to buy that furry blue sofa," said Chantal. "I could sew up the rip in the middle myself."

"If you need more furniture, how about that metal desk leaning into the ground?" asked Danielle. "The one with two missing legs?"

They stopped in front of the Esquire Tap. Fliers advertising upcoming bands and singers papered the glass door and prevented Danielle from seeing inside. "Not exactly upscale, is it?" she said as she pulled open the door and entered the two-story red brick building.

"Are you hoping to talk her out of dancing in adult clubs? Is that really why we're here?" asked Chantal, who stopped in front of a tall thin man who asked them for money.

"I want to see her in her work environment," Danielle said as she rummaged through her purse for money. "Do I think I can talk her out of stripping? No, I don't." Danielle handed the man ten dollars. "I would like to talk with her, though, one human being to another."

"I bet she'll be so drugged up she won't remember a word you say," said Chantal.

After the doorman took their money and carded Chantal, he looked at Danielle. "Ladies' night out?" he asked, his Adam's apple bobbing up and down.

"Right," said Danielle, and the two law externs followed the lights down the darkened hallway. They walked past a young man hunched over a colorful video arcade.

"What the—" he said and pulled off his baseball cap, revealing a receding hairline that belied his young face.

The hallway opened into a large dimly lit room where a DJ played country-and-western music. "Sounds like Rascal Flatts," Danielle said and kept walking.

"This must be the room where they dance," Chantal said.

"There's the stage." Danielle pointed and quickly stuffed her hand into her pocket. "This is like an adults-only fieldtrip."

A short waitress in her late thirties approached them. "Do you ladies want to eat?" she asked. When they nodded yes, she told them to follow her and led them up two steps into a room filled with round tables and chairs. Candles glowed from red glass vases set on each table. When they sat down, Danielle passed her fingers over a cigarette burn in the blue tablecloth. The table wobbled.

"This place almost looks like a regular restaurant and bar," said Danielle as she pulled her coat closer and looked around. "We must look like officers of the court tonight. We're both dressed in black."

"It's become a habit since we spend so much time sitting in a courtroom," said Chantal, looking across the room. "See the couple sitting on the couch in the corner, to the right of the stage? She looks bored and it's only 10:30."

Across the room, Danielle could see a skimpily clad young woman sitting on a furry blue couch. As she smoked, the older man sitting next to her slid his hand up her short skirt. Empty cocktail glasses circled their feet. The young woman dropped her cigarette into one of the empty glasses and motioned to a passing waitress. The waitress stopped, and when she showed the man a calendar of scantily clad women, he withdrew his hand, stood up, and grabbed his wallet. After spending his money, he sat down. The young woman on the couch smiled, grabbed his hand, and placed it back under her skirt.

"Not very subtle, is she?" said Chantal. "Spend money first, then touch me."

Danielle watched as the young woman spoke into his ear and nodded toward a door covered by a curtain. They both stood up, and the woman pulled the man into the dark.

"She's got the power going in," Danielle observed, "but who has it when they step back outside?" She paused. "I sound like a feminist."

"This place would make any woman a feminist," said Chantal. "Well. Except Nina."

"Feminists today only think about wage equality. So if the women working here make good money, they aren't concerned."

"No," said Chantal, "they don't much care what happens to the souls of these women. Do feminists even believe in souls?"

Danielle shrugged. "We'll have to ask Nina."

Chantal read the menu while Danielle looked at the stage. She saw men of all ages standing around or sitting on short barstools, waiting for the show to begin. Small white lights outlined the stage, which curved out into the room. "Look at the gigantic cutouts on both sides of the stage," she said. "They look like naked paper dolls."

The tableau in front of the stage reminded Danielle of a painting called "Nighthawks." Edward Hopper had painted a picture of an all-night diner where a few customers sat around a counter, staring into coffee cups. Here the men stared into glasses of alcohol and waited for a stranger to take off her clothes. Different settings but the same feeling of isolation.

Chantal closed the menu, and both women watched the action in front of the stage. A large bearded man with a beer belly caught sight of a scantily clad dancer walking by. He swiveled around on his stool, grabbed her around the waist, and pulled her to his chest.

"Chantal, your mouth is open," said Danielle. "I guess mine is too."

Chantal gasped. "Did he just put his fingers inside her panties?"

"I think so, and she doesn't look too happy about it."

"But now she's smiling like nothing happened!" said Chantal. "She's hurrying over to that table of college boys."

Danielle heard the rejected man yell at the woman's retreating figure. "What did he yell at her?"

"I think he called her a c-nt!" said Chantal.

"The college boys look as shocked as we are," said Danielle. "I didn't think we'd see forced sex in the open like that. Don't tell your grandparents I took you here. I feel terrible."

"Danielle, I made the decision to come. Besides, my grandparents know what kind of people I'll be defending or prosecuting." Chantal continued to watch the action around the stage.

"He's waving his glass around," said Danielle. "He must need another drink."

Danielle watched as a buxom waitress walked by, took his glass, and paused to get his order. The large man watched her walk away. As he waited for his fresh drink, he spun around on his barstool and faced the center of the room, his leg bouncing up and down to a private rhythm.

When the waitress returned with his drink, he placed the drink behind him on the stage. Before paying, he kicked out his legs, trapping the young woman between them. He rubbed her behind, which was exposed under her scanty skirt and thong. A gray-haired guy sitting next to him bent over and ogled her breasts (Please tone this down). When the two men started to argue over her, she broke free from their grasp and quickly walked away, a smile on her face.

"The customer must always be right in here," Danielle observed.

A thin blonde waitress approached their table. She wore short shorts and a tight black knit top with the bar's name stretched across her breasts.

"Ladies, what are you drinking tonight?" she asked. Her smile exposed two missing teeth at the side of her mouth, and Danielle noticed that the part in her hair revealed the truth about her blonde hair.

"I'll take a 7 Up," said Danielle.

"A Seven and Seven?" asked the waitress.

"No, just a plain 7 Up."

"I'll take one too," said Chantal, "and a cheeseburger with onion and pickles, and fries."

Danielle asked, "How many dancers perform tonight?"

"On weekdays, about ten. On weekends up to thirty," she said as she scooped up the menus. "Be right back, ladies, with your order."

To the right of the stage, Danielle saw a full bar lit by overhead red lights. The seats in front were all taken by men who drank, smoked cigarettes, and chatted with the female bartender, who joked with them.

"Do you see the naked Barbie doll sitting in the oversized martini glass?" said Chantal.

"Where?" Danielle asked.

"On the right side of the bar near the DJ."

Danielle observed. "The bartender is built just like the Barbie doll. Do you like the tattoos on her arms?"

Chantal shook her head. "I don't like tattoos on men or women, especially not on women, but I like the low-riding jeans and tank top she's wearing."

"The bartender looks about forty," said Danielle. "Hey, she shakes her ponytail the same way Amanda shook her hair in court."

The bartender checked her phone and looked out into the room.

"The place looks full," said Danielle. "Maybe seventy-five or so people are here."

Chantal sat up straight. "Look at that young woman at the bar. She's wearing a shiny black robe. The bartender just handed her something small. What do you think it was?"

"Probably drugs," said Danielle. "Wait a minute! That's Amanda!"

Danielle watched Amanda shove the object into her pocket and quickly walk through the door next to the stage.

"I figured she was into drugs," said Chantal. "You'd have to be to work here with all of these men pawing you."

"I wonder when she'll dance," said Danielle.

Around their table Danielle saw couples staring into menus. Another waitress dressed in shorts and an unbuttoned blouse and pushup bra brought an order of ribs and fries for the couple behind them.

"The barbecue ribs smell good, but who would bring a date here?" Chantal said.

Danielle lifted her glass and watched as red and blue overhead lights flashed across the stage. A siren went off, and a tall man dressed in a monkey suit and mask loped onto the stage. He turned on the handheld microphone. Danielle wondered if he would blow into it. He did.

"Welcome to the Esquire Pub, ladies and gentlemen," he said, his voice low and husky. "And college students," he added, waving his hairy arm in their direction. The college boys hooted and cheered for their university. Predictable, thought Danielle. When the boys settled down, the master of ceremonies continued.

"Get ready for some fun and excitement," he promised. "You have a fantasy? We have a girl. You want to spice up your love life? You've come to the right place. First up at the eleven o'clock set is a sexy cowgirl from the great state of Texas. She's gonna lasso your hearts and your other parts too. Short and sweet, but big where it counts. Put your hands together for Brandy."

Drums rolled, and a cowgirl from Texas took the stage, whirling a lasso. She snapped the rope on the floor and raised it into the air. Dressed in chaps and not much else, she tossed the rope to the side and bent over a chair, legs spread, her backside waving like a state flag in the air. The speakers blasted out "Save a Horse, Ride a Cowboy" by Big & Rich as she gyrated to the music. Danielle covered her ears when the audience erupted in catcalls and whistles. From behind the curtains, Monkey Man grabbed the chair and thrust an inflated phallus into the dancer's hands. She embraced the huge phallus, then rode it like a horse.

When the dancing cowgirl pulled off her cowboy hat and threw it offstage, the waitress appeared with Chantal's cheeseburger and fries and scooted it in front of her. From her apron pocket, she pulled a plastic bottle of catsup and dropped it on the table. "Excuse me," said Danielle, "but where do the stairs lead? Is there another dance floor upstairs?"

"Upstairs are rooms for private dances. If the dancers want to make extra money, they take customers up there. Can I get you anything else?" When both women shook their heads, she left.

Monkey Man introduced the second dancer, who took the stage when 38 Special's "Teacher, Teacher" boomed from the speakers. Danielle watched as a blonde young woman with long legs crossed the stage in a burlesque rendition of teacher attire. By the end of her song and dance, she was stripped down to the requisite pasties and G-string.

"Is she legal?" asked Chantal.

Danielle nodded. "Her free speech rights are protected, and she didn't say a word."

When the song finished, Danielle heard a drum roll. Monkey Man slid across the stage, stopped, and lifted his microphone. "Our next little girl comes to us all the way from California. She's just sweet sixteen and ready to please. Put your hands together for Sparkle!" he boomed, and AC/DC tore out of the speakers. Guitars and gravelly voices roared from dual speakers vibrating on both sides of the stage as the DJ played "You Shook Me All Night Long."

"Here she is," said Danielle as she watched the prisoner from the court strut across the stage wearing tall black boots with five-inch heels and a black pleated skirt with ruffles along the bottom. Under the skirt she wore a black bikini. A short black vest couldn't completely conceal thin black straps that crisscrossed her breasts. A black leather cap covered her jagged black hair; its large bill hid her eyes. The penitent in the orange jumpsuit had transformed herself into a motorcycle vixen.

The men sitting in front of the stage stood and cheered. Some whistled; others simply sat and stared. One man shot his hand into his pants pocket. The men at the bar smiled and toasted her with fresh drinks in their hands. "Hey, bitch," yelled a short stocky man. "I got something for you!" He thrust out his hips, rocked to the music, and laughed.

Sparkle looked down at the men below her who cheered her every move the way some men cheered their favorite sports teams. For the length of the song, she held them captive. Every eye in the place was on her. She gyrated her hips and strutted back and forth across the stage, tossing first her hat and then her skirt. Next, she tossed the vest, and finally she pulled off the bikini, exposing a black G-string.

"Good girl," said Chantal, "she's wearing the required pasties and G-string."

Danielle nodded. "She's following the law."

Chantal leaned over and said, "They really like her. You think she'll leave this? Seriously?"

Danielle shrugged.

They watched as the bearded man attempted to climb over the lights onto the stage. Sparkle put her black boot on his chest and pushed him back over the side of the stage. When he landed on the floor, the crowd roared. Sparkle walked offstage wiping her hands back and forth, like she had just cleaned up a big mess. Danielle saw the corners of Amanda's mouth turn up and thought the young woman looked pleased with herself, as if she had just reestablished law and order.

The woman sitting at the table behind them got up and walked to the ladies' room. Danielle stood up and said to Chantal, "I'm going with her. I don't want to be in the restroom by myself."

When she returned to the table, she said, "I saw one of the dancers snort coke in a bathroom stall. She asked me if I was a cop; must be the black attire."

"What did you tell her?" asked Chantal.

"I told her I wasn't, and she invited me to join her," said Danielle. "Have you seen Amanda?"

Chantal shook her head and yawned. "This is getting as boring as the court on a slow day."

After thirty minutes and several dancers later, Danielle watched as Amanda walked down the stairs with two men who laughed and joked with her. One man grabbed her breast while the other man felt her bottom. She waved them off and walked down the two steps from the restaurant to the main floor and over to the bar. Danielle wondered if the bartender would give her another packet, but instead she handed her a drink. Amanda gulped it down, and the bartender handed her another. Before she could finish it, an older man approached her. Taking his hand, she slipped off the barstool, smiled up at him, and stroked his chest. They crossed the floor and mounted the steps to the private rooms. Fifteen minutes later, Danielle saw Amanda descending the stairs with her client. Over his shoulder, he yelled, "See you around, bitch."

At 12:30, Amanda performed her first number again. At one o'clock, Danielle watched her walk out the stage door with Monkey Man, who escorted her to the exit. She stopped at the door and stepped out of her gold spiked heels long enough to rub her toes. She wore a dark coat and tight jeans. The black cap covered her head.

While Amanda chatted with Monkey Man, Danielle showed Chantal the package in her purse. "Did you buy her a present?" asked Chantal.

"Yes," explained Danielle. "I want to reach out to her, and I'm giving her something she will receive."

They stood up, stretched, and buttoned their coats. With Chantal, Danielle followed the young woman into the parking lot. Chantal asked, "Do you see that heavy man next to the building?"

Danielle looked back at the building and grimaced as she watched the man unzip his pants and flash Amanda.

"Hey, bitch," he yelled. "I'm comin' home with you."

"Not tonight, Harry," Amanda said. The man walked to his truck, got in, and started it up. He put the driver's window down, lit a cigarette, and glared at Amanda.

Danielle and Chantal followed Amanda. When Amanda became aware of the two women behind her, she looked over her shoulder.

"I bet your feet are killing you," said Danielle, stepping forward and reaching into her bag. "You were on your feet all night." She retrieved a pair of pink fluffy slippers and held them out to the young woman, who had turned around to face them.

Amanda didn't look at her, Danielle noticed, but above her head. "My feet hurt like hell! What's that?"

"A pair of slippers," said Danielle. "They're for you."

"Wait a minute!" Amanda said. Danielle watched the young woman's head roll slightly to the side. "I don't know you. What do you want?"

"You're right. You don't know us," said Danielle. "We saw you at the circuit court when you were there with your attorney. We wanted to see where you danced."

Danielle watched Amanda look at the slippers. "At the court?" she said, looking confused. "Pink is my favorite color. Are they for me?"

"Yes," said Danielle. "Here, take them."

Amanda looked around her, reached out, and took the slippers. "Okay, thanks," she said, swiping the slippers like a credit card. "That's it? You don't want anything?"

"No, we hope you enjoy wearing them. Have a good night," Danielle said as she started to walk away.

Amanda put her hand on her hip. "Wait! Are you two church ladies?"

"No," said Danielle. "We're law students. My friend Chantal here is going to be a public defender like your attorney."

"You don't want anything from me? You just go around giving gifts like Santa Claus?" Danielle watched her look around the parking lot. Amanda removed her hat and scratched her head.

"Just like Santa Claus," said Chantal. "So what do you think of the men at the club?"

"Are you kidding me?" Amanda said. "They're freaks! You seen how they act."

"Does Monkey Man make sure they don't hurt you?" asked Danielle.

"Hell, no," she said. "He says, 'Keep 'em coming back for more.' He don't care what they do, long as they spend their money. But I'll be outta here real soon."

"Where are you going?" asked Chantal.

"Vegas," Amanda said. "Gonna get a real good job in a show club in Vegas and just dance. This here is just a hustle club."

Danielle noticed that Amanda was looking at her quizzically. "This here is a hustle club," Amanda repeated. "You gotta hustle for tips. You want more money? You do private dances and sell stuff for the club."

"Oh, I understand," Danielle said.

Chantal added, "We hope your feet feel better."

Danielle started to walk away but stopped. "Will that guy in the truck follow you home?"

"Yeah. Harry follows me out every night," Amanda said, touching the fuzzy pink slippers in her hands. "Sometimes he's mean, but he spends a lot of money at the club so I treat him good." She put her hand through the slipper. "You better get out of here before my boyfriend pulls up. He gets mad when I talk to people. He'd really get mad if he knew you give me these slippers." She stuffed the slippers inside her bag and yelled at Harry. "Get lost, Harry. Here comes Randy."

Danielle watched as Amanda looked around the parking lot and then pulled out a pack of cigarettes. She lit one and stood by herself smoking. At the top of the bridge, Danielle looked back and saw a black Ram truck pull into the lot. Amanda walked over and climbed inside.

"Why do you care about this particular law offender?" asked Chantal as they walked over the bridge. "We've seen a lot of them this summer."

"I don't know," said Danielle. "If I looked like Amanda, maybe I would have become a stripper."

Puzzled, Chantal asked, "Why would you have gone down this path?"

"You know how Amanda's past is all over her?" Danielle asked. "Well, mine isn't. I look like a very straight lady from the suburbs."

"I guess you can't see my past either," said Chantal.

"I have a bad feeling about her boyfriend, Randy," Danielle said.

"He does fit the profile of an abusive male," said Chantal. "She can't talk with anyone or get close to anyone but him. She stuffed the slippers into her bag and zipped it up so he wouldn't see."

"Yes, and did you notice her face when she looked around the parking lot for him?" said Danielle. "She looked afraid."

Chantal nodded. "I've got a headache and I smell like onions and cigarette smoke."

"So do I, sister, so do I," said Danielle, "except for the onions."

Part Three

Several weeks later, as their externships drew to a close, Danielle called the Esquire Tap. Then she called Chantal. "I just called the Esquire Tap to find out when Amanda would dance this weekend," Danielle said.

"What did you find out? Is she still there?"

"No, she's not dancing anytime soon," said Danielle. "She's in the hospital."

"Would they tell you what happened?" asked Chantal.

"The woman whispered that her boyfriend beat her up."

"So you want to visit her, don't you?" said Chantal. "You want to make sure she presses charges against him."

"Yes," admitted Danielle. "Will you come along?"

Chantal was standing in front of her apartment building when Danielle picked her up that afternoon. "What did you bring for her this time?" Chantal asked as she closed the car door. Danielle nodded toward the backseat.

"Pink roses. Nice," Chantal said. "And pink is her favorite color. I still think you're a dreamer."

When they found the room, Danielle didn't see any visitors. Amanda sat in the hospital bed wearing a faded yellow hospital gown. The top of her head had been shaved and stitches held back her hair like a twisted barrette. Amanda seemed to watch her soap opera with the focus of a racecar driver. Danielle knocked on the door, and they entered the room.

Amanda looked up but Danielle could tell she did not recognize them. A golf-ball-sized welt protruded like a third eye in the middle of her brow, and Danielle winced at the sight of her black and blue eyes; one eye was nearly swollen shut. Stitches ran down the side of her arm, the one that held the remote, like the dividing line in a highway.

"We saw you dance at the Esquire," Danielle said. "We talked with you in the parking lot." Amanda lowered the volume and stared at them.

"I talk to a lot of people in the parking lot," she said.

"No, you don't," said Danielle. "You told us Randy didn't like it."

"We gave you the pink slippers," said Chantal, "and you thought we were church ladies."

"Oh, right," Amanda said as she looked at the flowers Danielle held in her hand. "Are those flowers for me?"

"Yes," Danielle said as she handed them to her. Danielle picked up the empty vase on the table next to Amanda's bed and filled it with water. "Here. You can put the flowers in the vase." She watched Amanda work to get all the stems into the mouth of the vase. When she did, she held the vase out in front of her, like a child who can't reach the table and hopes her mother will do it for her. Danielle took the vase and set the flowers on the table next to the bed.

"Did the club tell you where I was?" Amanda asked.

"Yes," said Danielle.

"So you want to know what happened, right?"

"No. We already know."

"Well, it was an accident. That's all," explained Amanda. "All my fault, and now he's in jail. And he didn't do nothing."

"Who called the police?" asked Chantal.

The young woman shrugged. "Probably some nosy neighbor."

"Do you have a place to stay when you get out of here?" asked Chantal.

"I'll go back to the apartment. He'll be out soon. I ain't pressing no charges 'cause it's all a big misunderstanding."

"Amanda, is this the first time he's beaten you?" asked Danielle.

Amanda ignored the question. "I can't dance. How am I gonna pay the rent?" She started to cry.

Danielle sat down in the chair next to the bed and handed her a tissue. "Do you want some water?" When Amanda nodded yes, Danielle filled a plastic cup with water for her.

Danielle waited for her to sip. "Do you know who gave you your name?"

"My mom, I guess," Amanda said.

"Do you know what your name means?"

"Do names have a meaning?"

"Yes, they do," said Danielle. "Chantal's name means 'a lovely song.'"

Amanda looked the way Danielle remembered her students always looked when she was about to tell them the end of the story, wide-eyed and expectant.

"Your name means 'worthy of love,'" explained Danielle. "You are worthy of love, Amanda, love that doesn't hurt."

Amanda cocked her head and looked at Danielle.

Danielle stood up from her chair. "I'm sorry you're hurting. You're probably tired and want to rest, so we'll leave."

Amanda leaned back into the pillows behind her and turned off the TV.

"Enjoy the flowers," said Chantal, "and take good care of yourself."

"Feel better," said Danielle as she walked out the door.

The two law students walked down the corridor to the elevator. "Are you crying?" asked Chantal.

Danielle dug a tissue out of her pocket and wiped her eyes. "I was afraid this would happen."

Chantal said softly, "Amanda isn't going to change as much as you would like her to."

Danielle inhaled. "I refuse to believe that," she said. But as she exhaled, she felt her shoulders drop.

The legal externs stood at the elevator door. It pinged, and a young and very good-looking man exited. He looked at Danielle and paused.

"Excuse me," said Danielle, "but aren't you Amanda Martinez's attorney?"

"And you are?" asked the representative of the court.

"I'm Danielle and this is Chantal." She inhaled the aroma of his very fine cologne. "We're both externs in Judge Acker's courtroom. We saw you with Amanda on Motion's Day a couple of months ago."

The man smiled and extended his hand. "I'm Shane Goodell."

"Amanda really looks bad," said Chantal. "I hope you can convince her to press charges against her boyfriend, Randy."

"That's exactly what I hope to do," said Shane. "Did you talk to her about not withdrawing her case?"

"No. We just wanted to see her," said Danielle.

"Amanda's mother is meeting me here," said Shane as he checked his iPhone. "We hope to explain how important it is for her to go ahead with a criminal case against this guy."

"I hope you and her mother are successful," said Danielle.

"Thanks, I hope we are too." Shane turned and headed down the hall.

"Do you think he and her mother will be successful?" asked Danielle.

"Hard to say," said Chantal. "She seemed really scared."

"Maybe he can convince her with his looks and fine fragrance not to withdraw her charges."

When the elevator arrived, they stepped inside.

Part Four

Paul, Judge Acker's law clerk, told her the news when Danielle walked into his office at the circuit court. "She's pressing charges against the boyfriend who beat her up," he said. "After the prosecutor took pictures of her injuries at the hospital, he called her attorney. He went to the hospital, and with her mother's help they encouraged her to press charges."

"Whose court was the case assigned to?"

"Guess."

Danielle smiled. "Amanda's boyfriend doesn't know what he's in for!"

Judge Acker stepped out of her chambers. "You heard?"

"Yes," Danielle said. "Oh, happy day!"

"I know you're happy," Judge Acker cautioned, "but don't forget how many abused women press charges and then don't show up for court."

"Yes, I know, but when she was in the hospital, she told me she wouldn't press charges because it was her fault. You know, the typical excuse. She's making progress."

Part Five

Danielle knew the statistics. But she hoped Amanda would not be one of the majority of abused women who backed out at the last minute.

The prosecutor was ready for the case. Paul told Danielle that he had been on call the weekend Amanda was in the hospital, had taken the photographs of her injuries himself, and would use them in trial. He stood a little over six feet, taller than the defendant—a white male about 5'10" and 210 pounds. Paul told her he often became physical with the defendants to show the jury exactly what had occurred to the victim.

Danielle thought Randy was a textbook case of an abusive male. He blamed the victim and presented himself as the responsible and reasonable person in the relationship. He was good-looking and very charming. The first day Randy took the stand, Amanda was not in the courtroom. She had not been there except for the day she testified, after which she never reappeared. But her mother sat through every day of the trial. Danielle saw her sitting in the center of the spectator section of the courtroom, her attention focused on the trial.

When the prosecutor stood up to question the defendant, he started by asking him to tell the jury what happened on New Year's Eve in 2012.

"See, I'm the guy who says, 'Stop arguing. Let's have a good time,'" Randy told the jury. "I had a couple of drinks, but Amanda, you know, she drank all night. She was slipping out to the bathroom to use cocaine."

"How do you know she was using cocaine?" asked the prosecutor.

"I seen her using in the women's bathroom."

"What happened during the drive home to your apartment?"

"I knew she was high. She drunk all night," Randy said. "I told her she shouldn't be driving no car after all that drinking, so I drove us home. On the way home, she tried to grab my phone. But I didn't choke her. I just put my hand on her neck to get my phone back. I said, 'Amanda, let go of my phone.'"

"How did she get the red marks on her neck?"

"Well, I didn't squeeze that hard," Randy explained. "I just wanted my phone back."

As Danielle took notes, she smiled as she wrote down the defendant's words. The prosecutor was exposing him for what he was.

"What did she do next?" asked the attorney.

"She spit at me. I pulled up to my place and said, 'Get your stuff. You're not staying at my place.'"

"Then what happened?"

"She argued with me in front of my car," Randy said. "Then she started running up the hill by my house, but slipped on the snow. I went after her because she was screaming."

"Did you punch her?"

"No, sir, because I couldn't catch up to her." Randy shifted in his seat. "When I did she was on the ground, screaming her lungs out. I tried to help her up, but she bit me on the hand. I said, 'Why you acting a fool?' I backhanded her. I tried to get her to stop."

"Are you telling the jury you slapped her?" asked the prosecutor.

"Yes, sir," said the defendant. "That's what I'm saying."

"Are you saying a slap made the knot on her face?"

"Yes."

"Who called the police?"

"I don't know. I didn't. When they got to my house, they didn't knock . . . just walked right in. That's against the law, ain't it?"

"What did Amanda put over her eye?"

"A bag of frozen vegetables."

"According to the tape of the 911 call, you told the responder that you had been robbed," said the prosecutor. "Did you say you had been robbed?"

"You know, some things about that night are kinda hazy, you know?" Randy said.

"Why did you run away from the cops when you got outside?"

"The cops wanted me to run. You know, they set me up. But I burned 'em; they were way behind me." Randy smiled, the memory of his victory fresh in his mind.

"Why didn't you stop when they told you to stop?"

"I didn't hear them tell me to stop. I could have jumped the fence," the defendant said, "but the big cop jumped on me with his full weight."

"Did you hit Amanda Martinez with your closed fist?"

"No, I just backhanded her to get her to stop screaming," Randy explained. "She was disturbing the neighbors."

"The pictures show an egg-shaped protrusion between her eyes. How could a slap make that kind of swelling?" asked the prosecutor.

"She kept falling down."

"Are you saying she fell on her eye?"

"Yeah, she fell down."

"Would you please stand and demonstrate on me how you hit her?" asked the prosecutor, who strode to the witness stand. Randy stood up and stepped out of the witness box.

"Show me how you slapped her."

The defendant lightly swung his hand against the man's face.

"That's how you hit her?" the prosecutor asked. "The jury can see the pictures of the victim in the hospital. Does a slap make a knot on someone's forehead?"

Randy didn't answer as the picture of Amanda's injuries flashed on the overhead screen.

"Now pick me up the way you said you picked up the victim," instructed the prosecutor.

The defendant walked behind the taller man and picked him up around his waist.

"If that's how you picked up the victim," the prosecutor said, "why was a clump of her hair missing?"

The defendant slunk back to his seat beside the judge.

On cross-examination, the public defender asked a few questions. Danielle wondered how he was going to be able to defend his client.

"Were you intending to injure?" Randy's attorney asked.

"No," said Randy.

"Were you intending to hurt the victim?"

"No."

"Why did you run from the cops?"

"I ran because I was upset. The cops was against me because I burned 'em when I ran."

"Were you ever on your back?"

"No," said Randy. "That one cop tried to pull me down, but he couldn't."

"How did the mud get on your shirt?"

"The cop must have put it there."

"No more questions, Your Honor," said the prosecutor.

Danielle watched Judge Acker give the jury instructions after closing arguments. Paul led the jury out of the jury box for deliberations.

Danielle looked around the courtroom. It was nearly empty. She had seen Amanda's mother every day in court and decided to look for her outside the building. Near the doors to the courthouse, Amanda's mother stood alone, smoking a cigarette. Danielle walked over to where she stood, rehearsing in her head what she would say.

"Hi, my name is Danielle," she said. "I'm a law graduate. I wanted you to know how much I admire your daughter. It took a lot of courage for her to go through with the trial." Amanda's mother just listened. Did she believe her, Danielle wondered. Would she think she was making fun of her daughter?

"This ain't the first time Amanda pressed charges, you know," the woman said, crushing the cigarette butt beneath her shoe. "I kept telling her she had to go through with it. She had to get rid of him."

"You're a good mother," Danielle said. "I respect you both."

The woman paused and looked at Danielle, but she continued. "Yeah, she finally did it. It's about time. That man was all charm on the outside but a monster inside." She turned and walked back into the courthouse to wait for the verdict.

Danielle was not surprised but immensely relieved. The verdict was unanimous on all counts: domestic violence, obstruction of justice, and filing a false police report. Judge Acker sentenced the defendant to the maximum ten years in prison.

— ∞ —

Danielle sighed as she walked past the roses to her car. The sun was setting on the other side of the courthouse, so the roses now bloomed in the shade. She wondered what Amanda would do now. Would she go back to dancing at the Esquire Tap or would she, like Hester Prynne, leave what was familiar and strike out on her own in another direction?

Hester Prynne left her native Boston but returned years later, and although she resumed wearing the scarlet letter, she created for herself a life of dignity and independence. Would Amanda do the same?

STORY CHANGES EVERYTHING

Genesis 2:16

You may freely eat the fruit of every tree in the garden—except the tree of the knowledge of good and evil. If you eat its fruit, you are sure to die.

Soundlessly the entrance doors closed. Opposite the entrance towered colorless walls bearing the imprint of bamboo forms into which concrete had been poured. The courthouse, a gift from the Chinese and designed by Wang Shu, confused the legal community and public as well. New York critics labeled Shu's design deceptively simple. Judges and prosecutors agreed the design was deceptive. The public agreed the building project successfully salvaged most of the materials from demolition sites around the city but remained unconvinced that the building was simple, accessible, or efficient. Perhaps a Midwestern town lacked the necessary sophistication to appreciate a gift so great.

In the middle of the concrete wall appeared a second set of double black doors, which slid noiselessly apart when approached. The doors opened into a large square room that housed the court's security system. Professionals and private citizens alike stepped onto a silent moving escalator after depositing suit jackets, briefcases, and other paraphernalia onto a conveyor belt that bowed beneath a large rumbling X-ray machine scanning each item.

Personal possessions, the identity cards of those entering the court, traveled along a belt that moved upward in a sinuous motion beside the temporary passengers navigating the legal system. A good number of these personal items were presented to their owners when the ride terminated. Missing items usually turned up during system inspections and made their way into the toolboxes of those checking the system. The remainder disappeared into the ethers of justice.

The belt traveled east, undulating like a serpent sliding through the grass. After depositing personal belongings and before stepping onto the escalator, every entrant passed through a doorframe designed to alert guards to contraband hidden in pockets and other retaining compartments. Today, nothing but nail files and clippers had thus far concerned the guards in charge of the court's security.

Once on the moving staircase, each passenger rose beside the conveyor belt, and although the sturdy building walls prevented influencing winds from entering the court, soft breezes brushed against each rider. In the spring, the fragrance of apple blossoms wafted through the air. Sometimes the air currents pushed the passengers in the opposite direction from the one promised by the guidebook, and men and women ended up in dark halls where they waited for specialty courts to open, often after the passing of two or more seasons.

More frequently, the escalator provided efficient passage from the courthouse entrance to the highest elevations in the building where hallways stretched into infinity, or so it seemed. Along these corridors, groups of lawyers stood in small clutches, whispering with their clients and anyone else wishing to be impressed or confused. Sunlight glared through irregularly shaped windows, casting harsh light on the faces of those standing in the halls. In the shadows above their hairlines, however, penumbras haloed the heads of the attorneys. In response to the persistent glare, both participants and spectators of the legal process donned large sunglasses to avoid the relentless light issued throughout the corridor. The court provided the glasses in baskets on each floor and in the public lavatories, along with a corresponding notice of their purpose and use. Pictures accompanied the notice. A disclaimer, printed in large red letters, appeared below the pictures and put the public on notice that responsible use of the glasses lay with the public, not the court. Those who wore the glasses rarely appealed the jury's decision.

A tall older woman turned and walked past the entrances to the courtrooms and headed for the nonpublic entrance used by the legal community as well as those aspiring to become a part of this most august profession. In law school, she was designated a nontraditional student, not because she attended part-time, but because she was several decades older than the majority of students. Her advanced years provided her with no advantages and several disadvantages. First among them, she experienced a decreased ability to retain black letter law, which slid silently out of her head during the night like excessive earwax. In the morning, a faint residue of black dust appeared on her pillow.

Second, she approached the cases she read with a perspective different from her classmates. Being older had provided her with an opportunity, though limited, to observe the impact of court decisions on society. She questioned whether the liberties created by the courts since FDR's administration provided true freedom or a slavish devotion to self. She had searched the Constitution for these new liberties but found them to be as elusive as the wind. But then again, she never claimed to keep up with younger minds and professors whose brilliance lit up the pages of dusty documents with the precision and clarity of recently sharpened knives.

She stopped in front of a black door after stepping into the zone of sight for the camera attached to the wall above the door. The attending secretary monitored this door, admitting or rejecting those wishing to gain entrance. A muffled buzzing sound allowed her to gain admission, at least into the corridor, not necessarily into all of the rooms beyond, most of which were locked. She opened the door and walked along an empty narrow hall that ended at the entrance to the jury room for court 17.

Long rows of additional black doors continued on each side of the corridor. To her right, black doors repeated without interruption. But to the left, one door stood ajar. She turned left, not resolutely but diffidently, still unsure of her surroundings and still lacking confidence in her own future in the law.

After several years, she still asked herself if she was ready. Ready for what, she wondered and sighed.

Since her divorce, she felt unsure of everything. Deciding that the best way to forget the past, was to take on a challenging career, she moved to another state and enrolled in law school. But she soon realized she didn't leave the past behind. During the last hour of three hour classes, she frequently found herself reviewing her marriage. She tried to pinpoint exactly when it had broken down and what she had done to cause her husband to leave her for a younger woman. She decided she had made a big mistake terminating her pregnancy. He said he didn't want children, but his new twenty something wife gave birth shortly after they married. She wished she could go back in time, and she wished she was finished with law school. She had completed over a month of a three-month externship. Two more months and then she graduated. Soon it would all be over. Then what?

Dressed in the requisite black suit, she strode to the open door, as if walking quickly would bring a quick end to the requirements of the Bar Association as well as to her dilemma. A small artificial red flower pierced her lapel, which she pulled at upon seeing the room empty. Behind the law clerk's empty chair, a window opened onto a semi-enclosed garden. She had never had time to gaze out of this or any other window. But finding the office empty, she drew near and looked outside.

She saw a lone apple tree lean away from the garden's door as autumn winds buffeted the enclosure, challenging the tree's integrity and threatening the position of the guard's cap. Stray pieces of paper swirled above the ground; perhaps a court document or two, she considered, lay among the debris wet from the preceding night's rain. But the guard did not stoop to pick them up. Not yet; maybe at the end of his shift.

The older student knew the story: the court had placed the man in the garden to tend and watch over it. The authorities warned him, "You may eat the contents of your lunch in the garden—but you may not eat fruit from the apple tree." Fair enough, he probably said to himself, and followed the decree, at least until a nubile young woman walked into the garden to escape the no-smoking rule inside the building. She figured the guard probably wondered if anyone had seen the lovely woman and the obvious smile on his face when she sat down on a marble bench, crossed her long legs, and lit a cigarette.

The guard talked and laughed with the lovely woman. The older woman who observed the scene in the garden wondered if the two met regularly and, if not, whether the lovely young woman would return. She had spent so much time talking with the watchman. The older student watched the guard pick up the smoked cigarettes and the apple core left behind. After hiding them in his jacket, he paused to look at the windows on all five floors surrounding the garden. The older woman moved to hide beside the window. Like the eyes of jungle animals, the windows watched the guard. She leaned her head and continued to stare. Despite the wind, he rubbed away the moisture above his mouth and she saw stains of sweat appear under his arms.

The extern decided not to report the woman smoking and eating, or the guard neglecting his duties as he engaged in conversation with her. She knew the regulation against eating those precious apples for she was aware of their history. The tree had been transplanted from the carefully tended estate of the country's third president. Monticello, an estate designed by Thomas Jefferson, had bequeathed this and other apple trees to courthouses around the Midwest. Jefferson himself had remained as unschooled about the proclamation against eating the fruit from this tree as the average citizen today. A voice arrested her attention.

"May I help you?" asked the court reporter who appeared at the entrance to the judge's chambers. She had pulled her white hair tightly into a knot at the back of her neck.

"Could you tell me where Paul is?" the extern asked.

"He's with the judge and the attorneys. Why don't you find the document you were working on yesterday and join the others in the courtroom? The inside door leading to the courtroom is unlocked," the court reporter said.

"Of course. Will court start on time?"

Before turning her back, the reporter smiled enigmatically. A faint smell of mothballs trailed her passage into the judge's chambers. Alone in the office, the older extern decided to join the others in the courtroom and carried her coat, purse, and computer with her because the jury room was closed to externs who used it as storage for personal belongings when a trial was not in session.

During a trial, the jury room was filled with citizens eighteen or older who stepped out of their private lives and into the court to fulfill their civic responsibilities and to determine the guilt or innocence of the defendant. Judging others enticed most citizens to show up.

She walked down the hall to the court entrance, inhaled once, and opened the door, nearly stumbling over a legal book placed against the door as a doorstop. She continued her progress into the land of law and judgment.

Today the court was filled with about a dozen law students busily working on court documents, at least when they weren't joking and bragging about how much they had had to drink the weekend before. The faces of female externs lit up when they described their tattoos and, when male externs were present, made provocative statements about their placement. Momentarily, each student bent over a personal computer.

As if on cue, the other students looked up at her as she squeezed her belongings past them to the empty chair at the end of the row. Each student held a delicious-looking red apple. The tallest extern, whose dress held her figure firmly in place, was seated in the middle of the row. She thrust her apple into her mouth and smiled as the juice ran down her face. The others did the same. When she saw the older woman's surprised countenance, her chin jutted upwards.

"What are you looking at?" challenged the young woman as she took another apple out of her purse and offered it to the older woman, who shook her head no. This extern looked exactly like her ex-husband's new wife; she even sounded like her!

"Those aren't apples from the courtyard garden, are they?" she asked naively, immediately regretting her simple question when the answer seemed obvious.

The young woman, disregarding the admonition, continued to crunch the firm, crisp fruit. Her eyes, not leaving the older student, whose body seemed to slouch into a question mark, held the older woman's stare. "Are you one of us or not?" she asked. Students sitting in the first two rows of chairs paused. Heads dropped; someone snickered. The young woman's companion placed his arm around her shoulder.

Dismissing the desire to remind them of character and fitness requirements needed to sit for the Bar, the older extern hurried to the seat at the end of the row. Paul opened the door to announce the judge's arrival. Placing half-eaten apples in their pockets or purses, the students and others in the courtroom stood. Paul trumpeted, "All rise."

Part Two

Chinese influence in courtroom décor had begun a decade ago, many decades after the progressive influence slithered into Supreme Court opinions. Blue or light yellow walls became decorating history as foreign as regular church attendance. Pictures of the State Capitol building during different seasons and times of the day no longer graced the walls but had been stored in a shed next to the parking lot. Single light bulbs now hung from the ceiling, casting shadows across unadorned dull red walls. A single red flag replaced the country's original flag and the smaller state flag. Flanking the judge's bench, Chinese Chippendale cabinets housed legal books referred to during disputes between lawyers. Pictures of Asian dragons papered the wall behind the jury, whose authority had waned in recent years.

A panel of twelve citizens, the jury was slated to yield its authority to a seven-judge panel of men called the supreme decision-making body, like those in China. During recent television newscasts, leading citizens and local politicians, giddy with excitement over the city's cultural and legal exchange programs, explained the changes occurring at the courthouse. Appearing at times to genuflect before the altar of diversity, those committed to the cause applauded the cultural exchange experiment.

Standing on a stage before news cameras, each one spoke more passionately than the one before. Like wallpaper, a group of international students stood behind the speakers, bussed into the capital by campaign operatives. These same upstanding and progressive citizens wiped off television makeup as well as their smiles when the reporters and cameras left the auditorium. The students returned by bus to their studies in engineering at the local university. Publicly, no one spoke ill of the new programs, the new courthouse, or the loss of the jury system. To some, diversity resembled the Egyptian idols worshipped by the ancient Jews who rejected Jehovah God.

Paul held the door to the courtroom open for the judge, and into her transitory domain marched Judge Havisham. The judge knew her days were numbered but carried on under the auspices of a higher unseen authority. Sniffing the odor of change years ago, Judge Havisham determined to be carried out of her court gasping her last breath. But before she submitted to the changes, she continued to perform her constitutional role with military rigor. It was rumored that in her chambers, she wore earrings shaped like American flags. But few openly confessed to the truth of these assertions.

During each trial, Judge Havisham insisted that the court reporter transcribe into the record every argument and piece of evidence; consequently, the decisions coming out of her court were rarely, if ever, appealed. Because Judge Havisham moved methodically through the proceedings, attorneys sometimes complained that coming into her court was like stepping into a black hole, at least for that day.

In keeping with her traditional routine, her black eyes examined the courtroom like the four corners of a contract and rested on the court reporter, whose glare bore down on the externs, silencing their chatter and bringing them to attention. Standing at her designated place, the judge wiped stray cobwebs from her bench and chair.

"You may be seated," she announced in a stentorian voice, then coughed. Grabbing a lozenge from one of several bowls placed around the courtroom, she ignored the plate next to the bowl that was stained with garlic sauce and hardened noodles, obviously the remnants of a recent meal.

"Paul," said Judge Havisham, "pass the lozenges. This place is too dry." Then she sat down, carefully arranging the black and red drapery of her stately robe.

Watching their leader, the students sat like dominoes. First one, then the next, fell backwards, until all of the students were seated.

"Where was the cleaning staff last night?' Judge Havisham asked. "Apparently they enjoyed their dinner at my bench."

As if on command, the externs laughed; everyone knew the cleaning staff had stopped cleaning this court since Justice Roberts, confused about his role as chief justice, rewrote the healthcare law, redefining a fine as a tax.

Today the judge's coiffure stood nearly a foot above her head whereas at the Personal Protection Order Hearings on Friday, it had risen a mere six inches. Piled atop her head and gleaming like Medusa's snaky locks, her black tresses shimmered. The towering hairdo was not propped up, like the economy, by an infusion of zero percent interest rates and inflated Chinese yuan, but by a metal framework through which her long black tresses swirled and twirled. On occasion, a curly lock refused restraint and twisted and turned, floating around the judge's very attractive countenance, creating a brief entertainment during the lengthy proceedings. Neither side ever objected.

It was day one of the trial, jury selection, and the attorneys and their clients would choose those who would sit in judgment of the defendant. The judge's towering hairdo centered the wandering attention of the attorneys and externs. She looked at the deputy standing next to the door through which the accused would walk and then down at the documents placed before her by one of the externs. She then flicked a long and errant black eyelash, which had settled gently on top of her gold glasses. The lash floated away from the bench and landed on the defense table where an experienced, if obese, attorney sat arranging his notes. His chest rose in anticipation. The lash appeared like heavenly reassurance.

"Let the jury pool in, Paul," the judge ordered.

Voir dire was about to begin.

Part Three

Although not all judges allowed attorneys the privilege of choosing who sat in judgment of their clients, most attorneys aggressively pursued the privilege, at least when they directed their time and attention toward their clients and not the new female attorneys, some of whom wore short tight skirts, fishnet stockings, and stiletto pumps. It was rumored that one young female attorney who had recently passed the Bar had become a courtroom hit when she wore black knit tops that she revealed beneath her suit jacket during a slow-moving trial. The knit apparel was embellished with curly leafed ferns adorned with gold sequins. The sparkling ferns rose from her waist to caress her bosom, regarded as large and firm by any gentleman's standards. But we digress.

To choose the best jurors, those most sympathetic toward a client, good defense attorneys gleaned what they knew about the process of choosing jurors by talking with them after trials. But not always. Sometimes they simply wanted to chat up a good-looking juror, hoping she had been impressed by their professional performance and would take a chance on an equally good performance with other parts of their bodies and in other rooms, besides a courtroom. Of course, elevators were always interesting.

Jurors enjoyed gossiping about the kinds of subjects discussed on entertainment shows, court TV, and CSI programs. Some even believed they were experts at judging human nature. They spent a lot of time exchanging views on the significance of the way a police officer rolled his eyes, and how offensive and annoying this was to them. During one trial, several jurors believed they had uncovered the true nature of the accused by counting the number of times he belched and the amount of flatulence he released into the courtroom. Not being privy to his personal medical history, they were unaware of his recent surgery.

Questioning prospective jurors had become an art form, one which the American Bar Association used to lure young attorneys to conferences in exciting locations where wine, sun, and casual sex could be enjoyed for the right price. The conference planners working for the Bar promised that attending the conferences would increase an attorney's skills and, by extension, her fees.

The prosecutor rose, stepped to the podium, and placed his notes on the flat surface before him. He had been a prosecutor for nearly a decade. Tall and athletic, he had once invited an accused domestic batterer to stand up and hit him the way he claimed he had hit his girlfriend on New Year's Eve. The jurors had seen the photos of the defendant, which revealed a huge knot between her swollen eyes and seven stitches below them.

This morning he looked over the jury pool in front of him and smiled. A diverse group of citizens sat before him: mechanics, professors, nurses, teachers, website engineers, and stay-at-home mothers, male and female, young and old, and of many races. Today the state was prosecuting a young man who had refused to take his girlfriend to an abortion clinic on the morning of her appointment and instead had locked her in his bedroom until the evening, when she promised not to abort their unborn child. The next day she went to the clinic alone. She was suing him for kidnapping; he was countersuing for breach of promise.

Clearing his throat, the prosecutor asked, "Juror number eight. How are you this morning?"

"I've got pneumonia, a fever of 102, and I need to go home."

Before the tall, handsome prosecutor could speak, the judge said, "Juror number eight is excused. Take care of yourself, madam." The sick woman smiled gratefully and left the jury box.

The court reporter replaced the sick woman with another name from the computer-generated list. A young man stepped forward to fill seat number eight.

The prosecutor continued. "Juror number two, how are you this morning?"

"I'm feeling better than that woman you just excused. But it sure is dry in here, and I can't hear half of what you're saying."

"Paul, give the man a cough drop and a headset and tell him to turn it up."

Once the man had fiddled with the headset to improve his hearing, the prosecutor asked, "Should a woman have the right to choose whether or not she terminates her pregnancy?"

"Yes. That's the law, isn't it?"

"Yes, it is. Should her partner be involved in her decision?"

"Well, they made it together in the bedroom, didn't they?" Snickering could be heard among the jury and externs as well. "You can't make them things by yourself." He looked at the judge, whose black hair slid quickly in and out of the metal frame.

"Is that a yes?" asked the prosecutor.

"Well, I guess so. Yes," said juror two.

"What if the man and woman aren't married? Does the father of the unborn have a right to help make this decision?" asked the prosecutor.

"If you ask me, that's the trouble today," explained juror number two. "Everyone does what they want, and if you can get it for free, why pay for it? Right?" More laughter drifted throughout the courtroom.

"Sir, is that a yes or no?" asked the prosecutor.

"Yes. That boy has his rights just like the girl," concluded juror number two.

"Thank you, juror number two," said the prosecutor.

Every extern kept score, guessing which jury candidate would be excused and which ones would stay. They all placed this man in the prosecutor's "dismiss" column. The prosecutor was going after this defendant because he wanted to raise the baby he had fathered. This young man thought his rights were equal to those of his girlfriend. The jury would see about that. The prosecutor continued.

"Juror number one, how are you today?" Before she could answer, he asked, "If a woman is not married and becomes pregnant, should she consider what her partner wants to do about the unborn baby?"

"If they've been together for a long time, yes," said juror number one. "There's common law marriage, right?"

"No, not in this state," said the prosecutor.

"Then I would say no," said juror number one. "A woman ends up taking care of it regardless, and labor is no joke. You can take my word for it." Sympathetic women smiled.

"Thank you, juror number one," said the prosecutor. "Juror number six, do you think the State has any business interfering with a woman's right to choose?"

"No," said juror number six. The externs placed juror number six in the prosecutor's plus column.

"Does the State have an interest in protecting a woman from a partner who wants her to have the baby?" asked the prosecutor.

Juror number six said, "Yes, the State should protect a woman."

"Juror number nine," asked the prosecutor, "does the State have an interest in protecting the rights of the man who has fathered the unborn?"

"Well, she can't make a baby on her own, now can she?" juror number nine said.

"Is that a yes?" asked the prosecutor.

"Yes." The externs placed number nine in the "excused" column.

"Thank you, sir," said the prosecutor. "Juror number ten, how are you feeling today?"

"Fine, thank you," said juror number ten.

"What do you do for a living?" asked the prosecutor.

"I'm a stay-at-home mother. I homeschool our four children," said juror number ten.

"Madam, should a woman consider her partner's wishes before she has an abortion?" asked the prosecutor.

"Yes," said juror number ten.

"What if the couple is not married?"

"An unborn child is created by two people who should decide together," said juror number ten.

The externs added another potential juror to the prosecutor's "excused" column.

"Juror number seven, good morning. Have you ever wanted to lock someone in a room to stop them from doing something?" asked the prosecutor.

"Only my mother-in-law," said juror number seven with a straight face.

"Would you ever lock your wife in a room?" asked the prosecutor.

"If I thought I could get away with it, yes," said juror number seven.

"Do you think people should control their feelings?" asked the prosecutor.

"Yes, but sometimes you can't," said juror number seven.

"But if you don't, the State steps in, right?" asked the prosecutor.

"Yes."

Questioning continued until 12:30 when the judge looked at the clock.

Suddenly, before she could call for a lunch break and dismiss the passive group seated before her, the courtroom doors flew open. Those in the jury pool leaned forward and gasped at the spectacle bolting into the courtroom. Spinning like a top, a whirling dervish sped into the court, then tumbled on an invisible mat before a bewildered audience. A sparkling sword, swinging rapidly from a leather belt circling his native costume, riveted every eye in the court. The dervish danced violently around the room, then stopped abruptly before the judge's bench. The older student sat back in her seat, marveling at the man's agility. Is my future in the law whirling around my head that fast, she wondered.

Unnerved, the judge merely nodded to the court officer, who stepped forward to apprehend the miscreant who had tumbled and danced one time too many in the judge's courtroom.

"Ladies and gentlemen, this is Roger. Roger has a history with this court," Judge Havisham began, but stopped. She decided not to reveal the spicy details of this history. "Officer, remove this man from the courtroom and call the county jail. Tell them to begin embroidering a pillow with Roger's name on it. He will spend the next several months there." She looked at Roger's serious face. "You have disobeyed your probation, sir."

"But Your Honor," gushed the dervish, "if I might have a word."

"One word, Roger," said the Judge.

"Your Honor, the law is spinning out of control."

"Who knows that better than I?"

"Your Honor, if I may…"

"No, Roger," barked Judge Havisham. "You may not speak another word in my courtroom." The judge looked up at the officer, whose worried face dissolved into a satisfied smile.

"Officer, take him away," said Judge Havisham.

The jury pool cheered. Judge Havisham stood, nodded to the officer, and said, "You are dismissed until two o'clock. Enjoy your lunch."

Part Four

During the lunch break, the older extern said, "Paul, I need to pull a file from the archives, but I don't know where they are or how to get there."

"No worries," said Paul. "The entrance is to the left of the stairs on the first floor. If you want to wait until I finish eating, I'll show you."

"Thanks, but I think I can find my way," she replied.

"Whatever works," he said. "The archives are easy to access, at least most of the time. Be careful of the occasional whirling dervish," he warned her and quickly added, "Don't worry. He's a solo act."

Feeling assured of her safety, she set out on her own with her iPhone and followed the stairs down to the first floor. The older student looked for the entrance to the archives but could not find a door next to the lower level. She looked around for directions or a map to the belly of the courthouse where old case law was stored. Vaguely, she remembered seeing a door earlier in the day when she walked up the stairs that morning. But before her first cup of coffee, she could not swear to the truth of anything around her.

Warmth from the heating duct below tickled her legs. She punched in the number for the law clerk's office but dropped her phone when she heard a door slam. Panic spread through her muscles. She froze. Leaning over, she looked down into the heating duct where she saw the pink cover disappear and heard it bouncing off the metal shoot that ended in the darkness below. While examining the metal grill covering the heating duct, she realized that the duct opening was large enough for her to slip through.

Looking around the busy first floor, she noticed the guards absconding nail clippers at an alarming rate. Those who had lost personal items pulled at their phones to type words of complaint about the strict court rules. Information about this intrusion into personal freedom immediately flew into cyberspace where it was received by sympathetic souls.

Eager to retrieve her phone, she considered using this alternative means of descending to the lower levels of the courthouse. After all, no one was watching and the phone couldn't have gone far.

Determined, she lifted up the grill, set it to the side of the conduit, and wiped her hands against the sides of her legs. How far down could the archives be? She used to be a gymnast and could easily twist and turn into the heating duct. Certainly she still remembered her former routines. Peering into the abyss and speculating on how far she would travel down to the lower level, she did not hear the steps on the stairs behind her, and this approaching person did not imagine anyone would stoop over an uncovered heating duct, let alone prepare to enter it. Unknowingly, he bumped her forward, into the future and into the dark passageway below.

She did not scream. She kept her eyes wide open as she fell into the conduit that accepted her passage easily, like a newborn gaining acceptance before the final squeeze through the birth canal. Slowly she fell through the dark passage that smelled of musty books and typewriter ribbons, her arms and legs banging against the metal passage like sticks against steel drums. She slid through the metal passageway, which was surprisingly pliant. Bright light appeared below her, but no gentle hands or forceps guided her passage into the subterranean cavern below. At the bottom, she spilled out onto a carpeted floor and spied her phone lying but a distance from where she lay.

She looked around and carefully stood up, checking for broken bones and additional aches and pains. Finding none, a sigh of relief escaped from her lips. She grabbed her phone, which had died, and cautiously looked around the small room. She could barely make out the figure before her, but when she squinted, she could discern the shape of a small man dressed in black walking toward her. As his pace increased, she stepped back to assess his person. He wore a traditional black robe and carried a large black book which he waved in her direction. On top of his small head perched a huge white wig that dwarfed his small stature. Abundant gray whiskers enveloped his frowning mouth. As he drew closer, she watched his whiskers move. A black spider struggled to escape. It tumbled onto his chest, spinning a silken string. It joined other spiders forming a web that surrounded the judge and a large timepiece suspended from a gold chain circling his neck. Brown caterpillars twisted into numerals on the face of the watch to reveal the time. "You're late!" the judge roared, examining his watch.

"Am I in the archives?" she asked, ignoring his accusation as she looked down upon his white head. She rose above him, bumping her head on a light fixture above.

"Step this way," he said and opened the door behind them. "Duck your head, please." On a mission, she followed.

Merely ducking her head was not enough, however. Before entering the next room, she had to drop to her knees and crawl behind his billowing robe from which emanated the aroma of pencil shavings and coffee. "Don't stand up until the next room," her guide warned. "The room beyond is cavernous, but the pathway narrow."

Indeed it was. She rose to her feet and turned to ask her gnomic companion a question, but before he could clarify her situation, he disappeared, leaving a trail of white vapor behind, a few scattering spiders providing questionable evidence of the little man's recent appearance.

The room around her hummed from neon lights radiating a rainbow of color. Huge college pennants floated above her head. But instead of reading college names, she read legal arguments glowing from their surfaces. She recognized statements from a controversial legal opinion. On a large pennant, she read: "A person does not include the unborn." On another she read: "Preserve and protect maternal health." On a third pennant, nearly as large as a bedsheet, she read: "the 'liberty' protected by the Due Process Clause covers more than those freedoms explicitly named in the Bill of Rights." Before she could say Justice Blackmun, she heard a clock ticking loudly and worried that a bomb might be waiting somewhere in the gloom.

Before checking her surroundings for bombs, she slipped on a pair of courthouse sunshades she had tucked away in her suit pocket. If they could protect against harsh light from the sun, perhaps they could reduce the glare from all of the neon lights. But the sweet sound of calliope music arrested her attention and checked the course of her intent to ferret out incendiary devices.

Beside the nearest bookcase she stood watching as a Cirque du Soleil performer descended from above. The corners of her mouth rose as she beheld the naked body of a man of indeterminate age pass before her just inches from her face. His curly black hair briefly touched her face, only to drift away beyond her reach. Inhaling slowly, she closed her eyes and breathed in the fragrance of spices and lime. When she reopened her eyes, she watched as pastel-colored lights lit up his smooth face. His full lips opened briefly, and he whispered her name. Her lips parted; she couldn't resist.

As his muscled figure swayed backwards and forwards, she gazed at his body twisting and turning until he rested upside down with his legs spread widely apart. She gasped. And his body started to spin. He rose above her, extended his arms, and swept an imaginary form into a welcoming embrace. She stretched her body upwards to become a part of his warmth and mystery.

He then regained an upright position, gently lifted a dove fluttering amidst his wavy locks, and snapped his fingers. The bird perched upon his strong fingers and opened its beak from which a pink and blue satin banner instantly unfurled before her. On its surface it read: "Personal liberties for women." She looked from the banner to his spinning person, trying to read the expression on his revolving countenance. The acrobat stopped, looked at her, and winked. Then he dropped his flag into her waiting hands. "Are you liberated?" he asked. Her chest rose and swelled. Her breathing quickened as she opened her mouth to speak.

"Yes," she breathed.

"Join me," he invited, extending his arms. "Join me if you wish." His lithe body dropped in front of her, and he gently drew his thumb over her lips and down her neck.

Moments passed before her excited companion jumped onto the nearby bookcase, which began to pulse and move. He took her hand as he pulled her gently toward his body. Bookshelves transformed into writhing bodies that groaned and moaned in pleasure. Her suit slid from her eager body, dropped beside the bookcase, and she lost herself in a swarm of slippery flesh, moving and twisting and moaning as the passion increased. At the peak of their pleasure, the sounds of a collective release echoed around the room. Lights flickered and dimmed. After the room became quiet, an unimagined power source reignited the neon display, which hummed and sighed. She slid out of the symphony of bodies and watched as they wilted and slithered off like snakes escaping a predator.

She sat up and buttoned her blouse. Reaching out her hands, she tried to capture the departing warmth and excitement of his body from the cold metal shelves of the bookcase. Then she curled into a fetal position, hoping to retain the fading pleasure before it disappeared completely. Circling her knees with her arms, she shivered. Their passion had expired. He was gone. Her personal liberties were intact and as comforting as a moth-eaten wool sweater.

The room grew cold. She stood, unsure of what had just happened. Around her warm neon lights glowed and then blinked on, then off. She watched as fragments of the opposing arguments passed in small but colorful neon tubing. Passionate memories still curled around in her head, eclipsing arguments written inside the musty books. She straightened her wrinkled suit, planted her glasses on her nose, and adjusted the frames around her ears.

She crossed to the opposite side of a room without walls where a stubby finger curled around a bookcase, beckoning her forward. Its size waxed and waned. A thin figure attached to the finger wiggled from behind a bookcase, emerged from the cold metal shelves, and motioned her to join him beneath a neon moon. His hawkish nose sniffed the air. Dressed in a shabby suit, his narrow-set eyes looked her up and down. He peered beyond her and around the room before pulling aside the lapel from his dusty suit coat. Inside his jacket, she saw buttons that glowed with the dissenting words of Justice Rehnquist. She focused her eyes and read them aloud.

"…no right of privacy here…";

"…that liberty is not guaranteed absolutely…";

and "The Court eschews the history of the Fourteenth Amendment…"

Once read, the arguments flew off the buttons and fluttered in the light until a tall man dressed in a wrinkled white shirt and tie caught the flying arguments and stuffed them firmly into a mailbox imprinted with the word "traditions" on both sides.

"Lies," he rasped. "Nothing but lies." After he spoke, his long nose grew several inches longer.

Certainly a kin to Ichabod Crane, the older student thought, as she watched his long fingers remove a mouse from the pocket of his khaki pants that floated above his ankles to reveal a pair of red socks. Ichabod's kin fed the small creature a bit of cheese and rubbed the top of its head.

"What is your position?" he asked.

Tilting her head up to address his towering frame, she scanned his face, looking for his eyes, the windows to his soul. Instead of a pair of eyes, she beheld a face resplendent with dozens of soft blue orbs. "Oh, of course, I believe in a woman's right to choose," she said quickly. Then for some reason she confessed, "But I have some doubts."

"Are you the reasonable man, then, the objective observer?" He laughed, but she didn't. Instead, she curled her lips into her mouth until they disappeared.

"Certainly you are old enough to have formed a stable opinion on the subject."

She shook her head. "Actually, I've been reconsidering my opinion."

"Ridiculous!" he snorted. "You betray your gender."

She held her tongue. Why argue with a professor whose opinions sat like crustaceans on the bottom of the ocean?

"I saw you examining the heating duct upstairs. You don't look like a typical student, now do you? Some worldly experience, perhaps, but behind the eight ball compared to the young ones, wouldn't you say?" He bent to study her face to glean its intent. "You took a long time getting here and you still don't know what you want, but come along."

He placed the mouse on top of his shoulder and walked ahead of her. Other furry creatures squirmed their way out of his pockets and pants, ran up his long back, which tilted forward as he walked, and affixed themselves to his shoulders. Their beady black eyes peered at her as she followed.

And he's arrogant as well, she thought. His arrogance took root inside her head. Although she struggled to pull out its roots before they spread and fastened around her mind, her efforts fell short. He was a law professor, after all, and she was not. He belonged in the law profession while she was merely a pretender, a fake, and a phony. She hurried behind him and wondered how she could get away.

No clearly marked exits appeared nearby. She continued to follow, but crossed her arms in front of her, turning the corners of her mouth down like a petulant child who refused to swallow her castor oil. He stopped in front of a row of bookcases, which repeated themselves like a vision in a Warhol painting; every bookcase looked the same, and there appeared to be hundreds of them, perhaps thousands. Lettering on the book spines differed only by one letter, the dates only by one hour.

"You see before you the slow progress of the law," he said. "Tradition holds fast, but not today. Soon personal liberties will expand and women will be as free as men. Now what is it you wish to examine? And why?"

The older student felt the poison of his arrogance metastasize like a cancerous tumor inside her mind. Her shoulders dropped, and her arms collapsed at her sides. "I don't remember, Professor."

"You don't remember?" he bellowed. "You don't remember?" His laughter echoed throughout the room and beyond.

Surely, she thought, the security guards upstairs could hear him. But no one came to her aid.

Her eyes darted from one bookcase to the next. The room felt like an accordion collapsing around her. Suddenly she stomped her foot and thrust out her chest. "Where is the door?" she demanded. "You are nothing but a bully!"

"You catch on fast," he said and examined her more closely. "You may follow me to my office where I will enlighten you further." The professor advanced, but as he turned to walk, his red socks snagged on the leading edge of the interminable bookcases and began to unravel. His socks became strings, and his pants unraveled and collapsed around his ankles. He was completely coming apart before her. The surprised professor gasped and ran behind the nearest bookcase, clutching himself between the legs.

On the floor, his shoes and the threads of his clothing hissed and smoked like oil on a hot griddle. A pool of black liquid formed in their place at the toe of her shoe. Unable to avoid stepping into the pool, she skidded across the floor like Sonja Henie and collided with a bookcase. But instead of bouncing off its hard surface like an eight ball on a pool table, she found that the structure softened and enveloped her.

Flashing before her eyes, she saw the preceding decades of her life. "I've made some big mistakes," she admitted as she checked her wrinkled suit for missing buttons and ripped pockets. She moved from side to side. Her bones had not broken. She licked her lips but tasted no blood. Nothing leaked or trickled from her body. She could still see. She had been saved a second time!

But where was she now, she wondered. Where were the bookcases and the judge, the flimflam and the professor, and the neon signs listing her personal liberties? Where were the legal decisions written by men of stature that defined her new rights? Where were the justices who sprinkled liberties into a woman's life like confetti from an open window during a parade? Without the law, how could she define who she was? Like Dante without his Beatrice, she continued alone.

Part Five

Ahead she saw an enormous gate. Music rang from an ethereal bell choir. Each note floated gently into her confused and worried spirit. She walked toward the imposing structure, defining the entrance to the place beyond. As she approached the iron enclosure, she saw a man sitting on the ground nearby. He rose to greet her as she walked nearer. His peaceful countenance offered her hope. He wore a long white robe and leather sandals. "Are you ready to enter?" he asked. She nodded. "I can see you have reasoned yourself into a corner." He waited for her to respond, but she dropped her head.

"I descended into hell back there," she confessed, wondering if he understood. "Just when I thought I had found all the answers in my personal liberties."

He nodded. "Yes, I know." He paused before describing what lay ahead. "What you will see beyond the gate may offer you comfort. My name is Caleb," he said and offered her his hand. She accepted.

"I too once lived in darkness," said Caleb, "but I was saved. I am here to guide you into a kingdom of peace where a Higher Power guides your steps." She straightened her shoulders and prepared to soldier on, determined to find the way. She was no longer the older student; she was an eternal student. Caleb took the lead, and she followed.

Inside the gate, she saw a vast crowd of people. Every nationality stood before her and a cacophony of languages assaulted her ears. Each one wore a white robe and stood in front of an imposing throne. The throne was made of lapis lazuli. Whereas the previous rooms contained dry, dusty books, this one throbbed with life. The air smelled fresh. While the previous rooms sat in cobwebs and dust, lit by artificial lights, a glorious presence surrounded her now.

Men in white suits stood before the throne. When a heavenly choir started to sing, the people surrounding her fell to their knees and sang songs of worship.

She asked her guide, "Who are these people?"

He replied, "They are you. They are the ones who died to their sins. They have washed their robes in the blood of Christ, and now they are clean."

She looked around her and saw images of her own face. One after the other sang praises to the Lord. She joined in when they prayed.

Suddenly the sound of trumpets filled the air. She looked up and on an overhead monitor she watched as hail and fire were thrown down onto the earth. A conflagration consumed the earth; trees, grass, and buildings burned. She watched a sparkling star fall from the skies and disappear into a silent sea. She smelled the salty brine and tasted it on her lips. Smoke rose from the earth, and locusts crawled from burning embers. In the distance she could see a rainbow emerge from the clouds and frame an angel who rose from the cloud. He broke the seals from the scroll in his hand and prepared to read.

"The Word is sweet," he said. "Take and receive."

She witnessed this great event. The angel leaned forward, out of the screen, and placed the scroll into her hand. He encouraged her to eat, and she tasted the sweetness of God's Word. She was healed.

Caleb guided her away from the throne and back to the imposing gate. Beyond the gate, she saw the elevator. Caleb motioned her to step inside. She did, the doors closed, and as the elevator descended to the floors below, she huddled in a corner and wept. Why, she wondered, did she have to go back?

The doors opened onto the corridor leading to the judge's chambers. She saw a disappearing coattail quickly turn the corner ahead. She couldn't tell anyone what she had seen, especially not what she had witnessed behind the gate, certainly not the other externs or her classmates. But she wouldn't forget. She had changed and could make her decision.

Part Final

She needed to sign out before leaving the court. Solemnly, she walked back to the law clerk's office, exhausted yet hopeful. She saw no one in the hall or inside the law clerk's office, but she heard muffled conversation and an occasional sound of laughter escaping from the judge's chamber. As she bent to find her name in the log book, she repeated her vigil at the office window and gazed into the garden below.

A blind woman and her guide dog entered the garden. When she reached the bench, she sat. Her dog waited for its release. The woman spoke a command, and the dog left her side to sniff the grass surrounding the tree. Beneath the apple tree, he lifted his leg. He returned to his master, who stood, patted his head, and put a treat in his mouth. They left the garden.

The untraditional student turned from the window and briefly closed her eyes. Yes, she was back in this world again where few understood the ancient history of that apple tree and the prohibitions surrounding it. In the garden it was separate and its prohibitions served a higher purpose.

She imagined herself walking the stage and accepting her diploma, but that's where her legal career would end. She had come to law school later in life, searching for a second career, a second life, another one after the mistakes she had made in the first. To her surprise, she had been searching for forgiveness, and it wasn't found in a law book or a courtroom.

The law provided no moral framework. Like a flower torn out by its roots, liberty lay motionless on top of the soil, its source unable to nourish, protect, or secure.

She signed her name in the attendance book and walked down three flights of stairs, wishing she knew then what she knew now.

Alone, she left the courthouse, her personal liberties wilting in her hands like a dead bouquet.

DONKEY CARE:
PLAY AND LEARNING CENTER

2 Chronicles 19:6

...and he said to them, "Always think carefully before pronouncing judgment. Remember that you do not judge to please people but to please the Lord."

O nce upon a time, there was a daycare center that strove to please everyone. It was called Donkey Care Play and Learning Center. The Supreme Director of Donkey Care, Mrs. Smith, worked hard to meet the needs of all families and children under her care and retained only the very best workers. Mrs. Smith told her staff, "I will not tolerate any employee who offends either the children or their parents. Our clients are always right, and so am I." Whether or not this policy was uppermost in the minds of her staff is not known.

However, those familiar with Donkey Care observed that Mrs. Smith went through childcare workers with the rapidity of a bullet train. Others said the bullet train comparison was grossly inaccurate. Mrs. Smith's Deputy Director said, "How fast does a bullet train actually travel anyway?" Before she was fired, the Deputy Director revealed, "Some of our colleagues are gone before we know their names. They pass through here like a train conductor; they punch your ticket and they're gone."

But most employees did notice how quickly the names changed on the parking lot placards. While no one knew for certain what went on in the privacy of special chambers or why the staff changed as often as a traffic light, everyone swore that the colors of their nametag badges switched with regularity. The Custodian, a young man whose physique rivaled that of Adonis, often helped the Supreme Director late into the wee hours. According to him, Mrs. Smith liked color. He said, "When she hires new staff, the colors change on our nametags. It's only January and she's used nearly every color in a supersized Crayola pack. Of course, I don't mind because I like all the colors." He paused. "Did I say that I liked helping Mrs. Smith?"

The Custodian, the various department deputies and assistants, and Mrs. Smith herself conducted their business under the auspices of the federal government. The daycare center welcomed children of all races, religions, and genders, before and after a sex-change operation. Even children of Tea Party parents could enroll; after all, a child couldn't help what cockamamie ideas rolled around in their progenitors' heads, like fiscal responsibility . . . Whoever heard of such a thing!

Recently, when Donkey Care admitted two new female children into the center room program, Mrs. Smith and her assistants expressed some concern. Would the little gentlemen welcome the little ladies or take umbrage at their appointments? After all, one little girl was already on the bench, and she fit in, especially with a little boy who disagreed with everything she wrote. Would she, Mrs. Smith wondered, have to take special action and treat some in the class a little more, shall we say, protectively? "We'll see," she told her staff.

In addition to the children and staff, the subject that concerned everyone was support. On point, of course, was that perennial issue: money. The Deputy Assistant of Accounting scrutinized the income of all prospective clientele, unless Mrs. Smith was friendly with the child's family or enjoyed a special arrangement with the child's father, in which case Mrs. Smith handled the billing.

Everyone at Donkey Care was equal, but some were more equal than others. Donkey Care Play and Learning Center claimed they followed best practices, and since this policy appeared in writing, prospective clientele believed the words printed in the daycare's brochure. After all, a reader could trust words written in black and white and accompanied by colorful photos. Admission to the center room or chamber, however, remained private, behind closed doors as it were.

These private doors were never photographed. Exterior photos of Donkey Care reflected iconic Washington DC. School pictures revealed a building similar to all the other government buildings built to serve the people. Donkey Care's stone exterior melded with the surrounding architecture, and except for the rainbow-colored sign outside on the green lawn, a tourist would assume the identical building housed yet another unnecessary federal department financed with taxpayers' dollars.

Inside was another story. Each brightly painted interior provided its own animal theme enhanced by flashing lights. For example, the green room featured lizards and frogs, the flaming coral room a flamingo that stood on one leg, and the blinding barn red interior a rooster. Every room struck a different pose like a fashion model during a photo shoot. After taking the daycare center tour, parents and children alike exclaimed, "Breathtaking!" or "Absolutely unique!" Every room was a hit. Every room, that is, except one.

At the center of it all stood two imposing Greek pillars guiding both staff and their charges to a room that resembled a courtroom, or a judge's chamber, or a law library rather than a unique space bursting with color and sunshine—and its own representative from the animal kingdom. While most visitors left the court like objects escaping a black hole, the invitees to this room, who played court and judges, found that the room mirrored perfectly an interior space stifled by the outside world of color, animals, and freedom. "I feel at home!" the little voices cried and eagerly ran inside.

That the daycare center existed at all was a boon to the capital of our country, but the fact that special little government boys and girls played court inside was a gift to every liberty-loving citizen who saluted the red, white, and blue. The daycare's services and reputation were the stuff that dreams were made of.

To protect that reputation, Donkey Care hired a General Officer of Telecommunications who devoted his entire day to creating, upholding, and protecting the image and reputation of the school. His position was also underwritten by the federal government. When interviewed, Mr. Foggybottom queried, "Who knows better than politicians how to manage a reputation?" He also strove to spread the school's good reputation around the world.

Before government authorities from the Third District stopped by with foreign diplomats, the General Officer of Telecommunications called an early morning meeting with the staff to make sure every Donkey assistant and deputy read from the same script when questioned by visitors with special license plates. At day's end, the General Officer acknowledged the best performances of those who sounded especially earnest by erasing any negative check marks disgracing the workers' evaluation sheets. On rare occasions, the Telecommunications Officer slipped a Twinkie into the waiting mouth of an exceptional worker like a mother bird dropping a worm into her baby's open beak.

While most government workers enrolled their progeny at Donkey Care, and each child was equally important, it was understood that some government positions were, shall we say, more important than others. The most special progeny, consisting of sons and daughters destined to become Supreme Court Justices, were separated from the other children, especially from those with an early interest in firearms and explosives. "Sometimes," Mrs. Smith said, "it is better not to mix oil and water, especially when the oil might contain questionable additives."

The important children arrived early, before the hodgepodge of other youngsters, to be organized immediately by the Deputy Assistant. Upon entry she lined up children alphabetically in a single file line and ushered the lads and lassies through a narrow corridor smelling of curdled milk, dirty diapers, and crayons. No child spoke or touched or even looked at any other child for fear of punishment which could be administered in one of two ways: one, not being able to change the words in the documents they reviewed; or two, not being able to play with the stuffed animals or same-sex dolls popular with children of all mental proclivities.

Occasionally the little ones in the back of the line tried to trip each other, but those in the front walked somberly to their esteemed destination like soldiers marching off to war. If a child complained about the smelly hallway, the Deputy Assistant reminded the miscreant of the lines of prisoners marching through the snow and ice in Siberia and demanded that the naughty child announce to the group that Donkey Care was the best.

Off to a special chamber, separated from the ordinary riffraff who picked their noses and sneezed without a tissue at hand, marched the nine progeny who knew they were gifted. Most of the time the children enjoyed the insularity of their playroom. But not always.

One such child, a boy of slight stature dressed today like Little Lord Fauntleroy in a royal blue velvet suit with short pants, occasionally objected to his high position on the court. Unlike the others, he was the chief and wore his soft brown hair curled under in a pageboy. Like the others, he had been reading since he was old enough to speak. His mother employed the methods of early Colonial mothers who taught their children how to read by using the Bible and prayer books in the home. He enjoyed reading, but when he was troubled he dropped his books and the legal briefs he reviewed and drifted to the windows where he stood watching the children playing on the other side of the wall of separation.

The boy's name was John, and it was rumored that his name belonged to someone important in the book his mother employed to teach him to read, the Bible. However, unlike John's mother, no one working at the school or in Washington DC had ever read this mysterious book, so the assistants concluded that the name's origin probably meant nothing, just like the book.

Several weeks had gone by since the introduction of the new lady students. The staff continued to monitor the interactions between the old and new students, but so far so good. As the Deputy Teaching Captain perused the room, approving of what she saw, she sighed and her shoulders relaxed. At least until she noticed that John had once again separated himself from his colleagues. He stood in front of the window, looking forlornly at the activity outside.

When the Deputy Teaching Captain saw John standing at the window gazing at two boys outside, she joined him. Together they watched the boys push and shove each other as they kicked a black and white ball across a large field. The Deputy Captain was so overcome by the inanity of their activity that she snapped her fingers and directed John's attention to the task at hand, which was to rewrite a long paper so the government could grow larger and more firmly entrenched in the lives of ordinary citizens, who sometimes didn't know what was good for them. She then took a sedative.

The children's task was nearly complete, so John needed to forget what was happening on the other side of the window, even though that pane of glass grew thicker with each passing day, eliminating permanently his contact with life on the other side. An audible lament escaped John's lips. If only he could forget.

The following day when the sun was especially bright, like the lights from flashing cameras, a large black dog appeared on the other side of the bulletproof windowpane. When little John saw the dog pacing back and forth, the Deputy Teaching Captain, who had observed John for the past year, wondered how John would respond to the presence of an important creature, possibly from one of the other branches of government, the one with all the power. She presumed he would pull back in fright, wet his pants, and hurry back to the reading chamber, which was a braided wool rug, circular in dimension.

Little John did precisely what she expected. Her young charge's pants grew darker at the crotch, and he ran to the rug where he dropped to the floor in front of the lengthy document he had been perusing, his little features frozen in fear. He tried to smile but gave up when he realized he didn't have the energy to dissimulate further. His response to the document lying at his feet required all the strength he could muster. He shouldn't change it. That much he knew. The score was even at four to four. But he knew he must, especially after seeing the big black canine that probably ruled the world outside this small chamber. "He looks like a king or maybe the president," John mumbled to himself.

The Associate Council Teacher rang a bell, signaling debate to begin, and all children sitting on the circular rug considered the brief before them. Elena and Sonia, the newest members of the court, and Ruth, the oldest, faced Little Lord John, who stared at the papers in his hands while considering how caterpillars turned into butterflies and escaped. He did not look at them.

Only Elena smiled, but sometimes her smile was like a false scent which a dog chased only to discover his prey had outsmarted him. Sometimes she smiled to protect herself from questions about her previous legal experience. She had none. She even smiled when she fell down or had to wait to use the potty. To soothe her self-doubts, Elena touched the little blackboard she carried like contraband in her pocket. Since John wasn't looking, she leaned over to Ruth and said, "Smart girls are cool." Ruth nodded in agreement. They both turned to include Sonia in their game, but she was busy admiring herself in a little hand mirror. Sonia surprised them by nodding at the mirror in agreement.

"Excuse me, Little Lord John," said Ruth, whose small brown eyes looked tired and crusted with sleep. "But we need to change the words."

"Yes," agreed Sonia, who placed her mirror beside her, lifted her red skirt and petticoats, and flashed them at their leader. "We can't pass the law," she sang loudly, "if the document says 'a fine.'"

The Associate Council Teacher inhaled suddenly and vehemently shook her head at the little girl whose dark eyes and long black braids disappeared behind the skirt and petticoats she held above her head. Sonia couldn't see the Associate Council's angry face through her undergarments, but she tilted her mirror and observed the scowl blooming like a marigold across her countenance.

Sonia ignored tradition, lifted her nose, and snorted like a donkey. She remained defiant for only a moment, then dropped her skirts to announce, "I'm better than anyone in this room by a long shot." Although no one challenged her, probably because each child had said the same thing at some time or other, Sonia liked to remind her colleagues of the facts, especially since she was new to the group.

"Not this again," complained Italian Sam, who shook his shaggy head and mouthed the words "Not true" to his colleagues. He looked at his companions through a curtain of stringy brown shoulder-length hair that refused to stay parted down the middle. "We don't question your right to be here, Sonia, so stop acting like a princess. And keep your petticoats to yourself and out of my face!" When he dropped his head to continue reading the document, his annoyance was obscured by that mop of unruly hair covering his face like drapery.

"That's right," agreed Anthony, a tall and bony child who looked younger than his years despite his attempts to appear older. It was rumored that every morning he lathered his hair with gel and brushed it up on top of his head into a faux-hawk. But by the time he got to daycare, instead of looking fierce, he looked confused and his hair resembled wilted spinach. "Change the word 'fine' to 'tax,' and hurry up, John!" he insisted. "I have to make poopie."

"You think you get to decide everything, don't you?" challenged chubby Antonin, shaking his curly head. "But you don't!" He sat next to Anthony and ignored every word he said as well as those spoken by his playmates. Before Anthony could respond, Antonin turned from Anthony and stuck out his tongue at his friend Ruth, who smiled and returned the gesture.

"When is snack time?" Antonin demanded. "We need snacks. I can't think without snacks."

Ruth clapped her hands and gleefully agreed. "Yes, snacks are good!" she exclaimed. At which point the Associate Council Teacher frowned and shook her head. Chagrined, Ruth stopped smiling and fell asleep.

As she started to dream about an evolving Constitution, her long black hair cascaded down the shoulder of Clarence, the other plump boy seated on the rug, who sat next to her. Her hair started to tangle in Clarence's braids, but Clarence shook himself free from their influence. Instead of examining his brief, he perused a picture book and fiddled with a rosary. Before falling asleep, however, Ruth peeked over his shoulder to look at pictures of NASCAR drivers in the book he studied. Those men don't look like the saints on his T-shirt, she thought. They are wearing helmets, not white robes and sandals. Ruth closed her eyes.

Observing Clarence, the Deputy Assistant said, "Clarence, are you reading about racecar drivers again?"

Holding his breath and not answering questions, Clarence waited to be accused.

"Please put your picture book away," the Deputy Assistant directed. "Are you finished with the brief?"

Relieved that he was not sent away to stand alone in the hall, Clarence nodded. He dropped the book and pocketed the rosary.

Clarence rarely spoke or asked questions. He preferred working alone and doubted if any of his colleagues really liked him since his entrance to the chamber was approved by a slim margin. The teachers, however, observed that the others accepted him and some, like Ruth and Antonin, played games with him, at least when Ruth was awake.

Ruth had dozed off but awoke when Anthony tickled her nose with his same-sex dolls and said robustly, not unlike a broken record, "Same-sex love for everyone!" Ruth looked confused. "What is a same sex?" she grumbled and stared at his grinning visage. Her small colleagues shared her confusion, tilted their little heads, and waited for an explanation. They had not yet figured out what equipment they each had, let alone how it worked, so they sat silently absorbing the undue burden of his enthusiastic pronouncements.

"Forget it then," said Anthony, abandoning his dolls inside the toy chest. "I'll go play with Stephen." Anthony skipped over to the standing globe where Stephen stood spinning the gigantic ball, his finger poised above it. Like a roulette wheel, it stopped. Stephen rubbed the bristles on top of his recently barbered head and leaned in closer to see where his lucky spin had come to rest. "Egypt!" he cried like a barker at a state fair. "We should study Egyptian law to decide the case before us."

"Not that again," complained Antonin. "You can't let go of those folks across the pond, can you?"

Ignoring Antonin's complaint, Stephen's reliance on ancient idols, and everyone else in the room, Clarence forgot his rosary and the book he was perusing about men dressed in shiny satin jackets imprinted with fearful designs. He stood up and walked to his private project. The Deputy Assistants watched him as he began tending a little garden of bean and corn plants he cultivated in Dixie cups.

Sometimes he accidentally dropped the seeds, newly developed by Monsanto, and they planted themselves beneath the heating element that zipped around the room between the walls and the tiles. One day after Christmas vacation, the children returned to see small stalks of corn swaying in the sunlight. Today, however, the plants were mere seedlings, much like the innocents in the chamber.

"Tell us what you are planting, Clarence," asked Stephen, who spoke a second time in French. "Expliquez, pour nous, vos plantes," Stephen repeated. But Clarence said nothing.

"Come on, Clarence, change your modus operandi and talk to us!" pleaded Stephen without ire.

"I'm not evolving!" said Clarence. He sat back on his heels like a football player ready to receive, his mouth firmly closed.

Since no one had a football or even knew how to throw one, they watched Clarence rock back and forth. He looked up, waiting for them to object. But no one said anything. Besides, there was just so much power the group could assert on individual members. The children soon lost interest and directed their gaze to Little Lord Fauntleroy, who stood at the window blowing his nose into an embroidered handkerchief.

Feeling the eyes of his classmates upon him, Little Lord John stuffed the hanky into his back pocket and turned from the window to face his silent interlocutors. Why, oh why, he thought, am I the leader?

He waited for their questions, but they silently watched him and wondered whose side he would join. Little Lord John didn't know what to do, but he knew he better do something and quick. Everyone was waiting. Plus, that mean black dog might come back.

"Hey!" exclaimed Samuel. "There's a big black dog pacing back and forth outside this window!"

"He's all black except for a white spot on his chest that looks like a bowtie," said Antonin. "He looks like a symphony conductor. I bet he weighs over a thousand pounds!"

Before the Deputy Assistant could object, the children raced to the window.

"More like a hundred pounds!" exclaimed Stephen, who started biting his nails as if they were candy.

"I don't care how much he weighs," said Samuel. "He doesn't scare me!"

Outside on the playground, John saw the big dog again. It was the biggest dog he had ever seen. He didn't know any dog could get that big! Every day that he and his playmates met to study the new document about doctors and nurses and who would pay their bills, he saw the dog pacing back and forth.

He even saw the dog after school before his mother whisked him away from the children who played in other rooms and laughed and screamed on the playground after lunch.

Yesterday he had pulled his mother's hand to direct her attention to the big dog, which was surprisingly skinny up close. But she calmly told him, "Don't look at the dog, John. It just wants to get your attention. Come along, dearest." And she lifted him carefully into his car seat in the back of her Toyota Prius.

But he thought differently. The dog had already warned him, not in so many words, of course, but with his eyes and mouth. Every day the dog snapped his teeth and drooled strings of slippery saliva. Nasty dog drool smeared the window. During naptime, John could hear the big black dog growling nearby. After naptime, the dog disappeared until a bell rang for dismissal. Then the dog returned to threaten him further. "What does that creature want?" he asked himself. "He looks like the boss of the world and growls like an emperor," John said softly to himself. He didn't think anyone could hear him, and even if they did, no one paid much attention to him unless he carried his gavel and gave them cookies.

John knew what he should do, but fear and a trickle of yellow water rolling down his leg prevented him from following his conscience. What if he did the wrong thing and the dog attacked him! Or chased him away from Donkey Care! Where would he go?

He watched his colleagues smile and wave at the dog. Sonia gave the dog a thumbs-up. Then she and Elena and Ruth all held hands. The boys stuck their hands in their pockets.

"He must be the dog in charge," said Sonia, who had turned her back to the window to view the dog reflected in her mirror. "He acts like a president!"

"Look at the apricot poodles dancing beside him!" cried Ruth. "They must be his little helpers."

"Oh, look!" said Sonia. "The big dog is sniffing their butts!"

The diminutive girls left the window quickly, hiding their faces in embarrassment. Though small, each little darling wondered how it must feel to be a tiny poodle and have a big black dog sniff your butt! They squealed in delight as they ran to the bookcase to check the status of the last document on their docket. Had they agreed or not? All they needed was a number bigger than four.

Little Lord John noticed that after the big dog sniffed the backsides of the diminutive prancing poodles, the dog continued to pace, ignoring his entourage like they were empty food and water bowls.

"Ooh!" squealed Anthony. "He lifted his leg and peed on them!" The boys laughed, but John, who remembered his calling in life, quickly stifled his own levity because he, Little Lord John, might be next. He also must always provide leadership for his fellows, who were laughing so hard one of them broke wind. John's face sobered and within seconds the boys appeared as staid as the marble columns heralding the entrance to this hallowed sanctuary.

"It smells in here," said Antonin. "Can we open the window?"

"If someone opens that window," warned Anthony, rubbing the two miniature boy dolls he kept in his pocket against each other, "that big dog might jump in here and eat us all!" As he stuffed the dolls inside his shirt and close to his heart, he brought his argument to a close by stating, "Every doll has a right to privacy."

"I dissent," said Antonin. "Put those dolls back inside the toy chest and stop rubbing them against each other." Anthony knew his day would come, but it wasn't today. He threw the dolls into the toy chest, but his aim was off and they landed on top of each other at the center of the circular rug.

"That dog is just a big bully!" exclaimed Samuel. "He just wants to scare everyone so they think like him. If you let him scare you once, you'll end up on a slippery slope!"

"Let's take a picture of him," suggested Ruth. "Do we have a camera?"

"We should have cameras in here and outside, so we can watch ourselves work," said Elena. "Then we could see the big dog even when we're doing our work."

"No court cameras!" rebutted Stephen.

"Forget the cameras," interjected Ruth. "It stinks in here, and my civil liberties are being trampled upon by the person who needs to use the bathroom. I must speak up when I am being marginalized by flatulence."

But before one of her companions could defend her by making reference to the evolving Constitution that could be used to create new rights the way Monsanto created hybrid seeds, the children heard the melodious refrain of a Brahms lullaby sung acapella by someone in their midst. Turning toward the source of this musical interlude, they saw Antonin standing on top of the toy chest, his little mouth open, his eyes closed. The children stood transfixed, at least until the dog jumped against the windowpane and barked. Undaunted, Antonin continued to sing.

"You don't scare me!" affirmed Samuel, pointing his finger at the dog. "I don't care if I'm the only one, but I vote to ignore you."

"Look!" cried Sonia. "The dog is on the ground, and his legs are sticking straight up."

"Is he sleeping?" asked Ruth, yawning.

"Maybe he's under a spell," said Elena, checking her little blackboard for an answer. Finding none, she smoothed her short brown hair and smiled. Or maybe he's bored like I am, she thought.

Antonin stopped singing. "The dog is enjoying the music, but don't be deceived, dear Ruth." He jumped off the toy chest and placed a pudgy arm around his best friend. "He is assuming a position of surrender, but if we open the window, he'll attack. He's not what he appears to be."

Antonin tapped John on his shoulder, and the boy in blue turned around. "Come on, John," insisted Antonin, "it's time for snacks and chocolate milk."

"I don't want any," said John, scowling at the boy standing next to him. "Leave me alone. I need to think."

"You aren't thinking," said Antonin. "You're just pouting." Antonin opened his mouth to say more, but his friend Ruth tapped him on the shoulder.

"You're it," Ruth squealed and took off running.

But Antonin remained standing next to the boy whose small frame ensconced in royal blue couture and blending into the blue curtains nearly made him invisible. "Do you want to play tag?" Antonin asked.

"Can't you see I'm otherwise occupied?" pleaded John.

"You can't catch me, tubby," said Ruth, who bonked her friend Antonin on the head with a stuffed elephant retrieved from the toy box. "I'm the fastest one in this room!"

"No, you're not, shorty!" countered Antonin, grabbing John's personal copy of Black's Law Dictionary out of his pocket. Like many law students, Antonin threw the book across the room. John glared at the tenor. "You really should be more considerate, Antonin," he called to the happy pair as they ran circles around him.

He made up his mind. He would do it! He would agree to go along. By default, he chose the easiest path. To get along, he changed the word. Now maybe his playmates would finally believe he really did have a heart. Maybe then the big black dog with the bowtie would never come back, although he doubted it.

He retrieved his dictionary and placed it in his private cubicle identified as such by his name. He then swept up the brief, lying in wait on his napping rug, changed the word, and dropped the document in the out box. He stood quietly and watched the score jump to 5:4. The other side had won, of course, but now maybe the threatening dog would go back home where he belonged.

"Maybe we should call this law Scotus Care," said Antonin when he saw the score change. "I do believe that words no longer have meaning."

"Don't be sad, Antonin," said Ruth, comforting her friend by handing him a peanut and his favorite stuffed elephant. "Someday maybe you and I can go to India and ride on a real elephant together. We can eat peanuts and give the elephant some as well. What do you say?"

"You're so tiny, you would probably blow away," said Antonin. "But that sounds like a plan."

"We could leave this daycare center for good and travel the world," said Ruth. "What do you say?"

"I say I'm not leaving. I'm staying in this chamber until I'm not running on all eight cylinders," Antonin said, "and I agree with Samuel. I'm staying until that big black dog with the white bowtie is gone, all the way gone."

"I'm staying on the payroll too," said Stephen, "just like my dad."

The big black dog did leave. As soon as John changed the word, the big dog trotted across the playground where its cheering fans awaited him with open arms and doggie cookies. He walked past his entourage, and they quickly followed in his footsteps.

"We should install thermal imaging above the dog house and watch what he's up to," suggested Samuel, "but maybe that's illegal."

"No cameras here or there," warned Antonin. "That would not be legal under the Fourth Amendment without a search warrant."

"You're right," said his companions in unison.

"Let's get back to work," said Ruth. "What's next?"

The Deputy Council Teacher pointed to the circular rug, and the future justices sat. She handed each one a new brief, and the youngsters began reading.

They all lived happily ever after, at least most of them, much of the time.

WHILE SOME MAY, OTHERS MAY NOT

Zechariah 7:11

Your ancestors refused to listen to this message. They stubbornly turned away and put their fingers in their ears to keep from hearing.

Karlee was relieved to be back home. A last-minute decision had placed her in New York with her husband, Bill, who was in the city for a few days on business. She thought it would be fun, a change from the grind of law school, but instead of being exciting, she found the heat and humidity, the traffic and crowded streets and sidewalks enervating. While energy pulsed through its streets, New York remained an enigma; Karlee couldn't sense the soul of the city. Its residents moved through the streets too quickly and the tall buildings made her dizzy and unsettled.

Bill had no spare time. He had warned her that he would be working long hours, but Karlee thought he was exaggerating. He wasn't. She outlined the cases and reading assigned for the week and watched old movies.

When she and Bill landed, she stepped out of the plane and inhaled clean Midwest air. She considered kneeling down and kissing the ground but decided that Bill would wonder if she was suffering from law school derangement and suggest she drop out of school and choose another profession. When they arrived home from the airport, she changed her clothes and kissed him instead of the ground and drove to school.

Her Con Law class met on Thursday evenings. Despite the fact that she was always prepared, she felt nervous. She never knew when she would be asked a question on topics like the Equal Protection Clause, which seemed to be applied according to the whimsy of the Court. One case in particular had been especially puzzling: *Railway Express Agency v. New York*. She decided to do some research about the case in the library after class.

The stairwell in the library was silent as she climbed the empty staircase, noting the bare walls beside the stairs. No somber eyes of former law school presidents or deans assessed her progress, no flyers of upcoming events grabbed her attention. She didn't even observe an angel going up and down the wooden staircase offering her an invitation to another kingdom, one ruled by spiritual laws, not the ones made by politicians and upheld or struck down by the courts.

She quickly found the book she needed, although it had been shelved in the wrong place. Would this article about a statute written in New York City be as flat as the outlines of property she viewed in old deed books in the vault at her grandmother's court office? She wondered. Would this article be written in clear, clean, but unremarkable prose? Or would it provide a riot of figurative language or a dissonant Prokofiev symphony at variance with her senses? Would the article tingle her senses like the frigid ice water in the red Coke machine outside her grandmother's office? She used to shiver when she pushed her small hand and arm into the deep metal box to retrieve a miniature glass bottle of Coke.

She sat down at a long wooden table and opened the book. After consulting the table of contents, she found the article. On the first page, she viewed an old picture of New York in the 1940s. Flipping through the pages, she saw black Packards and Plymouths shaped like huge bullets parked beside curbs inside caverns of tall dark buildings. The streets looked nearly empty, despite what the city's brief stated: that the city streets of New York were tangled with traffic due to trucks hired for the sole purpose of driving around with advertisements painted on their sides. After all, many of the men were overseas fighting for freedom. Who was driving these trucks for hire, the ones that carried no cargo?

She began reading the following article that was unlike any she had read in a book on the law. Perhaps because her senses were starved for an exciting text, she may have rewritten some of the article as she read. To this day, she isn't sure.

In the 1940s, traffic snarled in New York City, but when was that news? Complaints poured into City Hall and into the Offices of Borough officials. Grade school children wrote letters of protest, complaining that they often missed dinner waiting for the trucks to deliver the latest Captain America or Archie comics or a fresh supply of Bazooka gum cigars, Jolly Ranchers, and Black Cow candy bars. They couldn't wait to buy the new trading cards with pictures of Joe Di Maggio, Ted Williams, and Sugar Rae Robinson and make it home for dinner on time. If they waited for one, they missed the other.

Nuns wrote that they were late for mass, and bar owners wrote that their beer deliveries arrived when their taverns were filled with thirsty customers who needed to be served, not told to wait for the trucks to be unloaded. Owners of drug stores with soda fountains and their ice cream loving customers showed up at City Hall to complain that deliveries of certain flavors, like chocolate, never made it to the local drug stores.

Customers, who had stood in line for forty odd minutes on a hot and humid summer night for their weekly chocolate fix, raised their fists and threatened great bodily injury. Soda jerks reported their customers' recalcitrance to authorities, but these reports were quickly denied by indignant customers who claimed that ice cream reminded them of their childhood. When reporters and cameras left ice cream shops, ice cream lovers and soda jerks engaged in pinching contests that left scores of ice cream aficionados and soda fountain employees scarred for life. All because there was too much traffic!

To say nothing of the pasta delivery trucks that arrived late to restaurants in Little Italy where members of certain crime families blew out the tires of the trucks and peppered their sides with holes the size of a rat's head. Something had to be done. Ambulances arrived so late that the elderly forgot what medical condition they claimed was a dire emergency and asked to be taken to the movies instead.

Karlee looked around the library. She thought this article was quite entertaining.

City Hall tried to reassure residents, and residents tried to feel assured. But how long can a pregnant woman wait to deliver or a marching band wait to march? In ballparks across the city, batters stood at the plate, ready to swing, but where were the pitchers? Where were the softballs? They were stuck in traffic! And the hard and soft baseballs they threw from the plate slept soundly inside hot trucks, and waited patiently to be unloaded by men with ropey muscles wearing brown wool pants, vests, short-sleeved shirts, and brimmed caps.

Across town, puppies were half grown by the time they reached pet stores, and first graders were ready for second grade by the time they skirted traffic jams caused by delivery truck drivers. Stalled at red lights, these mesmerized drivers ogled colorful photos plastered to the sides of trucks revealing young brunette women with short wavy hair and rosy cheeks who held a cold bottle of Coca-Cola. New Buick Road Masters, Packards, and Nash Ramblers rolled into showrooms so late that they were tagged as last year's models. All because of advertising on the sides of trucks tying up traffic but not delivering any goods!

Things were in a fine state of affairs, to say nothing about the competition. How to get a leg up in your business, that was the real worry. What were a few ice cream lovers covered in black and blue marks or a few disappointed, spoiled children compared to the advantages your competition gained by advertising his product on the side of a truck rented for the sole purpose of advertising his product?

Businessmen all over the city pondered the challenge of overcoming and defeating their competitors. In the wee hours of the morning, business competitors stared at the ceiling, sweat dripping down their faces because a delivery truck had lost its load of window fans, and the machines now lay at the bottom of the East River or smashed against the side of a building, all because a truck driver had been distracted by a Twinkie painted on a truck roaring down the street. Residents claimed that at night they could hear those fans oscillating at full speed. Stranded, these trucks lay out of commission, gasping for an opportunity to traverse the public streets of the city with advertisements on their vehicles.

The drivers of trucks carrying goods prayed for a guaranteed legal right to spread commerce throughout the city's five boroughs while their trucks lay impotent at the bottom of the river, all because their drivers had become enthralled by an advertisement for sliced Polish ham with cherries on top driving in the opposite direction.

The devil was in the details, or so it was said. But in New York in the '40s, the devil was in the colorful advertisements that assaulted the eyes of the truck drivers who rode around the city all day and night to deliver goods. Bright pictures of Ex-Lax, Rice-a-Roni, and Camel cigarettes plastered the sides of trucks for hire as well as delivery trucks, riveting the attention of drivers and pedestrians alike.

While crime was down, accidents had risen to such a degree that the adding machines used to tally the number of traffic accidents and ambulance trips to local hospitals exploded. On the desks of accountants up and down city hall smoldered the remains of machines requiring large rolls of white narrow paper. Frustrated, they stuffed Dutch Master Cigars in their mouths, the kind they saw advertised on trucks snarling traffic. No one could keep up with the accident rate in New York City. It was not the best of times; it was the worst. Dickens didn't know everything.

And what about the problem of signs and advertisements created to attract the attention of taxi cab and bus drivers! Or the focus of drivers in cars whose attention wavered only to be sucked into an ad for Campbell's tomato soup—the public swore in written affidavits that they could smell and taste the tomatoes—or onto a moving billboard portraying a loaf of Wonder Bread with those cute red, yellow, and blue balls on both sides of the loaf?

Citizens testified they could taste and smell the freshly baked bread—with baloney and mustard, of course. But the police commissioner said advertising on vehicles, used only for advertising, constituted a threat to drivers and pedestrians alike. If allowed to continue willy-nilly, surely the Allied Forces would lose the war.

Colors and gloss, shapes and primitive graphics designed to capture the eye and the beholder's heart threatened to undermine the country's GDP. It was so bad driving down a New York street that drivers began wearing screens around their heads to isolate them from the tempting distractions created by a picture of Aunt Jemima, who was in reality Nancy Green, a former slave. The most popular device resembled a catcher's mask, but wealthier drivers, or their chauffeurs, wore Army helmets to protect the wearers from sensual enticements outside their vehicles.

Public safety became the new mantra for aspiring politicians. To maintain their power and show the public their elected officials actually worked behind those polished mahogany doors at City Hall, the police commissioner promulgated a law which they claimed would reduce traffic hazards. It stated:

No person shall operate or cause to be operated, in or upon any street an advertising vehicle; provided that nothing herein contained shall prevent the putting of business notices upon business delivery vehicles, so long as such vehicles are engaged in the usual business or regular work of the owner and not merely or mainly used for advertising.

Several dozen exceptions followed. Of course, there were exceptions. There always were. No law ever written in the history of mankind was written sans a list of exceptions. For one, second cousins could drive the trucks for hire that carried no freight. So could students, immigrants, and barbers. Just like the Bible; there were good guys, those suffering from palsy or demons, and those just looking for the best place to fish. But it all boiled down to the trucks that businesses used solely for advertising purposes, and not for deliveries—and of course to union payoffs.

Payoffs must be underscored. New York was a big place, so everyone expected a little money would be handed out in the alley or passed under the table. The law stood adamantly opposed to drivers who traipsed around the city tantalizing pedestrians and drivers alike without being able to satisfy their longings because their trucks were filled with hot air and not real goods.

Business owners whose trucks delivered goods, in the normal course of business, wanted the sole right to plaster advertisements on the sides of their delivery vehicles. They accused the drivers who hauled around hot air in their trucks of causing all the problems. These vehicles, driven in the course of a day, usually by nonunion drivers, were the ones causing all the accidents and late deliveries, the ones advertising Hormel Spam and smoked fish without any on board; trucks that did not deliver any goods were verboten. Period.

So there. It was done. The law was written. As Professor Sager, an esteemed law professor at an equally esteemed law school, said, "... a state may treat persons differently only when it is fair to do so." Whether or not the sage professor had received a financial kickback is a concern that misses the point. We must further dismiss Justice Reed's dissent in which he argued "that to sustain a law based on such a 'whimsical' distinction was essentially to render the Equal Protection Clause 'useless in state regulation of business practices.'" Reasonableness, the clarion call of the judicial system, did not stand a chance against the unions and the businesses that hired them; Justice Reed should have saved his pen and paper.

A lawsuit followed, but when was that an unusual occurrence? A motion against the city was filed by Railway Express Agency, a company that operated about 1900 trucks in New York City and sold space on the exterior sides of these trucks solely for advertising purposes. The plaintiff defended its right to distract drivers and pedestrians alike with advertisements painted on the sides of their vehicles, like the painted eyelids of Jezebel just before she was thrown over the balcony. And, in general, of promoting business for a price while not delivering the goods. But the court claimed it was not the court's function to pass judgment on the wisdom of the city traffic regulation.

The defense stated that Railway compromised the safe passage of New Yorkers who walked or rode to their destinations. Their brief contained no statistics revealing the number of accidents caused by companies putting advertisements on their hot air trucks compared to the number caused by advertisements for products actually inside the truck and promoted for a price.

The brief read by the justices further claimed that the hireling could be put into a class by itself and be dealt with differently from those companies acting on their own. Equal Protection under the law had its limits, after all, and the city believed that the courts would decide their case based on practical considerations provided by experience rather than upon theoretical inconsistencies. Money was not mentioned in either side's brief.

On Wednesday truck drivers gathered around the parking lot behind the Supreme Court of New York where the case was being heard. Those who drove for companies that hired out their empty space for a price walked to the far side of the lot, smoked Camels, and discussed the fate of their employment. Those who delivered goods for individual companies that also sold goods, mostly union members, stood under a maple tree, wiping the sweat from their brows and eating red hot frankfurters dripping with mustard and sauerkraut from a nearby vendor whose cart was covered by an umbrella. The two groups shot occasional glances at each other. At four o'clock a whistle blew, but none of the drivers boarded their trucks and left the parking lot. And the police turned the other way.

At five minutes past the hour, the back door to the courthouse opened. Court reporters left, their equipment trailing behind them like lost puppies. All of the drivers silently watched as the plaintiff's gray-suited attorneys, whose danger antennae had kicked into high gear, donned sunglasses, walked out into the bright sun, and quickly fanned out across the parking lot in the direction of local bars. When they returned, they held cold bottles of Budweiser dripping with beads of water. As they drank, they thought about the arguments they would assert against the city and pressed the bottles against their hot faces.

Finally, three defense attorneys who represented the city emerged wearing black suits. Three law clerks stumbled behind the defense like goslings following a mother goose. One of the prosecutors, whose rioting red hair grabbed the attention of truckers, waved to the prosecutors, then danced in place, lifting his knees up and down. A union trucker named George yelled, "Hey, boys! It's a clown with red hair!" Nonunion truckers eating hotdogs watched as the guardian of justice swung open his suit jacket, revealing golf attire beneath the black folds. Attached to his belt, a putter swung at his side.

The three short defense attorneys, each impeccably dressed in starched white shirts, bowties, and perfectly tailored gray silk suits, formed a short chorus line. They watched as the prosecutors threw their empty beer bottles into the bushes and marched over to the trucks with cameras in their pale hands to take pictures. Each man's dark hair remained in place and perfectly coiffed, although the wind had started to pick up. After photographing sufficient evidence, the city's defenders left their cameras near the courthouse door and reunited to form a second chorus line opposite the tall prosecutors, who stood with dignified posture.

With no warning, the prosecutor with the rioting red hair lifted his foot and kicked the baldheaded attorney standing next to him on his backside. He then tore away from his fellows and darted quickly behind a nearby tree where he stuck out his tongue. "Did you see that, Tony?" asked one of the nonunion truckers, whose mouth provided a view of quickly chewed food. "What the hell?" his friend replied.

The truck drivers watched as the defenders of truth jerked up their legs and pumped them up and down. Remaining in place, they growled and grunted, then took off after the red-haired man, whose tongue continued to dart in and out of his mouth like a Mexican lizard. As they ran, two of the prosecutors pulled out bats and plastic cudgels hidden in the mysterious folds of their gray jackets, and when they stood in front of the red clown, they patted his head then swung their weapons down on his storming red pate. Red squealed, scratched the pavement like a horse ready to charge, and said, "Hey, boys. Look over there!"

When his opponents turned to look, Red ran around some bushes until the opposing counsel chased after him. Then he stopped, reversed course, and ran in the opposite direction until he smacked into his opponents, sending their hefty bodies rising up into a wind current that carried them to a nearby trashcan where they landed with a resounding crash.

"Boys, we have a public duty to perform," said George, and he and his buddy lifted the defenders from the confines of their entrapment. Other truckers walked over and removed the chop suey sticking to their silk jackets with chopsticks, conveniently left for just this purpose, and wiped away the mustard oozing down their foreheads. The public defenders clapped their arms around each other, bowed to their liberators, then scurried back into the fray.

Barking like frenzied dogs, the line of defense attorneys circled a lone prosecutor who stood defiant in the middle of their circle. The adversarial nature of the American justice system was playing out in a parking lot. The sound of cheering grabbed George's attention. He looked up at the courthouse where he saw the cleaning staff and security guards leaning out of open windows and cheering their favorites on to a victory. George and his buddy watched as employees exchanged money, then cheered for their favorite team three floors above the hallowed halls of justice.

Spectators were viewing litigation in its purist form, and they held their breath as the prosecutors whooped like Indians, tapped the black-suited defense on their shoulders, and yelled, "You're it!" A passerby stepped forward to get a better view but was trampled as the public defenders led a chase around the parking lot near the drivers for Railway Express. George grabbed the innocent man and helped him stumble into the shade where he soothed his startled nerves with a Fanta grape soda, handed to him by a quick-thinking legal assistant.

The crowd watched as the shortest, heaviest defense attorney—wearing a black suit, a favorite of the employees cheering from the windows, and nicknamed Defender Lift because he wore lifts in his shoes—reversed direction and swerved in and out of the pack of wolves behind him who continued to chase the truth. He skipped to the center of the parking lot, stopped, pushed back his suit coat, and revealed a red belt cinched below his waist and pulled tight like the knot at the bottom of a balloon, the kind held by the birthday boy at his party. He pulled a bugle from his side pocket, placed it carefully to his lips, and blew with all his might.

Immediately the wheels of justice stopped spinning. The frisky wind lifted his short body, reduced to half its size after his exhalation of so much hot air, and carried it up and over the trees. A few truckers yelled out, "He's over here!" George turned to see Defender Lift, his body tightly squeezed into a cannonball, hit the waters of a fountain dedicated to the men and women who daily uphold the rights guaranteed to us by our Founding Fathers. Waves splashed and rolled, but the buoyant Defender Lift quickly emerged. Several able-bodied men lifted him from the fountain water, but he removed these helping hands and charged back to the fight for justice occurring in front of his wet face.

Those who made their living from the conflicts of others stood in a circle facing each other. One of the prosecutors stepped away from the group and ran toward a truck loaded with goods, but he didn't proceed very far, for unbeknownst to him someone had dug a hole and covered it with leaves and dead flowers from the courthouse garden; he fell into it, hands and arms first.

His posterior wiggled for freedom until the public defenders hurried over to extricate him from the trap. Ready for the opposing counsel's feint, the upside-down prosecutor struck out his legs and feet, and like a donkey protecting a flock of sheep, kicked his opponent into the flowerbed near the courtroom entrance where he sat like Little Jack Horner.

Someone from the courthouse windows blew a whistle. Without fanfare, the conveyors of justice strode to the curb where they all sat down in front of a large truck displaying a picture of Betty Crocker. They turned to view a sign behind them portraying a man smoking a Camel. To their left, they observed a blue-eyed blond child eating Kellogg's Cornflakes from a brightly colored bowl. "This gets confusing," said one of the attorneys. They all agreed.

Hearing a second whistle, this time blown by the head custodian still standing at a window, the attorneys stood, bowed to each other and the onlookers around them, and walked back to the courthouse amidst shouts and cheers. George and his buddy lit firecrackers. The prosecutor with the rioting red hair quacked and led the way to the back door of the courthouse where he opened the door through which his fellows followed him inside like ducklings pursuing their matriarch.

The court upheld Section 124 of the Traffic Regulations. After several appeals in state court, it was reviewed by the Supreme Court. In a unanimous decision, the Court ruled against Railway Express, a company that leased trucks for the sole purpose of advertisement.

———— ∞∞∞ ————

Karlee closed the book, checked its publishing date, and decided, at least for the night, that law was an amazing field of study. She thought she returned the book to the shelf.

However, when she returned to the reading room after a quick call to Bill, the book was nowhere to be found. In its place on the table, a puff of smoke rose, not unlike the steam from hot New York streets after a summer rain.

THE TRASH CAN SPOKE

Psalm 42:5

Why am I so discouraged? Why is my heart so sad? I will put my hope in God! I will praise him again—my Savior and my God!

Psalm 27:10

Even if my mother and father abandon me, the Lord will hold me close.

T he streets were empty, the neighborhood quiet. In the past couple of weeks, the temperature had soared, the humidity as well, so the kids stayed inside in front of fans and TVs, while the gangbangers waited until the sun went down to stand on the corners and look for trouble. After a busy night, pimp-mobiles parked in the shade while the source of their incomes rested up in darkened, air-conditioned rooms. It was Sunday.

A nondescript van, no longer shiny, moved through the neighborhood as unobtrusively as a fox avoiding a predator and stopped in front of an apartment building. Its surface looked like it had been washed with Spic and Span, the shine a mere memory. Most of the residents on the West Side viewed the van and its driver with curiosity rather than mistrust. But not all. The driver wasn't selling drugs or women, but clearly he was selling something. Statuettes lined the van's dashboard, the windshield recently repaired after a gang member sailed a rock through its pristine surface. "We don't want no bullshit Jesus in the hood," he had yelled. Instead of yelling back, the driver replaced the windshield.

The figurines looking out of the van windshield remained in place and the driver undeterred. Every notable man and woman of faith stood on display in front of the clean glass windshield, washed daily by the van's owner. The biblical figures on the dashboard viewed the activity on the streets as they had viewed those activities for two thousand years. The figurines knew what they saw and knew that it displeased God.

From Moses to Rachel, the small statues stood, mutely reciting ancient history. This panoply of God's servants graced the van, attracting the attention of believers, skeptics, and the curious alike. Moses carried the Ten Commandments, Peter held the keys to the kingdom, Daniel stood beside a lion, and Jonah waited at the mouth of a whale. Joseph displayed his multicolored robe and John the Baptist wore a goat-hair vest. Ruth held her mother-in-law's hand and Elijah carried dry bones. In the center stood Jesus in a white robe, a lamb on one side, a child on the other.

On warm afternoons, children asked the driver if they could play with the dolls. Mothers looked at the driver, an older man in his fifties, and took him for a crazy zealot. They pushed the backs of their children forward and kept walking, even if the little voices begged to touch the people of the Bible.

Some residents of the community turned away from the red van and those figurines whose eyes saw what they did. Others figured Jesus wouldn't take them after all the sinning they had done. They did not turn inward to examine their feelings or ask for forgiveness. Instead, they tuned out. Some climbed to the roofs of neighborhood buildings where they viewed the cityscape before them, like the Israelites viewed the giants in the Promised Land. They saw the giant clusters of grapes dripping with abundance but outside their reach. Drugs satisfied their cravings while alcohol deadened the pain of seeing too much abundance, close, but so far away.

However, two sisters weren't afraid and stepped forward to talk to the driver about his display. Their gram told them his name was Mr. Curtis and that she worked with him at the post office. The girls understood what he was selling. They had bought it themselves. They liked Mr. Curtis and his faith figurines because they had big dreams. A Bible lesson ignited their faith. Shamika wanted to be a teacher and Tamara, her younger sister, dreamed of being a lawyer. They told their gram they wanted to make something of themselves. Their gram said, "You better plant your seed and tell the Lord what you want. He sittin' high, but He lookin' low." Encouraged by their grandmother's words, the girls came close to the driver's window and asked him about the Bible people.

Mr. Curtis handed each sister a figurine. "Lemme ax you some questions," he said in an accent hailing from Alabama. "What these dolls teach you?" When the girls hesitated, he said, "All in all, they teach love. You know, so I'm gonna say you wouldn't do nothin' wrong to yo neighbor."

The girls had been taught about loving their neighbor, but Tamara worried what those neighbors might do to them. She dropped her eyes but listened as Mr. Curtis continued. "I be seein' yo fear. But the Lord, hey, He wit you. He got yo back. Like my daddy tole me, 'You gotta stand up quick.'"

Tamara looked up; she felt her face turn flat like cardboard until Mr. Curtis explained. "That mean to stand up fo God, and He stand up fo you. You know what I mean?"

They knew because their grandmother, Miss Mildred, took them to the Baptist church a couple of blocks away from where she stayed. Gram told Tamara that they had a ride to church this morning. "Mr. Curtis, he be carrying us to Ebenezer Baptist. We all goin'. Well, everyone 'cept for your mama. You, me, Shamika, and Mr. Curtis."

Tamara pressed her nose against the windowpane in the living room of their third-floor apartment. Her willowy frame bent as she peered out onto the street. "Shamika," she whispered, "you better hurry. Gram and Mr. Curtis, they be lookin' this way."

"Girl, don't point. I know where the street is. You better check yoself. You know Gram don't hold with no bad grammar." Tamara was about to object but remained silent when she saw Shamika smile. Both sisters spoke two languages: street talk and the English taught in school. Tamara returned Shamika's smile and watched as her older sister paused in front of the mirror to check her hair one more time and then rub her finger over both eyebrows.

Bibles in tote, they scanned the living room once more for bottles, cups, and cigarette-laden ashtrays, the detritus of their mother's life, then closed the door. The living room now revealed no sign of the noisy party the night before. Since she was young, Tamara had listened to party noise at night. She and Shamika had learned to sleep through it. It was easier now with the ear pods in place, a gift from Mr. Curtis. Tamara locked the door and hurried after her older sister. She knew the day was off to a good start; no one had urinated in the hallway.

"Don't you girls look fine," their gram said as they slid open the door and climbed into the backseat. "Those dresses fit real nice. Orange is a good color for caramel-skinned girls." Their gram faced Mr. Curtis and continued, "You never know what you'll find at Goodwill." Tamara watched her gram lift her head, like some rich lady who bought only the best. "The only difference between Goodwill and Sears is basically the price. Ain't no other difference," Gram concluded.

"Shouldn't be mo' than eighty-nine to the penny," said Mr. Curtis. "That's what my daddy say."

Gram nodded in agreement. "Ain't that a fact. Can't pay no mo' than what they worth."

Mr. Curtis glanced over at Tamara's gram. "You sure yo folk ain't from Alabama, Miss Mildred?"

Old-school gospel music played on the radio. Tamara liked it when Mr. Curtis sang along. From the backseat she watched his animated face in the mirror above the dashboard. He was a handsome old man, she thought, and reminded her of the artist Aaron Douglas, whose picture she had seen in a book about Harlem Renaissance artists. Both men brushed their gray curly hair straight back from their faces and wore a moustache and rimless glasses. Second to the law, Tamara loved the arts. She enjoyed going to the school library during Black History month to read books about the accomplishments of her people. Someday, she decided, she was going to be in that book.

"Shamika, your hair looks real nice. You too, Tamara. Did Rhonda perm your hair?"

"Yes, ma'am," the girls responded, their voices lilting like songbirds.

Shamika explained, "Mama took us to the salon last Tuesday."

Gram touched her own curly gray head. "Real nice and wavy. You be stylin' for sure. Maybe she could do mine. Is your homework all ready for the new week?"

In unison, the girls responded, "Yes, ma'am!"

Tamara saw Gram give a shake of her head and press her lips together. She knew Gram felt blessed. Gram turned back in her seat. "Now say hello to Mr. Curtis," she said. "He's carrying us to church this morning to hear Bishop Thomas speak."

"Good morning, Mr. Curtis," said Shamika. "Thank you for picking us up this morning. Sometimes the bus is late."

"It be a pleasure," he said in a mellifluous baritone voice and continued singing along with the radio. "'Your grace and mercy brought me through, I'm living this moment because of you . . .'"

Gram exclaimed, "Why that's Franklin Williams and the Mississippi Mass Choir!"

Mr. Curtis nodded, then asked, "Shamika, fo sure you ready to graduate. And, Tamara, you comin' on along, ain't that the case?"

Tamara answered, "Yes, sir. I'm coming up right behind Shamika next year."

"I wanna say, you walkin' down the aisles for commencement?" he asked.

"Yes," replied Shamika, "and Tamara signed up to assist with the ceremony. Her tutor, Erica, is one of the graduation speakers."

Gram nodded. "Her tutor and Tamara pray after every study session. She's a Spirit-filled girl. Ain't that right, Tamara?"

"Yes, ma'am. But the librarian told us we couldn't pray together inside the school," Tamara said, her brow pushed down in frustration. "We pray anyway when she's not there. I thought we had free speech in this country."

"Maybe not in school," Gram said.

"That's not what the Constitution says!" Tamara exclaimed, sitting up straight.

"I declare, Tamara," laughed Gram, "someday you gonna change the world. You watch!"

"I wanna say, them kids in school need Jesus the most," declared Mr. Curtis. "What you gonna study at the community, Shamika?"

"I'll take general classes at the community college and then apply to a four-year college. I want to be a teacher, and Tamara wants to be a lawyer," said Shamika.

"You be pickin' yoself up by the boots," said Mr. Curtis, nodding his head with the music. "You must be hittin' them books pretty hard."

Tamara wondered if Shamika would tell Mr. Curtis how they managed to study in a house filled with their mother's boyfriends.

"Yes, sir," explained Shamika. "We get home real fast and study, before Mama has her company." Shamika moved up in her seat, placed her arms on the back of the front seat, and continued. "You know those locks you gave us, Mr. Curtis? They work real well on our bedroom door, the bathroom door too."

"Every girl needs her privacy. Ain't that right, Mr. Curtis?" said Gram.

"Yes, ma'am," he replied as he slowed the van in front of the church. "I be droppin' you ladies in the front and be wit you in a shake."

Tamara unfastened her seat belt and watched Shamika jump out and run to the front of the van to open the door for their gram. Tamara carried Gram's purse. They walked slowly to the church entrance. Tamara knew Gram's arthritis was bad and said a quick prayer for her healing. "Long as I plant that seed," Tamara whispered to herself.

Tamara paused as she held the door open for a family coming up behind her. Inside she saw Miss Vivien greet her gram. As the stocky woman welcomed those around her, the multicolored feathers in her hat bobbed to the rhythm of her speech. "Sister Mildred," she proclaimed, "you blessed with them gran' babies. Look how grown they be."

Tamara's grandmother lifted her chest. "Don't I know it, Sister Vivien. Both of them girls is saved and Spirit-filled!"

"Praise the Lord!" replied Sister Vivien.

"Don't you know, my girls be the Lord's blessing. Shamika graduates in June and goes to City College in the fall," Gram said.

"Shamika, she favor her mama, but Tamara must favor her daddy. Tamara still wants to lawyer. Ain't that the case?" asked Sister Vivien.

"Yes, she has her heart set on defending God's people, and Shamika wants to be a teacher. I keep praying for their mama, but so far the Lord ain't said a word."

"You keep prayin' for that girl, Sister Mildred," Sister Vivien declared with a stamp of her foot. "The Lord works in mysterious ways; you never know when He be movin' in a sinner's life."

Tamara saw Mr. Curtis make his way through the lobby and join Tamara's gram and Miss Vivien. "Mornin', ma'am," he said. "I wanna say that hat has all the colors of God's rainbow. It looks real dignified."

Tamara wondered if Miss Vivien would take offense, but she smiled at the tall handsome man. He extended his hand, and she noticed that he wore a wedding band. Tamara saw her face fall, but the woman kept on smiling. Gram introduced him to Sister Vivien, who listened as he spoke. "My fine wife, Roschel, be blessed," he explained, "for the Lord is wit her. Next time I come, you gonna meet her."

Sister Vivien replied, "I'd be mighty pleased to meet her, Mr. Curtis. Mighty pleased."

Tamara had never heard Mr. Curtis tell anyone his wife had cancer. He believed the Lord would heal her, but so far she had never seen the woman at church or out riding in the van with Mr. Curtis. Gram told her that she had been a beautiful woman in her day, but the cancer had turned her high yellow complexion into white tissue paper. The cancer had spread to her bones, and she weighed 90 pounds. Sometimes Tamara felt confused by Mr. Curtis's insistence that his wife would get healed when she only seemed to get sicker. However, she admired his faith and positive spirit.

Tamara heard the doors to the sanctuary open and watched Mr. Curtis move quickly down the aisle to find seats toward the front. She could hear the band tuning their instruments and see the choir line up in the hall. Tamara hoped for a word from God about her future after high school. Could she make it in college? She wondered. Would she be accepted into law school? She wished she had Mr. Curtis's faith. He never doubted that the Lord would answer his prayers. Sometimes Tamara wondered if the Lord had time to hear hers.

Tamara looked around for her sister and saw Shamika standing next to the sanctuary doors talking to William, a boy she and Tamara knew from church. Gram said he was sweet on Shamika. They both attended the church youth group and had enrolled in the local junior college, but their sights were set on a four-year college after that. Tamara wished William had a brother her age who wanted to go to college. Not many boys in her neighborhood talked about going to school after they graduated.

When they walked into the sanctuary, Tamara paused to watch the light stream through the big stained-glass window. Just like the window in Carlos Palmer's painting, the colors glowed and splashed onto the floor. She saw women rush here and there, smiling and talking with friends while the menfolk sat in the pews. Young boys in starched white shirts and girls in pastel dresses with full skirts trailed their aunties and grandmas. She noticed thick Sunday papers and Bibles marking the seats already taken by those who had arrived early but stood gossiping with friends before the music started. Some of the menfolk stayed for both services, sat in the pews between times, and caught up on the news.

Tamara felt the Spirit spread through her body. Excitement, like hot wires, charged the atmosphere and animated the faces of all she saw, except for the little boys who tugged at their starched shirt collars when their elders weren't looking. Tamara sat down next to Mr. Curtis and looked around for her sister, who was still smiling up at William by the sanctuary doors.

Gram stood nearby and nodded in agreement with Sister Vivien. She's probably encouraging her gram, Tamara thought. Gram had been praying for years for Tamara's mother, her only child. Tamara questioned whether the Lord heard those prayers because nothing ever changed. While Gram prayed with tears in her eyes, Tamara prayed with doubt in her spirit. Her mama had been in the life for as long as she could remember. The girls mostly avoided their mother and instead asked the Lord to make a way for them in college.

The band started to play, the choir walked in, and those still standing hurried to their seats. Tamara joined the congregation that stood swaying side to side to the music. They sang along with the choir until the choir director grabbed the microphone, stomped his feet, and belted out "Take Me to the King," a praise and worship song that got everyone moving. She watched Mr. Curtis tap his foot and sing to the Lord like he knew Him as a friend.

Across the aisle a short woman in a purple suit and matching hat rose up from the pew, dropped her head, and stretched out her arms. She raised her legs and started spinning around toward the front of the church. Tamara thought she looked like the woman in Annie Lee's painting called "Holy Ghost." Just like in the painting, the Holy Ghost filled this church woman with joy, freeing her soul of all fear and pain. Tamara felt the Spirit wash over her, so she stretched out her arms, pointed to the ceiling, and called out to the Lord. "Praise the Lord!" she shouted.

After church, Mr. Curtis drove them home. When the van pulled up in front of their building, Tamara saw her mother sauntering down the street, swaying her hips from side to side. Tamara wished that she favored her light-skinned mother, who looked like a movie star. She saw a shiny black car pull over to the curb. Her mother must have known the driver, she thought, because she smiled at him. But then her mama smiled at nearly every man she met. When Tamara had asked Gram why her mama didn't have a job and had more boyfriends than a dog has fleas, Gram said, "Child, your mama fell in love with her beauty instead of the Lord. Too much beauty can go to your head."

Tamara watched the man move away from the steering wheel and slither over to the car door. His windows were down, so he placed his ring-covered hand on the door and looked up at her mother. He sat squinting into the sunlight but continued to gaze at her mama. When her mother saw the van and Gram's frowning face, she waved off the driver and approached the van. Tamara pushed open the door and hurried out onto the sidewalk.

"Mama, who was that?" she asked.

"Child, you ain't my mama," her mother scolded.

Tamara persisted when she saw the bag her mother carried. "Why did you walk to the store, Mama? Shamika and I did the shopping yesterday."

"You didn't buy everything I need," she said. "You forgot to buy eggs, and I got me a taste for biscuits." Tamara saw Gram looking at her mama.

"Shamika," her mother ordered, "take these groceries and run upstairs. Change your clothes and make me some breakfast. I want sausage and grits too."

Shamika clambered out of the van and took the plastic bag, looking inside. Tamara started thinking that maybe they'd have a family breakfast until she saw Shamika's face cloud with disappointment.

"Well, Mama, you took my girls to church," Tamara's mother complained, "so now they spout that Jesus crap. You brainwashin' my girls."

"I took you to church too. Remember?"

"And what did the Lord do for me, Mama?"

"He gave you two wonderful girls."

"Yeah, two big mouths to feed."

"The welfare feeds those girls," Gram said. Tamara saw Mr. Curtis tapping her arm. "But you feedin' and clothin' them. They hair look real nice."

Tamara saw her mama look quizzically at Gram, then turn away from the van and lift her hand like a drill sergeant to point at the walkway to the door. Tamara waved goodbye and quickly walked ahead of her mama to unlock the outside door. As she opened the door with the key around her neck, she wondered if her mama would one day walk through the gates of heaven. Tamara had asked her grandma that question, and Gram had said, "Only God judges the saint and sinner alike. Just make sure you be ready for the Judgment Day, Tamara."

In a breathy voice, Tamara said, "We heard a guest pastor this morning at Ebenezer Baptist."

"Yeah, well, I don't want to hear about it. Just go upstairs and change your clothes," her mama said, then paused at the landing and looked at her younger daughter. "Someday, Tamara, reality gonna bite your butt."

Maybe it will, Tamara thought. Maybe it will.

Part Two

City high schools provided their honor students an opportunity to visit local courts, hospitals, and businesses. Career Day was a huge success with the juniors and seniors alike. Tamara told her sister that she and Erica would observe a case in the Court of Appeals involving a high school valedictorian whose diploma had been withheld.

"Shamika," Tamara explained, "Erica's mother said this girl invoked the name of Jesus the night of graduation, and they pulled the plug on her microphone. After the ceremony, the principal made her wait in his office alone without her family or friends." Tamara took a breath, then continued. "Can you believe that?"

"Did the court go along with the school?" asked Shamika.

"Yes, the lower court ruled in favor of the school, so the girl's parents are taking it to a higher court."

She then told Shamika what she said to her guidance counselor. "She asked me if I was interested in being a nurse's assistant. But I told her I wasn't interested in bandaging up folks' problems in a clinic. I told her I was going to be a lawyer and defend the rights of Christians to speak in public about the God who really does the healing of our problems."

A smile lifted the corners of her sister's mouth. "You said that? Girl, you somethin'. Someday you'll be standing before a judge and jury saving the world from the devil." Tamara wondered if her sister was teasing her. But Shamika proved otherwise when she put her arm around Tamara's shoulder and pulled her close. "I'm proud of you, girl," Shamika said.

Tamara liked to study. Gram told her that hard work came first, and dreams followed. She thought that made sense even though her mama said dreams were for suckers. Mama also complained that Tamara asked too many questions. "You need to stand back and listen. I'm being honest with you. You gonna end up pregnant just like me." Tamara listened but had other plans.

She and Erica had signed up to visit the Court of Appeals where Erica's mother tried some of her cases. Her mother was meeting them in Judge Komensky's courtroom. The students filed out of the building and boarded the buses. Tamara sat next to Erica and asked, "Have you ever been to the courthouse with your mother?"

"Yes. I have watched my mother defend her clients, and I understand why she likes her job. She helps women get out of bad marriages and makes sure their husbands provide enough money for their kids' support."

Tamara wondered who her daddy was because her mama never spoke of him. She didn't even know if she and her sister had the same daddy.

"I want to practice family law. How about you, Tamara?" Erica said.

"I want to defend the rights of Christians, but I don't know if I'll be able to go to college like you. You won a scholarship, didn't you?"

"I was blessed, yes. But you don't need to be a valedictorian to get a scholarship. Talk to Mrs. Martin about it."

"But she's not my counselor."

"Send her an email and ask for a pass during your study hall. Since I tutor you at that time, I could go with you. But you need to take the first step. I know you can do this, Tamara. You have good grades and belong in college." Tamara felt her eyes water and looked out the window at the large courthouse where men and women in dark suits with briefcases hurried toward the door while others stood near a large container pulling on cigarettes and looking up at the sky.

Part Three

It was time to go home when Tamara and her classmates arrived back at school on the bus. Walking down the empty hallway to her locker, she reflected on her day at court and wondered how it would feel to stand before the judge in a fancy suit and be called Counselor. Could she be the first of her family, she wondered, to stand on the right side of the law?

At her locker she stopped and squinted in the glare of the sun. The numbers on the lock blurred, so she raised her arm to block the sun's harsh rays that bore through the window like a drill through a lead pipe. Instead of feeling excited about her day in court, she suddenly felt alone and uncertain. Her mouth felt dry and she felt sweat slide down her back. She looked at the blank walls and empty hallway and listened as the lights buzzed above her. She felt trapped, as desperate as a cornered animal.

Tamara opened her locker, grabbed the water bottle from the top shelf, and drank. The water tasted warm. She put her books into her book bag in the order of the classes she would study that night and wondered which way she should leave the building to avoid running into Rashad.

As she shrugged into her book bag, she saw him approach like a stealthy panther hunting its prey. His eyes traveled up and down her body. His lips parted and he pressed his upper teeth onto his lower lip. He rocked his head back and forth to some rhythm beating in his head. "Lookin' fine, mama. Where you been?"

"I went to the Court of Appeals for Career Day," she replied, knowing that if she didn't talk to him, he'd get angry and accuse her of thinking she was better than him. "You think you all that," he'd say. So she tried to deny who she was and blend into the neighborhood. But it didn't help. She still felt trapped by their hatred of her.

"You a dreamer, Tamara. You ain't never gonna make it out of the hood," Rashad said, spitting his words like discharge from a wound. "All that hope and change ain't nothin' but bullshit."

"Maybe you're right," Tamara said quietly.

He stood in front of her and quickly glanced around. Miss Shandy stood at the door to her classroom. She scowled at Tamara, but when she saw Rashad smiling and winking at her, she nodded and went back into her classroom. Tamara stood unprotected at her locker and felt like Ishmael in his dinghy, adrift in the ocean.

Tamara said nothing when Rashad knocked her book bag onto the floor and pushed her up against the locker. He grabbed her around the waist and pulled her close to his body. She flinched when he pressed his crotch against her buttocks. "You and me, girl," he breathed into her ear, "got to get together." He forced her hand onto his groin. "Feel good, don't it?" He jerked her around, and she gritted her teeth when he forced her to face him. "Look at me, girl," he demanded, holding her chin firmly in his hand. "You think you somethin'. But you just a ghetto bitch. I'll get your cherry; just watch."

Tamara pushed his hand away from her face and pulled back. "I have to get home, Rashad," she sputtered.

"Yo mama gets it on with all the homeboys, Tamara. You gonna be just like her."

"She'll kick my butt if I go out with anyone. You don't know her. She puts her cigarettes out on my arm if I'm late."

Rashad looked at her. "You a story, Tamara."

Tamara struggled to free her right arm and shoved the sleeve of her suit jacket up to her elbow. "See this!" she hissed. "You think I burned my own self?"

Rashad stepped back. "Okay. I see."

Behind Rashad, Tawana stood with her hands on her hips. "What you doin', Rashad?"

Rashad held his arms out straight like a patrol boy protecting children at a red light. He shook his head. "I ain't doin' nothing but helpin' this girl with her lock."

"You a story, Rashad Griffen. I know it and you know it. Everybody know it."

Tawana came closer to Tamara and poked her chest. "You listen up, bitch," she warned, so close that Tamara could smell her strong perfume. "Rashad is my man. Don't even think about gettin' in his pants 'cause I will kick yo ass! Take that to the bank." Tawana wiped her hands and stepped back to assess her competition. "You got a suit on, but you ain't nothin' but a skinny-ass bitch." She pushed Tamara into her locker but dropped her hands when she saw Shamika.

"Lookee here! Yo sister. Now we got two bitches with an attitude in this here hallway."

Shamika bore down on the intruder, and she and Tamara watched as Tawana ran to catch up to Rashad. They sauntered down the hall together, Rashad's hand sliding down her back to her backside.

"You okay?" Shamika asked, patting her younger sister's warm, damp face.

"Sure. He was just passing time when Tawana showed up," Tamara said as she gathered up her belongings.

"He was doing more than passing time, Tamara. Your hair is messed up. Did he feel on you?"

Tamara's shoulders dropped. "Yes," she said softly, "and I feel dirty."

"Look at me, Tamara. You're a good girl. Rashad can touch you on the outside, but he can't touch you on the inside. Come on," Shamika said as she rearranged her sister's hair.

"Miss Shandy knew what he was up to, but she just walked back into her classroom," Tamara complained as she pushed her books into her book bag.

Shamika took a mint out of her backpack. "Here. It'll make your breath fresh, and you'll feel clean inside."

Tamara put the mint in her mouth but stopped in the middle of the hall and looked into her sister's face. "What am I going to do when you graduate, Shamika?"

"We'll think of something. One day at a time, Tamara."

Part Four

It was Tamara's turn to take out the garbage. Before leaving the kitchen, she surveyed the stairs and alley, then stepped out onto the back porch, grabbing the plastic bags. Down three flights of stairs she walked to the cement area where a large trashcan stood. Her eyes darted around the alley, and seeing no one around, she pulled the bags across the ground, lifted the garbage lid, and hefted the bags into the container. She dropped the lid, stepped away, and looked around.

Further down the alley she saw two boys smoking weed in back of the corner garage. Tamara wondered what happened to their dreams. She had seen her mama's report cards and certificates; she knew she had been an honor student. What happened?

She sniffed the air and smelled something besides garbage. Tamara lifted first one foot, then the other. Dog mess! She had stepped in it with both feet!

As she wiped her shoes in the grass, she noticed some long, dirty white objects. They weren't baseball bats, she thought. They weren't thick enough. They looked like bones. "Oh, God," she said out loud. "Please don't let that be a skeleton!" Without breathing, she lifted the garbage can lid and pushed it around in the weeds. In front of her she saw bones that appeared to be moving. Stepping away, she remembered the Bible passage she had read the night before about the valley of dry bones. It was one of her favorites.

She felt herself falling into its words, and instead of the alley she saw an empty, lifeless valley covered in dry bones. The air was dry, the ground sandy and broken. Her heart sank in despair.

Softly the bones rattled. She watched them come together and attach themselves. Muscles attached and flesh formed over the bones. The bones stood up and became a complete skeleton! Skeletons surrounded her. All hope wasn't gone! The bones stood up and began marching. The alley was filled with an army! Tamara remembered the vision the Lord showed Ezekiel in the valley of the dry bones. The Lord had promised to open the graves and cause the people of Israel to rise again. She would rise with them! A voice interrupted her vision.

"Hey, Tamara! We got some unfinished business to tend to. Come over here, girl. I'm gonna take you up to the roof." Rashad stood in the middle of the alley smiling and rubbing his crotch. He started to unzip his pants but stopped when the pot smokers urged him on. He strolled over to where she was standing.

Tamara pulled her shoulders back and picked up the garbage lid. She took a deep breath, lifted it above her head, and slammed it into Rashad's face. "Get away!" she screamed. "Don't you ever think you'll take me on the roof. I'm not like my mama!"

Rashad touched his face and saw blood on his hand. "You bitch! I'll cut your face." He stooped and picked up a piece of broken glass.

The two stood glaring at each other, squaring off like good and evil. The kids smoking dope stood watching, waiting expectantly for a fight to break out. No birds sang, no dogs barked, no babies cried. Tamara focused on Rashad's eyes. She repositioned the trashcan lid in her hand and crouched down, preparing for his attack. But instead of the sound of Rashad's shoes twisting and shifting on the pavement to reposition for his second attack, she heard noises coming up out of the garbage can.

A growling sound rose from the trash barrel. Tamara jumped, and Rashad's eyes and mouth opened wide. The barrel hissed, and a loud banging erupted from the metal container. It lifted up off the ground and rolled toward Rashad. Tamara held her breath. She stared at Rashad, and Rashad stared at the trashcan. "What's in there?" he asked.

"Go and see," Tamara said. "Go and find the dead bones of your life, Rashad. But watch out! The devil might creep out of there and pull you in."

"Girl, you crazy," he said, leaning forward and gasping for air. He placed his hands on his knees and looked up at Tamara. "You got your grandmama's covering," he said, realization coming on him like a floodlight, "and I ain't messin' with the devil for a piece of ass." The boys in front of the garage started to chant, demanding that Rashad take action.

"F-ck you!" he yelled. "You crazy-ass bitch. Stay away from me." Tamara held her ground and watched Rashad's eyes shift from the trashcan back to her. He took another step back into the alley, tripped, and took off running, holding up the waist of his baggy pants. When he reached the street, Tamara saw him turn left. "Rashad disappeared like the Road Runner in the cartoons," she said softly. "He's not as tough as he thinks." She picked up the lid and placed it on the trashcan. But before going upstairs, she saw the old red van turn into the alley and a small pale woman sitting in the passenger seat.

"Tamara, what are you doing down there?" yelled Shamika. "You better get upstairs and fast."

"No, come on down. Mr. Curtis is here, and I think his wife is with him."

Part Five

The honor society always assisted with graduation practice, so Tamara had volunteered to help. She stood in the main aisle of the auditorium with other honor students and nodded to each row of seniors when it was time for them to stand and walk up to the stage. Tamara counted nine students sitting in the first row. Her tutor, Erica Calder, sat at the end.

"Do all of the valedictorians have a copy of their speech?" asked Miss Shandy, Tamara's guidance counselor.

The students nodded and one student raised his hand. "We have just sixty seconds, right?"

"That's correct, Jason. When your name is announced, stand and walk up to the dais on the stage. Remember to speak slowly and clearly into the microphone."

The back door to the auditorium opened, and two guidance counselors walked in with the assistant principal, Mr. Lewis, and sat at the back of the auditorium. One of the women was Mrs. Martin, Erica's counselor. Tamara waved at her. They had met with Erica last month, and she had given her a lot of information about scholarships, something Tamara's own counselor had not done. Tamara sat down in the front with the other volunteers. She wondered what Erica was going to say in her speech. A minute wasn't very long to thank everyone who helped you.

She listened as students thanked the school, the principal, and their parents. Some students turned the spotlight on themselves by talking about their personal interests and dreams for the future. Tamara wondered who she'd thank.

The students had voted to have a local pastor and rabbi say a prayer at graduation, but the principal vetoed their ideas. Erica's mom explained that the Supreme Court prohibited prayers at school-sponsored events. Tamara felt sad and confused because the prayer had been a tradition for years. Gram told her that Bishop Thomas had given the prayer when Tamara's mother had graduated from this high school. So much had changed. "Tradition don't count for much these days," Gram said and Tamara agreed.

"Erica Calder," the class president called. Tamara lifted her chin as Erica, her friend and tutor, walked up to the podium. Erica looked down at her notes briefly, then out into the empty auditorium.

"Tonight is a milestone for every graduate seated before you. We have all worked very hard and with the grace of God have made it to this place in our lives. We think back to all those tests we studied for and wonder how we studied and prepared week after week, month after month for four years. My Savior, Jesus Christ, helped me. He encouraged me when I wanted to quit. Jesus heard my prayers and gave me the strength not to give up. I hope you come to know Him and His love."

The students applauded, and Erica walked to her place on the risers and faced the auditorium.

Mr. Lewis popped up from his seat and walked quickly to the stage where he stood and faced the graduates. Tamara was sure he was frowning because his hands were on his hips. "Erica, step off the risers. I want to talk with you. Do not leave with your classmates," he said firmly. Then he addressed the entire class. Tamara cringed as he spoke. "Erica was told that she needed to write a different speech, but she didn't listen to directions. Give me that speech," he commanded.

Tamara watched Erica separate from her classmates and hand Mr. Lewis her speech. He grabbed it from her hand and ripped it up. Then he walked over to the trashcan next to the stage and threw the speech into it. He returned to the center of the stage and inhaled. As his chest swelled, stretching his shirt across his chest, Tamara thought she was watching the Incredible Hulk.

"Hey, there's smoke in the trashcan!" yelled a boy standing near the door. The students watched as smoke rose from the trashcan. A loud moan echoed in the auditorium, and some of the girls screamed.

Mr. Lewis quickly scanned the group before him. "Who made that noise?" he demanded. Tamara stared as Mr. Lewis motioned to the student at the end of the first row. "Go check the trashcan for a fire." But the student remained frozen where she was. "Somebody thinks they can play a prank, but they won't get away with it," he ranted. "Did someone walk through the side door?" When no one responded, he glared at the guidance counselors. "Weren't those doors locked before rehearsal?"

Miss Shandy stood up. "Yes, the doors were locked. I checked them myself."

Mr. Lewis shook his head. The bell rang, but no one moved. "I'll find the person who set up this prank. Erica, you stay here. The rest of you may walk quietly to the lunchroom." Tamara left the auditorium with the seniors. When Tamara found her sister, Shamika told her to go to class. "I'll wait for Erica and sit with her," she said. Tamara hurried down the hall.

Tamara pondered the meaning of free speech. She thought the Constitution guaranteed free speech. Maybe that right didn't apply to students in public school. But then why could her classmates bash the government and the president in class? They had free speech to talk about politics. Why couldn't students talk about their faith? She wondered what Erica was going to do. Would she change her speech?

Part Six

Tamara awoke before the alarm went off. She wiped her forehead. She could hear the air conditioner running in her mother's bedroom. Graduation started at 6 p.m., but Mama and her friends had celebrated a day early. Seniors didn't go to school, so she let Shamika sleep. She unlocked the bedroom door and looked into the living room. It was empty! "Thank You, Jesus!" she whispered and got ready for school.

Tonight was the big night. Tamara and Shamika were waiting on the sidewalk when Mr. Curtis's van pulled up to the curb later that day. Gram smiled and told Shamika she looked lovely, but she didn't ask where their mama was. When Tamara asked if she'd be there, her gram told her not to worry.

As they approached the school, Tamara watched the girls walking into the school. Next year, that's going to be me, she thought. They wore their Sunday dresses and high-heeled shoes. Curls rolled down their backs, fluttered at their ears, or were held tightly on top of their heads. Most of the boys wore white shirts, dark pants, and Michael Jordan kicks. Mr. Curtis dropped the girls off at the door. Gram said she would sit with him and meet them afterwards in the cafeteria where refreshments would be served.

The girls walked quickly down the hall next to the auditorium, and Shamika lined up with her classmates. She carried her graduation gown until William hurried across the hall to carry it for her. Tamara watched William hold the gown as her sister put it on. I bet they get married, Tamara thought, and decided William would be a good brother-in-law even if he did take away her only sister. One day at a time, she told herself.

In his speech, the principal told the graduating class that it had been one of the best classes in the past ten years. He said that he would miss them but knew they would make themselves, their families, and their school proud as they moved ahead in life. The PTA president spoke for what seemed like ages. Finally, Tamara would hear her friend's valedictory speech. Tamara saw Erica's mother and the rest of their family sitting near the front. She even saw her mama sitting with her boyfriend in the front of the balcony. He must have told a joke, she thought, because her mother was laughing.

The class president stood to call the valedictorians to the podium. Finally, she would hear Erica's speech. When she asked Erica what she planned to say, Erica told her she would hear soon enough. Tamara saw Erica sitting straight up in her chair and thought she looked ready for battle.

"Our last valedictorian is Erica Calder," said the student announcer.

Tamara pushed forward in her seat and watched Erica walk to the podium. It looked like she was trying to hide something in the folds of her gown. At the podium, she looked straight ahead like Joan of Arc at the stake. The audience waited.

"You may not know it," Erica began, her voice loud and clear, "but our Constitution does not guarantee free speech for students in high school, so I cannot thank Jesus Christ for helping me achieve my dream of becoming a valedictorian. This is a state-sponsored event, so I have to stuff my gratitude toward my Savior, Jesus Christ, down my throat." Erica paused.

"But the Supreme Court," she continued, "has upheld the right of those who practice Santeria, also known as voodoo, to sacrifice chickens and goats during their religious services. Let's see if the High Court upholds my right to sacrifice a chicken as part of my valedictory speech."

The audience leaned forward in their seats, all eyes riveted on Erica as she retrieved a rubber chicken at her side.

Tamara held her breath as she watched her friend pull the head off a rubber chicken. Fake blood exploded onto the stage and Erica's graduation gown. The audience gasped as the red liquid dripped from Erica's nose and down the front of the podium. Then Erica spun around and sprayed the red liquid onto her classmates, who must have thought it was parade confetti because they laughed and cheered.

Squawking noises blasted through the sound system. The principal waved to the band director, who stood up, but before he could raise his arm to focus the band's attention on him, pandemonium broke out in the auditorium. Tamara covered her ears as the graduates whistled and shouted like they did at a basketball game when their team beat the competition. Parents chanted, "USA, USA, USA!" Tamara saw her sister look from right to left as if she were seeking an anchor she could throw to steady the ship. The formerly dignified seniors sitting patiently for their diplomas jumped up in their seats and started singing the national anthem. Cymbals crashed and the band followed.

Erica Calder joined her classmates, who lifted her up onto their shoulders. Tamara stood smiling. She believed she had just seen a second Tea Party, not in the Boston Harbor, but right here at a public high school in the center of the Midwest.

Mr. Lewis walked over to the graduates. He reached out to grab Erica, but her classmates kept her above his reach. He shook his fist at her, but the principal took his arm and led him off the stage. Tamara watched the graduates march off the stage and down the center aisle. They cheered and whistled. Tamara left to find her sister, and the auditorium emptied out.

The girls found Mr. Curtis's van in the front of the school.

Gram was the first to speak. "That girl has the power of the Lord inside her. Did you know what she had up her sleeve?"

"No, ma'am, I did not," said Tamara.

Mr. Curtis grinned. "Now that be a preacher woman! I ain't seen no one like that 'cept fo Dr. Martin Luther King!"

"I wouldn't want to be nowhere else," said Tamara's mother, "except at that graduation, even if you didn't walk down the aisle, Shamika."

"When you graduate from college, Shamika, we'll see you walk," said Gram.

"Looks like you fillin' her head with mighty big dreams, Mama," said their mother.

"What do you want her to do, Tanya . . ." But Tamara saw her Gram's mouth close as she pressed her lips together.

Her mama continued. "You better get those notions of graduating college right out of your head," she said as she climbed out of the car. "Get upstairs and change your clothes. I've got something special for you, Shamika. Goodnight, Mama. Goodnight, Mr. Curtis. I hear you brought your wife over here last week."

"I sure did. She better and better each day, gaining weight too."

"Well, I hope to meet her one day. Goodnight, and thank you for the ride and for taking my girls to graduation—" She hesitated. "And to church. Maybe I'll go with you next time."

Part Last

Tamara asked her sister if she could see her diploma, but Shamika said the diplomas were still at school. "Mr. Lewis withheld every senior's diploma until some parents threatened to sue. So the principal told us we could pick them up tomorrow," she explained as the girls and their mother ate ice cream and cake together at the kitchen table. Mama had ordered a strawberry cake with

Shamika's name on it. Tamara took a picture of the cake and Shamika sitting behind it with the camera William's family gave Shamika for graduation.

Tamara said, "Erica won't get her diploma until she writes her classmates an apology. She called me and said that Mr. Lewis called the police. He ordered her to his office after the auditorium had settled down. She had to wait for him without her parents, counselor, or friends." Tamara wanted to lick the frosting off the cake box but didn't.

"Were her parents mad at her?" Shamika asked.

"Well, they stick up for her, but I don't know what they thought when they saw the police with Erica in the principal's office," said Tamara. "I pray the good Lord chooses me to defend valedictorians like Erica and free speech." Tamara looked at her mother, who was preoccupied with her phone.

"Mama, can we have a second piece of cake?" asked Shamika.

Their mama nodded. "You go right ahead. Tonight's a big night. My first baby just graduated from high school and is headed for City College in the fall! Your gram is right. I am blessed."

Tamara expected her mama's boyfriends to come over that night and celebrate, but no one did. Later when Tamara turned out the lights, the girls lay in their bed discussing the changes in their mama. "Do you think she'll really come to church next Sunday?" asked Tamara.

"I don't know," said Shamika, "but my graduation is a milestone in Mama's life. When your first child graduates, you aren't a young woman anymore. It's a turning point for a mother."

"Do you think she'll give up the party life?"

Before Shamika could answer, Tamara's phone vibrated. She sat up, swung her legs over the side of the bed, and listened to her gram's voice. After she said goodbye, Tamara sat quietly, her legs dangling over the bed.

"Girl, tell me," her sister pleaded and sat up beside her. Shamika took Tamara's hand. "Was that Gram?"

Tamara nodded. "Mr. Curtis's wife passed."

"Oh," Shamika said quietly in the dark.

"Maybe it's for the best," Tamara began, but her heart wasn't in her words. "Now she's not in pain anymore."

"I guess," Shamika said. She grabbed a tissue from the night table and blew her nose.

The sisters sat in the dark together. Tamara couldn't hear any noise from the streets, just the hum of their mama's air conditioner.

"Let's pray," said Tamara. "We can pray for Mr. Curtis and his loss, and that his wife is carried home to Jesus."

"And that our mama comes to church next Sunday," Shamika said and folded her hands.

Tamara exhaled, her breath seeking relief from her mother's failed promises. Maybe she will change, she thought, and she too folded her hands.

Seeing things imperfectly, through the cloudy mirror, the girls bowed their heads and prayed. Someday they would understand.

CHICKENS: NOT JUST FOR EATING

Jonah: 2:8

Those who worship false gods turn their backs on all God's mercies.

Part One

J udge Vanderhall sat up in bed. He popped up like a jack-in-the-box released on Christmas morning by an impatient toddler. However, in his dream it wasn't Christmas morning, and he wasn't a toddler. Since the trial, which challenged the *Smith-Lukumi* decision, he had had recurring dreams of beheaded chickens, bloody chickens, and squawking chickens struggling to free themselves. In the dreams Santeria priests gripped their necks and then decapitated the chickens to increase the frenzy of worshippers spinning around to thundering drums. The judge knew what the Constitution stated: the government could not unduly burden the practice of religion. Thus, under the auspices of the Court, the killing of chickens and goats continued. The meeting of two opposing currents, he thought: one religion founded in light, another in darkness.

He questioned the Court's decision and wondered why the justices couldn't find a legitimate government interest that would survive strict scrutiny. Surely the justices could find a government interest and protect animals from inhumane treatment. While animal rights groups had not been strong enough to lobby effectively in 1993, they were stronger now. Some days the law burdened him, especially on the days when his patience had been stretched thin.

Judge Vanderhall knew he was not a patient man, despite what some woman at church had told him. "I've watched the proceedings during PPO hearings," she had gushed, "and you have the patience of Job!" His wife, Diane, would never say something so mindless. She knew how sitting through personal protection hearings week after week knotted his stomach. He complained to her week after week about how annoying the complainants could be.

Every Friday a few residents demanded protective orders against a neighbor who sat on his porch and looked at them, or a boyfriend who wouldn't move out when a relationship ended. Last week, an ex-husband appeared in his courtroom because his former wife wanted him to call before he stopped by. He refused. Instead, he climbed through the basement window of his former home to get a suit. Not two calendar weeks later, the man reappeared in his courtroom—this time as an attorney prepared to defend a client who broke into his ex-wife's home to retrieve his fishing equipment. Judge Vanderhall wondered if the attorney had considered the similarity between himself and his client. Probably not. The woman at church may have been right. Like Job he was tested.

His friends told him he was aging gracefully. He questioned their sanity. Losing your hair at the age of forty did not require grace, only bad genes. His five-foot-nine stature had not been diminished by poor health or sloppy posture despite the fact that he sat all day. Since passing the Bar, he had not gained more than five pounds. Perhaps the stress of presiding over trials and courtroom soap operas had helped him stay reasonably fit.

On Fridays he couldn't eat. In the courtroom, he maintained his composure even while listening to family members accuse each other of stealing ladders and then hiding them under their porches. Secretly, he wanted to knock their heads together. Diane had made him take up golf and continue playing tennis, both of which he resisted, but she had made arguments for both activities he couldn't refute. His wife was clever that way.

He objected. "I don't like listening to grown men complain on the golf course, Diane," he said. "They don't pay me for my time."

"Learn to ignore others, Judge," she said.

"That's what you tell the kids," he asserted, but she wasn't embarrassed after being caught.

"Ignoring others is wise counsel for us all," she said and went back to fixing dinner, a meal replete with good nutrition but lacking in desserts for him. Diane strictly oversaw her kitchen and everything in the house.

He refocused on the problem at hand. Damp bedding trapped him and curled around his legs like braids wrapped around a Swiss girl's head, the kind of blond, yodeling children he and Diane had seen in the Upper Peninsula last summer and found so obnoxious. Okay, he had found obnoxious. Diane, on the other hand, had found them sweet and innocent. After they listened to the children sing and yodel, the children hung around Diane like globs of whipped cream. Even on vacation his patience was tested.

In the early morning gloom he couldn't see the difference between the sheets and the blankets, and he couldn't reach the lamp to shed some light on his situation and clear his mind of the dream. He kept seeing a voodoo priest throwing shells across a table. Compounding the problem, his wife wasn't in their bed; he felt the warm place where she had lain. He heard the toilet flush and the faucet run. Diane walked out of the bathroom, and he watched her turn on the fan and open the window. He noticed her face was flushed.

If anyone was aging well, it was Diane. She looked just like she did when they met, nearly thirty years ago at a church youth group. Her trim, petite figure often caused much younger men to turn and stare. During the coffee hour at church, he overheard women tell her how lucky she was that her skin was nearly wrinkle free. Before her accident, she walked every day and usually had a tan, even in the winter. He didn't ask her if she dyed her hair; he didn't think wives had to tell their husbands everything.

"Why are you sitting up?" she asked. "You look like someone fighting the rapids in a kayak."

"I can't move," he said, sighing loudly.

She walked over to his side of the bed and bent to unwrap the sheets and blanket from his legs. "What happened? A bad dream?"

"No, I didn't have a bad dream," he said as he watched her hands deftly remove the impediments to his freedom. "Thanks."

"So what were you dreaming?" she said gently. He appreciated how she was careful not to entrap him with aggressive questioning. She never sounded like the attorneys he had to listen to every day. He had listened to their brilliance for the past twenty years, not quite as long as they had been married. She sat beside him.

"This time," he explained, "I was in a room filled with burning candles. A priest was giving me a reading to see if someone had put a curse on me. He threw a bunch of shells on the table, and then, the next thing I knew, the whole place caught fire. The priest escaped, but I couldn't get out because a gigantic scorpion blocked the door. Don't laugh."

"At least you got your answer," Diane said. "Someone put a curse on you."

He started to think about who would put a curse on him, but stopped when he saw her looking at him. "You don't believe that nonsense, do you?" he asked.

Instead of responding, she turned her head and left the room. "What are you doing now?" he asked her retreating figure. She returned with a glass of water and a damp washcloth.

"Here, drink this—it's not a potion made of scorpion powder, just water." After he drank, she gently wiped his damp brow, the way she used to wipe the brows of their children when they were sick. He wondered if Diane was thinking about the time their young daughter brought her a warm washcloth. "Mommy," she had begged, "do my head like you do Daddy's."

"Thanks," he said. "You were awake too. Were you dreaming about magic potions and blood rituals?" he taunted, but she remained impassive. They had both read up on the religion of Santeria and learned that the practitioners burned candles to attract energies that they directed against their enemies. They learned that, unlike Christian priests, who never promised their confessors that they could control God, voodoo doctors exchanged money for promises. They claimed they could take revenge against a person's enemies.

The local paper described how the voodoo priests traveled north to the Midwest and took their shells and powders with them. Haitian immigrants living near town had begun sacrificing animals, raising alarm and anger in an area populated by farmers, academics, and animal rights activists. He read that both groups, residents and Santeria believers, were picketing today in front of the building where the blood rituals took place. Neighbors complained of the noise, cruelty to animals, and the smell of rotting carcasses in the church's dumpster. The neighborhood association filed a lawsuit, and the case landed in Judge Vanderhall's court.

Diane returned to the bedroom and said, "We should be grateful Chango didn't burn up the bed!"

"What time is it?" he asked. He could see the clock but asked her anyway.

"Just after four. Why don't you go back to sleep?"

"No. If I did, I'd oversleep."

She leaned over and kissed his balding head. "No, you won't. You sleep. I'll get up now and wake you when it's time." Gently, she pressed his shoulders back into the pillow, and he submitted.

"Take your cane when you go downstairs," he reminded her.

She closed the door, grabbing her cane as she left.

Part Two

Dressed in black trousers, a starched white shirt, and a gray sweater vest, the judge sat in the breakfast nook. At the oak table he bent over a bowl of granola mixed with plain vanilla yogurt. "Do you want your coffee now, or will you drink it in the car?" Diane asked.

"Now is good. Are you having cocoa?"

She nodded and smiled. He knew she loved anything chocolate. He asked, "Are you going to the airport today?"

"Yes, we're picking up Aunt Grace." She brought their cups to the table and sat down next to him.

"Who's going with you?" he asked, trying to sound nonchalant about her escapades.

"The usual group. I'll show you what we're wearing," she said, put down her cup, and left the room. When she returned, he groaned.

"You aren't wearing that, are you?" he asked, shaking his head.

"It's cute, isn't it? Aunt Grace loves chickens."

Instead of something reasonable, he thought, like jeans or slacks with a university sweatshirt or a windbreaker, she wore a yellow chicken costume with a detachable head that she put on as she stood before him. Big rubber chicken feet covered her feet. When she stood up, he watched two feathers float to the floor.

He turned to see if she was watching him. She wasn't; she had bent down to admire her rubber feet. Whatever possessed her family, he wondered, to begin a tradition of wearing costumes to the airport when they picked up friends and relatives. Sometimes the group had to take several vans to get everyone to the airport. She even convinced church members to wear costumes and join the group. At least they weren't going to the local airport where someone might recognize her. He dreaded seeing her painted face and costumes in the news and imagined seeing her on TV, telling the reporter who she was. "Hi! I'm Judge Vanderhall's wife. This morning the judge picked out this chicken costume for me. It's his favorite."

He got up from the table. Clucking, she chased him around the kitchen and out to the garage. "You forgot your coffee. Cluck, cluck, cluck . . ."

Without looking at her, he backed out of the garage and drove his Smart car around the vehicles pulling into his driveway. He stopped long enough to watch the antics unfolding on his property and to check for tire treads on his immaculate lawn. He saw Diane standing near the lilac bushes. Her arms akimbo, she yelled, "Hey, Merle! The judge is a fuss-budget, isn't he?" She shook her head. "But I still love him."

She yelled so loudly he looked next door to see if his neighbors were on their patio. The older couple wasn't outside, so he shouted, "Stay off my lawn with those vans, Merle!"

Both vehicles parked near the garage door. Merle, the driver of the blue van, was Diane's favorite cousin. The judge watched him wave and smile when he saw Diane. "You look great!" he said. "Are you ready to hit the road?" Before she could answer, the occupants of the vans, clucking and laughing, spilled out of the vehicles and onto the carefully landscaped lawn. Two of her sister's children ran up to Diane and asked, "Is it Halloween?"

"No, it isn't Halloween!" he yelled, and drove off scowling. Heading to a main thoroughfare, he remembered the last time Diane's sister joined the group. She had dressed like a hooker, and airport police had arrested her for solicitation. Diane thought it was a hoot, but the judge didn't think so. "Were her kids with her?" he had thundered. When she told him the truth, he ranted and raved. "Don't you realize you're contributing to the delinquency of minor children?" He had raised his voice until he noticed she was humming and examining her fingernails.

He tried reasoning with her. "You aren't going to the airport again, are you? Dressed in costumes?" She did not respond. She listened carefully to everything he said without interrupting or arguing with him. But a month later when Uncle Jim returned from Hawaii, she joined the group and headed for the airport. This time she was dressed like a hula dancer. At least no one was arrested.

"When Uncle Jim walked out of security," she explained, speaking rapidly, "I placed a lei around his neck and kissed him. Judge, I thought he was going to cry."

Before he could object, she continued. "Then Uncle Jim laughed and everyone clapped, even the people waiting to board a plane." Diane pulled out a lei and put it around his head. When she turned her back to start making dinner, he removed it.

"Strangers asked if they could go home with us!" she said, her eyes lost in memory. "It was a great day. I wish you had been with us." Earlier that morning, she had reminded him of the Uncle Jim adventure, but promised him that today would be even better. He wondered what those words forebode.

Several blocks from the circuit court, the judge saw groups of protesters. One group chanted about animal rights and carried placards showing pictures of mutilated animals. According to the paper, the protesters carried signs with pictures taken at Santeria rituals in Florida. The article he read stated that the religion had its roots in nature and natural forces.

At the church in their Midwest location, these "roots" of nature were being thrown into the parking lot dumpster where they had dripped down the sides of the huge container and landed on the asphalt parking lot, ripening in the afternoon sun. An inquisitive child had brought the "roots" home to his shocked and confused grandmother, who took pictures to show her daughter and son-in-law. When her daughter came home from work, she called the police, who took more pictures for the county prosecutor.

The judge slowed as he approached the activity. On the right side of the street, he saw the other group of protesters in front of the building they rented. He observed some of the Santeria believers holding up candles while others distributed brochures advertising botanic soaps and scorpion powder. He watched two women weave in and around the cars, handing brochures to the drivers. Passersby learned that the soaps and powders broke spells. Halted at the corner, the judge saw two adolescent boys riding their bikes to school watching the scene before them, their eyes bouncing from one side of the street to the other. Their confused faces captured the meeting of two opposing currents, each side pushing to be heard. The judge checked his watch; the boys weren't late.

At a red light the judge stopped and watched with everyone else. An older Haitian woman approached his environmentally safe car and handed him a brochure. He took it and read that the soaps and powders broke spells. The light turned yellow, so he placed the pamphlet on the seat next to him.

When the light turned green, he pushed on the accelerator, but nothing happened. Instead of making a smooth transition from stop to go, the car sat inert. This had never happened before. The car had always performed well under normal conditions. He tried restarting it. Nothing. He tried again. The engine turned over but quit. On the next attempt the engine started, but the car shook. A few seconds later it exploded. Helpless, he sat and watched a fire erupt from under the hood. Suddenly, the hood blew up into the air. With a loud crash, it landed on the pavement. The sound of the explosion reverberated in his head.

The protesters shouted for him to get out. While the judge saw their alarmed faces watching the fire engulf the tiny vehicle, he sat frozen in fear. One of the animal rights activists dropped his sign and rushed to the car. He pulled open the door, unfastened the seat belt, and grabbed the judge, who stumbled out, dazed but coherent.

The judge assessed his rescuer. "Didn't I sentence you to two years in prison last week? What are you doing out running the streets?" he demanded, his eyes peering into the face of his rescuer. Recognizing who he had just pulled out of a burning car, the young man didn't wait around for words of gratitude. He fled.

"It nearly killed me!" the judge said to the boys sitting on their bikes. The vehicle touted for its environmental friendliness, he thought, nearly killed me. He considered the irony. "Wait until Diane hears about this!" he muttered, remembering how she laughed when he brought the car home. She called it a clown car and refused to ride in it. Once again, he thought, Diane knew more than he did.

With the other spectators, he stood on the sidewalk gazing at the car as it burned like melting wax. He heard the roar of an approaching fire truck's horn and watched as the racing vehicle sped around the corner. Someone had reported the fire, he thought, while his own smartphone burned inside the car with the brochure advertising products used to break spells. Looking around, he wondered where they sold these potions.

A police car pulled around the corner and stopped beside the burning paraffin. "Judge Vanderhall? Is that your car?" The judge stood up straight as if to challenge the officer to make a joke.

"Yes, that's my car," he snarled. "Isn't it obvious?"

The officer knew the judge and said, "Get in. I'll take you to the courthouse." The judge hesitated before getting into the backseat. "Sorry, Judge, but there's no room up here in the front. You know computers take up the entire passenger side of the vehicles. There's no room in front for a second man." When he saw the judge's face in the rearview mirror, he added, "Don't worry, we're almost there."

"Don't drop me in front," the judge warned. "Drive around in back."

Despite being only a few minutes late, Judge Vanderhall fumed, believing his entire schedule had been thrown into a tailspin. However, he walked into his courtroom on time as he always did.

At one o'clock, the judge heard a knock on the door to his chambers. His law clerk walked in and placed a bag of food from a local restaurant on his desk.

When the stolid protector of the law unwrapped his sandwich, he exclaimed, "Chicken! Why did you order me chicken?"

"Your Honor, it's Thursday. You always order chicken on Thursday. Does all the talk about wringing chicken necks—"

The judge held up his hand in warning and dropped his head. "Stop! Go out and get me something else. Tuna would be good."

The law clerk grabbed his jacket and joined one of the externs waiting for the elevator outside his chamber. The judge opened the door to his chamber and listened as the two young men talked. The extern spoke first. "Why do you work for him?" he asked. "Judge Vanderhall is a curmudgeon. Everyone complains about him."

"He's not that bad," defended the judge's law clerk. "He's just a little surly at times."

"At times? Are we talking about the same guy?"

"Why don't you tell me how you really feel?" his law clerk responded. The elevator door opened and the young men entered. The judge stood at the door, imagining the scene in the restaurant. The waitress would undoubtedly say, "For Judge Vanderhall?" His law clerk would nod, and she would say, "Tuna on wheat, hold the tomato, lettuce, and mayonnaise. Pickle on the side." The judge knew his orders were as predictable as his scowl.

The judge understood that few externs had jobs lined up after graduation. Law students graduated with a pile of debt. Sometimes they felt testy. He knew. He and Diane had taken the first offer to come his way. He had seen the externs sneer at him when they left his courtroom. Sometimes, he thought, they looked remarkably like him.

Part Three

That night the judge joined his wife in their sitting room later than usual. Sammy, his cat, sat grooming himself in the judge's chair. Before sitting down, the judge picked up the large tiger cat and gently placed him on his lap.

"He's been waiting for you," Diane said as she stroked Muffins, the calico cat that sat on her lap and cuddled in her arms at night after the judge had fallen asleep. He had never told her, but when the lights went out Sammy also jumped on the bed and curled around his bald head. He assumed she knew of Sammy's nightly visits and appreciated that she never mentioned it to him. He and Diane rescued them from the city's animal shelter. He had encouraged her to adopt them because their kids lived so far away.

The two cats purred, nearly in unison, as he and Diane stared at the gas fire. The warm fire brought them back together at the end of the day. They had the gas installed when the original fireplace developed structural cracks. Although there was nothing like a real fire, when it went out you nearly froze on the way to bed. A wood-burning fireplace sucked the warm air right up the chimney where it escaped into the darkness.

He and Diane discussed the problem and opted for a change. The gas fire kept the evening chill at bay as they sat in front of it as well as when they made their way to bed. But they missed hearing the crackling and popping of burning logs. When the sun set, the wind invaded their sunroom through lead glass windows that were as old as the house, but the heat released by the new gas fireplace stayed in the room. They both lamented the loss of their wood-burning fireplace, but now that it was warm, the judge enjoyed the room even more.

They sat quietly, reflecting on the events of the day. He figured Diane was thinking about Aunt Milly and the scene at the airport. She told him about the airport shenanigans when she picked him up at the courthouse, how Aunt Milly's face had lit up, and how some of the other passengers wanted to go home with their group. The usual.

"The chicken costumes were a big hit with Aunt Milly, Judge," she told him. "Milly laughed until tears streamed down her face! The other passengers clapped and some even took pictures. One of the passengers was a reporter, Judge. We may be in the paper." He looked at her beaming face, felt horrified to think that his wife's picture might appear in the paper, but said nothing. Since her accident, he found it difficult to complain when she appeared so joyful. She was like an eager child on Easter morning, he thought, hunting for her Easter basket.

"Did you find another car?" she asked, the sound of her voice breaking into his thoughts.

He looked at her. Hearing no sarcasm in her voice, he said, "Yes. A new Prius is less than the Smart car. I decided against the Chevy Volt.

I've heard their batteries have caught fire, and I've had enough of putting my life at risk while I'm saving the planet. Thanks for dropping me at the dealership."

Outside, they could see the moon rise. They watched its steady progress as it ascended over the trees. He saw her eyes fixing once again on the tree splintered during a recent storm. Its branches were missing, and it ruined the appearance of the yard.

"Diane, are you looking at that damaged tree?" he asked. She nodded. "What do you find so fascinating about it?"

"Judge, I see it standing alone in the dark and think about Anne Hutchison, the woman who believed in the doctrine of being born again. She created a different kind of storm inside her church. No one listened to what she had to say." Diane looked at her husband. "You listen to the defendants in your court, don't you?"

"You've sat in my court; you know I do," he said. "Maybe I listen too much."

"I'm glad you do. No one listened to Anne Hutchison. She was tried for sedition and banished. After leaving her home, she and her four children were massacred in Indiana." The judge watched her shiver in spite of the fire's warmth. "But she stood up for her beliefs, Judge."

"Are you sure you don't want me to cut down that tree? It doesn't have any branches or leaves. It doesn't look like anything else in the yard."

"I'm sure. I don't like everything matchy-matchy," she said. "Besides, it reminds me of how bravely our ancestors defended their religious beliefs. We don't do that anymore."

"Can't we defend our faith without having to look at that ugly tree?"

"No," she said. "We need a visual reminder to stand up for our beliefs."

He considered what she said as he watched a few stars twinkle. He heard something rustling in the bushes outside. "It's probably a raccoon," he said.

"The moon is so full you can see everything in the backyard!" she exclaimed.

He looked at their yard, which was still filled with a sandbox, swing set, and picnic table. The croquet set was in the garage.

"My favorite moon is a Clair de Lune moon—you know, the crescent," she said.

He nodded and wondered when they had last listened to Debussy. "The city orchestra doesn't play Debussy anymore."

"Not since they hired that new director who features Brahms, Beethoven, and Bach," she said, finishing his sentence.

"When was the last time we went to the symphony?" he asked.

She shook her head. "I don't remember. I'll call tomorrow about tickets. Do you still prefer Mozart?"

He nodded. "Do you remember where we went on our first date?"

"The one with the church youth group?"

"No, our first one alone. We went to the symphony, but I can't remember what we heard."

She smiled. "We heard Debussy and Ravel."

Captured like a whisper in time, he saw her face when she was nineteen, nearly twenty-five years ago. Leaning over, he kissed her. "I remember the first time I saw you. I liked the way your eyes twinkled. I thought you were excited about our date."

"I was. You were the first boy I dated seriously," she said.

"You were serious about me? What did you and your brothers do to the boys you weren't serious about?"

"Nothing. They were too boring."

"Nothing?" he asked, continuing the conversation they had come to enjoy. "You were twinkling like fireworks on the Fourth of July because you were a prankster. You attached tin cans to the back of my old sedan, remember? You and your brothers. I should have run for the hills then." He shook his head and nearly smiled.

"Yes," she said proudly, "and you would never have had any fun. You would have married Shirley Vander Galien and written scholarly law articles your whole life." She looked over at him. "Do you want some cocoa?"

When he nodded, she got up and stood behind him. She cradled his head against her breasts. Leaning over him, she kissed his forehead, his cheeks, and his mouth. "I loved you then, and I love you now."

He didn't move. He watched Muffins follow her out the door but resisted the desire to do the same.

Part Four

The Santeria challenge had landed in his courtroom. He hadn't been surprised. Controversial cases were not an anomaly in his courtroom. For two days local newspaper reporters watched jury selection, and TV reporters filmed voir dire. He never liked having to open up his courtroom to the news media; the atmosphere turned into a circus, which reminded him that Diane was going to the airport today dressed like a clown. At least his wife had not appeared in the local paper dressed like a chicken.

Before the trial began, the judge heard that the defense attorney stopped the prosecutor in the hall and told him he would accept a bench trial. The attorneys texted him immediately. The judge knew that a jury from this area would rule against the church despite the Supreme Court's ruling that slaughtering chickens and small animals could continue. The defense probably figured that out as well. The church could appeal, but thus far the ACLU had not stepped forward with any help, legal or financial. A trial and an appeal would cost the Santeria group a lot of money they probably didn't have. The public defender didn't have a lot either, and while a highly publicized trial would get his name in the papers, the case would take up a lot of his time that he could spend on clients with larger bank accounts. The judge knew that the defendants' attorney would argue for time, place, and manner restrictions and hope the judge had an open mind. But the judge knew he did not have an open mind, whatever that meant.

The attorneys stood before Judge Vanderhall's huge desk. No stray papers peeked out of the many files stacked on the desk. Next to the public defender stood the county prosecutor. They had come to an understanding before entering the judge's chamber. The prosecutor could live with time, place, and manner restrictions. The outcome seemed a foregone conclusion, but when the judge looked up and told them to sit, the public defender's breath caught in his throat.

"Counselor, define the time, place, and manner restrictions to which you and the prosecutor have agreed," the judge commanded.

"Your Honor," said the public defender, "as argued in *Church of the Lukumi Babalu Aye v. Hialeah* . . ."

"Cut to the chase, Counselor," said the judge.

"The Santeria church does not conduct their ceremonies on regular days, Your Honor, but according to the lunar calendar. A regular schedule would interfere with their practices."

The prosecutor stepped in. "Your Honor, we consider it reasonable to allow the church to practice their animal sacrifices on Saturdays between the hours of 8 and 10 p.m."

The judge leaned back in his chair. "Counselor, that schedule does not take into account the church's proximity to a city park and school. In addition, several stores, restaurants, and bars line the streets on the south side of the building rented by the Santeria practitioners. To the north are single homes and an apartment building. Any restrictions to commerce along Water Street would be considered unconscionable by the Chamber of Commerce," the judge said as he built his argument.

He continued. "Homeowners have the constitutionally protected right to possess, use, and enjoy their property whenever they wish as long as their enjoyment of that property does not infringe on the rights of others. The owner of private property has exclusive and absolute rights to it, sans genet. No one wants to see flies swarming over chicken corpses left to rot on the asphalt surface of a parking lot."

The two attorneys remained sitting. They both assumed that some restrictions of the practice of Santeria were well within the letter of the law and that the church could resume its sacrifice of animals.

"The defendants here knew or should have known the city health codes regarding the disposal of dead animal carcasses," the judge said. "None of those regulations were followed here. I rule in favor of the home owners."

The judge stood, nodded to the men before him, and remained standing until they left. He said quietly, "Someone else can uphold *Lukumi*." He sat back down at his desk, grabbed a folder from one of the piles on his desk, and wondered if he should have been more open-minded to the progressive philosophy that all religions were the same. He would tell Diane when he got home.

Part Five

"Now what are they doing?" the judge moaned as he approached the driveway to his home the following day. He saw the same two vans he had seen yesterday morning backing out into the street. Neither driver appeared to be looking for oncoming traffic. He honked. Merle looked his way and waved, then took off with a big smile on his face. "He's still wearing that rubber nose. He looks ridiculous!" the judge complained aloud. "He needs a job, and he needs to keep his wife in line like I do." He tisked, pressing his tongue against the top of his mouth.

After he parked the new Prius inside the garage, he walked into his spacious yard. Near the back where the treehouse still perched in the oak tree, he saw his wife dead-heading flowers with clown makeup all over her face. "What was Merle doing here again?" he said as he walked toward her. "He was still wearing that ridiculous costume."

"Oh, Judge. We just returned from the children's ward at the hospital. The kids asked us where the circus was," Diane explained. "He and Shirley always bring candy."

"Oh," he grunted. "So what's for dinner?"

"We'll eat at the church. It's Community Night. We can stay for the missionary's talk if you're not too tired." She placed the basket of dead flowers in her husband's hand. "I heard on the radio that the case was dismissed."

"They don't waste any time, do they? The reporters must have interviewed the attorneys when they left my chamber." He looked at her and reached for her hand, enfolding it in his. He slowed his pace as they walked to the back door.

"Merle said the Santeria group is a public nuisance," she said. "I agree. Voodoo is not a religion but a trap for the ignorant."

"So Merle's not a progressive," said the judge. "I thought he was."

"Merle cares more about kids than he does politics," said Diane.

"Your cousin and his wife must bring a lot of cheer to those sick kids," replied the judge after considering what Diane had just said. "I'm glad you went to the hospital with them."

"I think we do," agreed Diane. "Sometimes the kids get sad when we leave, but since Merle retired, he says he can take us to the hospital more often now."

"I approve of these hospital trips, but don't get any ideas. I'm still an old fuddy-duddy," he promised. "What are they serving tonight at Community Night?"

"They're having lasagna and salad. I'll go change."

"Did you wear a big red nose like Ken?" he asked. "When I saw Shirley and Merle pull out of the driveway, they were still wearing theirs."

"Of course," Diane said, smiling. "We all did, both in and out of the children's ward."

"You said a missionary will speak after the dinner. Where's he from?"

"It's a couple. The mission is in the Dominican Republic, but they work with Haitians. The church helps support this couple and their plans to build a church. We can ask about Santeria and the magic potions," she suggested. "I won't mention anything about the trial."

"The trial will be yesterday's news by the time you get that makeup off and we drive to the church," he teased. "Why don't they build the church in Haiti?"

"It takes forever to get the required building permits," Diane explained. "It's easier on the other side of the island."

"Maybe that's why Haiti's economy is so bad. Aren't they the poorest nation in the Caribbean?" he asked.

She nodded. "Let's ask the missionaries what they think of voodoo. Maybe it's more ingrained in the people than the statistics suggest. Catholicism is supposed to be their national religion. Did you dismiss the case because of the law or because of what you think of Santeria?"

"Both," he said. "Come on. Get changed."

Part Six

He watched Diane sign them both up for the mission trip to the Dominican Republic where the Osterhousens served. He and Diane would live in a settlement for the Haitian workers called a bothy and help build the church. He would sleep in a dorm with nine other men, and she would stay on the other side for women. During the day they would all help mix cement, which he knew from previous trips was a difficult job. They would lay cement blocks and secure them with rods. Because they had visited other third-world countries, he knew what to expect. No golf, no gourmet meals, no air conditioning, and no white sand beaches, except from a distance.

One month later, their plane landed in Santo Domingo, the capital of the Dominican Republic. Scanning the airport, he saw no chickens, circus performers, or cowboys and cowgirls, just tourists dressed in typical vacation attire. He and the mission group retrieved their luggage and then walked outside to wait for Terry and Jennifer Osterhousen to pick them up.

The judge waited with Diane in the shade of the airport's overhanging roof where a nice breeze blew from one side of the open airport to the other. The cool air dried the sweat he felt running down his back and forehead. "I like how open the airport is," he said to Diane. She nodded and continued to scan the road for the mission van.

"There's the van," Diane said, "and they're on time!"

Terry pulled up to the airport and stopped. Jennifer greeted the missions group while Terry helped the men load the luggage into the van. The judge observed that both Terry and Jennifer were tall. Jennifer was as tall as he, but Terry was much taller. Jennifer's hair was braided, and Terry's was hidden under a baseball cap. The judge whispered to Diane, "He's probably losing his hair and trying to cover up his bald spot. I refuse to cover up mine."

Both missionaries wore cotton shorts and loose-fitting shirts. The judge thought they looked comfortable in their surroundings.

"Terry, how far is the mission from the airport?" asked the judge.

"The ride will take about thirty minutes," Terry said. "We'll drive through the country, which is pretty flat, and with God's grace we'll arrive safely and on time for a dinner of black beans and rice."

"I'm starving," said Lucy, a friend of Diane's. Everyone agreed.

The road to the settlement was bumpy and unpaved, but not impossible for the van to pass over. "I can smell the ocean from here and see a little stretch of beach," Diane said. "Lucy, did you see the beach?"

"Yes, and I can smell raw sewage. It's really hot, much hotter than I expected it to be in May," she replied. He and Diane had known Lucy and Bill for several years and had traveled to New Orleans with them after Katrina hit.

The van stopped, and the judge watched as two young boys led some cows across the road. The boys waved and smiled at the visitors to their country. Further down the road, the judge observed a schoolyard where male students, dressed in uniforms, played soccer. Two nuns stood by, watching their game.

"Do girls and boys attend the same schools?" asked Lucy.

"Most of the children of both genders go to Catholic schools here in the Dominican Republic," Jennifer explained. "On the other side of the island in Haiti, most children do not attend school. Over half the population of Haiti is illiterate. The United Nations Human Development Index ranks Haiti as the poorest country in the western hemisphere."

Terry continued. "Over two-thirds of the people lack formal jobs. The average family lives on less than a dollar a day. Some come over to the settlements for work, but the people here do not welcome them."

"Why not?" asked Diane.

"The Haitians are looked down upon because their skin color is darker than the Dominicans, and they have no money," explained Jennifer.

"We had to get vaccinated for the trip," said Diane.

"Yes, you have to have a cholera vaccination before traveling here because of cholera outbreaks. Travel agencies recommend travel insurance as well," said Terry.

"Are most Haitians Catholic?" asked Lucy.

"The official religion is Roman Catholicism, but the country's real religion is voodoo. The majority believe in voodoo and practice it in some way," explained Jennifer. "But those who come to live and work at the settlement are Christian."

"While it's easy to be a Christian back home," said Terry, "it requires real faith in Haiti. To believe that Jesus watches over them while living in such poverty requires deep conviction. These believers will help you appreciate how much we have been blessed living in the United States, and their faith will humble you."

"In fact," said Jennifer, "the Haitian Christians will probably give you more than you will give them."

The judge wondered if that was true. The people were so ignorant. What could they possibly teach him? And they were too poor to give.

Before sitting down to eat, the missions group showered. One faucet attached to the wall provided cold water for nine or so men. The judge sucked in air before walking into standing water beneath a water fixture that ran like the tap water in his grandmother's sink out in the country. After a hot, dusty ride from the airport, it was better than nothing, he thought, but not much better.

After dinner, the Haitian workers sat in rows on wooden benches under a few trees and learned Scripture. The missions group sat with them. Pastor Terry recited a line of Scripture and then stood next to the first row of congregants and recited it a second time. They repeated the words. Then he stood next to the second row and repeated the same line. The second row repeated what he had said. After each row of Haitians recited the original line, they all repeated it again. Soon everyone had memorized this line of God's Word.

At the end of the week, the church conducted a foot-washing ceremony for those who had come to help them. Two Haitian workers knelt down before each of the men and women in the missions group. Ramone, an older man, knelt before the judge. As the poor man removed the judge's sandals, the judge lowered his head. The older man dipped his cloth into a metal bowl of water and washed the feet of a man who did not know what it was like to live in poverty. The poor Haitian spoke the words of the Savior both men knew and loved. "You must do as I have done. In the name of the Father, the Son, and the Holy Ghost, go in peace. Return to the island soon, for we are brothers in Christ."

Judge Vanderhall felt his eyes water. He rubbed at them before Diane noticed and wondered how this man's faith had grown so strong.

Before flying back to the United States, the missions group toured the capital city of Santo Domingo where they walked along sidewalks, careful not to step in holes the size of Midwestern potholes after winter. At least twice a day, the electricity flickered and went off for a few hours both here in the capital as well as at the mission.

"I don't see many tourists in the city," the judge commented to Diane. "Do you think the tourists ever see the poverty in either island?"

"Probably not," said Diane. "They're out playing golf or soaking up the sun. I hope you didn't get too much of it."

"I'll be fine," the judge said. "Don't worry."

When they returned to the settlement, the judge broached the subject with Diane. "Do you think we should find a voodoo church and attend a ceremony?"

"Are you serious, Robert?"

"Yes. Maybe I am not being open-minded about their unorthodox practices. I need to see for myself," he said. "Would you come with me?"

"Let's talk it over with Pastor Terry," said Diane. "I'd like to ask him what he thinks of a trip to see a Santeria ceremony. He should know whether it's a good idea or not."

After the judge spoke with Terry, he watched as their host approached the elderly man who had washed the judge's feet. Pastor Terry talked with Ramone and pointed to the judge and Diane as he spoke. Ramone listened with his eyes to the floor. The judge noticed that the elderly man answered Pastor Terry's questions, but then looked askance at the American couple. Ramone shook his head and wandered off.

That night Pastor Terry called a taxi after warning the judge to be careful. He also prayed for their spiritual protection.

About nine that night, the judge helped Diane into a dented taxicab smelling of cigarettes. He greeted the young driver and noticed how the man studied them. "You know what you doing, Mister?" he asked. "You want I take you to Santeria?" When the judge nodded, the man turned around and drove them across the border into Haiti. The judge knew what he was doing. Lots of tourists visited a Santeria service. After all, he reasoned, the Supreme Court had given the religion its stamp of approval. Santeria was just one of many religions.

The cab stopped outside a low wooden building with a tin roof. The judge saw the driver look toward the entrance to the building. He rolled down his window, lit a cigarette, and looked back at the two Americans. "You be careful, mon," he said. "I wait here." When the judge opened the taxi door, he could hear the pounding of drums.

"I wait for you," the driver repeated. "Be careful what you doing."

"We won't be long," said the judge as he closed the door to the cab. He held Diane's arm as they climbed up a path covered with sand and broken shells, its uneven surface stamped with the signature of poverty. Neither of them spoke as they neared the yawning entrance to the building.

Looking neither to the left nor the right, the judge entered the building. As he and Diane walked into the darkness, he felt his wife press against him. Tightly, he held her hand, vowing not to let go. The room they entered was smaller than his courtroom; he squinted until his eyes adjusted to the dim light. He saw older practitioners standing in the back, lining the room's periphery. They chanted as each worshipper fingered a strand of beads in her hands, oblivious to the worshippers moving rhythmically around the room.

Dangling from the rafters above his head, a single light bulb hung suspended by a long cord; it cast a dim light and outlined the shapes of figures undulating to frenzied rhythms. The pounding drums obliterated his thoughts, and his reasoning emptied onto the floor. The judge watched the darkness swallow up the writhing bodies, later releasing a naked arm, a laughing mouth, a head wrapped tightly in a brightly colored scarf. A fetid smell forced its way into his eyes and nose, clinging to his thin shirt like turpentine.

The judge pressed toward the center of the room where he stopped, surrounded by believers in Santeria who revolved around them like planets blocking the sun. Frantically the women and men danced to pounding rhythms. The judge watched Diane gaping at the figures dancing around them as they moved like a mysterious current whirling about a vortex. In the darkness, the judge struggled to maintain his equilibrium in this sea of unknown forces. A sharp and pungent odor of sweat crawled up his nose. He felt dizzy and struggled to breath. He continued to watch, his eyes held captive by an energy beyond his control.

The judge felt invisible as he and Diane stood trapped in the midst of the ceremony, unable to move. He heard voices chanting. A woman shrieked. Dark bodies buckled, then rose. The frenzied worshippers slowed the tempo of their movements, their eyes lifting to the front of the room where a priest suddenly appeared. He felt Diane's hand slip from his; he strained to find her, but she had disappeared into the shadows. The worshippers surrounding him pushed him toward the priest, and against his will he moved with them. They held candles and chanted words he could not understand. They circled the voodoo priest and swayed as they watched him. Above him, the judge heard chickens squawking and wings flapping. And then he did it.

The judge watched as the priest raised a frantic bird into the air and wrung its neck, then severed the head from its twisting body. He threw the carcass to the side, lifted the animal's head and drank. Looking over the heads of the dancers, he flicked his wrist. Blood flew off the severed head and sprinkled the believers who spun around him. Droplets of blood spattered the judge's skin. He rubbed frantically at his face and quickly closed his mouth. The drums pounded, and he looked up. He saw the priest reach out and grab at another chicken that squawked and flew into the rafters seeking safety. The priest, of indeterminate age, tore the bird from its perch and ripped off its head. The judge gagged. The room started spinning, and he struggled to find his balance. In the doorway, he saw a young boy fight his way up to where the priest stood. A small goat trailed after him, and he pulled at the rope as he pushed through the frenzied crowd.

The metallic smell of blood overwhelmed the judge as he pushed his way to the entrance where Diane leaned against the wall; he pulled her out into the humid night. He directed her toward the taxi and stumbled, alone, into the weeds where he bent over and retched. As the contents of his stomach emptied onto the ground he felt the innocence in his soul depart.

Diane lifted him up, and the judge stood unsteadily and waved to the taxi driver, who rushed from the cab. Feeling the presence of the man next to him, the judge leaned on his shoulder as they made their way to the taxi. He prised open the door and collapsed into the backseat. The judge remembered the warnings, but his curiosity had pulled him like thread into the fabric of evil. Without wisdom, they arrived. Without joy, they left.

"Mister, Santeria is no game," the driver said. "I try tell you. You gringos think is like Jesus. But no; you seen the devil!"

Part Seven

He remembered nothing about their trip to Miami or the second leg of their journey back home. They found their suitcase, and with backpacks securely in place, the judge and Diane walked through the underground parking lot where he had parked his new car. But before he could open the trunk, he looked at Diane, who stood beside the passenger door. He tried to talk but felt himself fold onto the cement floor.

188 | VICKY WALL

He woke up in a hospital bed. Diane was on her phone talking with their daughter, assuring her that her father was going to be just fine. "If you want to fly out, of course, do so. He had sunstroke, but he's not dehydrated now." The judge watched as Diane paused to listen. "No," she continued, "he refused to wear a hat. You know how your father is." He heard her mention something about the weekend and hung up.

"How do you feel?" she asked as she stroked his forehead. "Don't get up. You're hooked up to an IV. You were dehydrated."

"What happened?"

"You collapsed in the parking garage. I called an ambulance and followed it here to the hospital. You had sunstroke."

A nurse walked into the room. She looked at him and took his temperature. He waited for her to scold him, but she said nothing.

"Has the doctor examined me?" he asked.

"Yes, and your vital signs are normal," the nurse said. "Trips to third-world countries can exhaust even the strongest people, even the young. You'll be fine and back at the courthouse next week."

When she left, he saw a tall, broad-shouldered man pause at the door. Diane greeted him with a smile and invited him into the room. "It's good to see you, Pastor Ken," she said.

"I was in the neighborhood, Robert, and thought I'd drop in to visit the sick and foolhardy," said the pastor as he walked over to the bed.

"Pastor Ken, please come in and sit down. I'm going downstairs for cocoa. Want some?" Diane asked. He just shook his head.

When she left, Pastor Ken pulled up a chair and sat down next to the hospital bed.

"Why are you here?" asked the judge. "Did Diane call you?"

"I'm here," said Pastor Ken, "because someone forgot to put on all of God's armor to stand firm against the strategies of the devil."

The judge lifted his hand in self-defense. "I was just following the law, Pastor Ken. The Supreme Court upheld the practices of Santeria, so I figured they knew what they were doing. But Santeria is not just another religion. The Court was wrong."

"Yes, Diane told me about that decision and the recent case in your courtroom," Pastor Ken said. "The Supreme Court justices were victims of a belief in pluralism just like the Pharaoh in Egypt who believed in multiple gods. Maybe the justices didn't bother to read Exodus like you didn't bother to read Ephesians 6."

"But there's nothing I can do to stop it."

"God doesn't ask you to change Court precedent, Robert, or save the misguided," Pastor Ken said. "Moses couldn't change the Pharaoh's hard heart, and you can't change Court decisions. As Habakkuk says, 'The law has been paralyzed.' But you didn't paralyze it."

The judge listened to his pastor's words, knew he had spoken the truth, yet he felt helpless. "I've lost my confidence. I'm not sure I can continue to sit on the bench."

"First of all, your faith has been attacked by powerful forces. You need to rebuild it. Start by reading your Bible every day. Build yourself back up in God's Word. Second, stay out of dark places where they practice voodoo. Third, God is still in control. He, not you, will throw the wicked into the fiery lake of sulfur." He rose and stood beside the judge's bed. "Let's pray, Robert, for God to remove any evil attachments to your soul." The judge bowed his head.

"You always were an ordinal numbers kind of guy, Ken," said the judge. "First, second, third. But thanks for setting me straight."

"Look whose back to tuck you in?" said the pastor when Diane appeared at the door. "Here's your compass, Judge. Are you taking him home tomorrow, Diane?"

"Yes. Thank you for visiting, Pastor Ken. We'll be in church this Sunday."

The next morning he felt strong enough to go home. A hospital attendant pushed his wheelchair to the hospital entrance where Diane would be waiting for him. Instead of insisting that he didn't need a wheelchair and getting into an argument with the young man, he expressed his appreciation. He said thank you to the volunteer who assisted him, got up out of the wheelchair, and walked to Diane's car.

On the drive home, he told Diane what he was going to do. "I'm going to write a short letter to Ramone, the man who washed our feet. That man knew who he was. Like John the Baptist, he made himself smaller so Jesus could become bigger."

"The missionaries were right, Robert," Diane said. "The Haitians gave us more than we gave them."

"Ramone has so little compared to us," the judge said. "But he has so much."

"I saw Jesus when he washed our feet," said Diane.

"Me too."

"Let's send Ramone a gift, maybe a shirt," she suggested.

"That's a good idea. What else have you been thinking?"

"I've decided not to buy a new car," she said. "I'm going to send our car savings to the mission."

"Okay," the judge said. "What about your stash in the kitchen cupboard? That money you use to buy cocoa and chocolate with?" Diane turned sharply toward him. "Will you sacrifice your chocolate money?"

"Robert!" she scolded. "I can sacrifice my new car, but never my chocolate."

When they entered the house, Diane turned to the judge and said, "Let's go upstairs. Two kitties are waiting to welcome you home."

"Two kitties?"

"Okay. One kitty will welcome you; the other will simply stare."

The judge followed his wife up the stairs, wondering if she would be there the next time he forgot who he wanted to be.

* In memory of Diane Ball *

JUST ASK

James 1:5

If you need wisdom, ask our generous God, and he will give it to you.

Isaiah 65:1

I was ready to respond, but no one asked for help.

After reading the announcement, Karley groaned. She peeled off damp running clothes from her willowy frame and swished into a terrycloth robe and flip-flops. Before grabbing a bottle of water from the refrigerator, she pulled the scrunchy from her ponytail, leaned over, and swept her long blonde hair into a towel. The washing machine was set for a small load, so she tossed her damp clothing in and added some detergent.

When she walked outside on the deck, she nearly tripped over Rehnquist, her 60-pound jogging companion, who lay stretched out in the sun. Before joining him, she snatched up her iPhone to call her sister. The sun felt warm and comforting as she scratched Rehnny behind his ears, kissed the top of his warm head, and waited for her sister to answer. It was Saturday.

Without preamble, she demanded an answer from her older sister. "Can you believe this, Abby?" said Karley as she set her jogging shoes in the sun. "Another wedding in Texas in July."

"Is that what it is? I haven't opened the mail yet," said Abby, not bothering to stifle a noisy yawn. "Why are you surprised? Weren't you expecting another marriage? Hold on. I need coffee." While Karley waited, she got up and refilled her dog's water dish.

"Are you still in bed?" asked Karley when she heard Abby slurping her coffee.

"Yes, Greg took the kids swimming and let me sleep in. Now, back to Cousin Cheryl. You know she likes to get married," Abby reminded her, "and she likes to change husbands every five or so years. She's due."

"But it's in July—again!" said Karley, her exasperation mounting. She walked back into the kitchen. "I love our cousin, and I love Texas. I even love July, just not all together."

"Well, we have to go, don't we? Mother would want us to represent the family. Besides, aren't you curious about the new man?"

"After the last one?" asked Karley. "Working for the post office for twenty years doesn't make you an interesting person. Unless you write novels before you go to work like Hawthorne, and he worked at a customs house."

"Her last husband was a bit boring, that's true," agreed Abby, "but he loved her. He probably still does. And you forget that trips to Texas and weddings are a good excuse to buy clothes and shoes. You always leave out the best part, the chance to update your wardrobe."

"I suppose," said Karley, examining the rundown heels of her jogging shoes. Why did her sister always forget she and Bill lived on a tighter budget than she and Greg did?

"Back to Cousin Cheryl's pending nuptials," said Abby, laughing. "Do you remember her last wedding on the golf course? When lightning struck during the reception?"

"And the bridesmaid passed out when Cheryl said 'I do'?" said Karley, laughing at the memory. She wiped her eyes, wet from flashbacks to the comedy of errors. "Why doesn't she ever get married in traditional settings like a church?"

"Come on, Karley. How many times has Cousin Cheryl entered into the holy state of matrimony? What church would marry her?"

"I'm sure many churches would marry her," said Karley. "There aren't any rules anymore."

"Nowadays, people want rules they are comfortable with."

"Yes, folks want flexible rules they can change so they can do anything they want. I used to live like that," said Karley. "What a disaster!"

"Well, you don't live like that anymore," said Abby. "Now, about Cheryl's wedding."

"In the month of July, outdoors, in Texas," said Karley. She knew she was perseverating but couldn't help herself. She stood up, threw the plastic bottle into the recycling bin, and glanced at the stack of bills she needed to pay.

"We do love her and we have to support her, don't we?" asked Abby. "And hope this one sticks."

"If we continue to attend her weddings," said Karley, "she may think we approve of her divorces."

"I don't think we should judge Cousin Cheryl. But we do need to pray for her."

"Well, if we do decide to go, I'd like to see the Ten Commandments monument on the grounds around the State Capitol," said Karley, anticipating a less than positive response from her sister.

"Well, that sounds boring." Abby wasn't shy about speaking her mind. "Besides, isn't it illegal to display the Ten Commandments in public?"

"In most situations, yes," said Karley. "In this case, the Supreme Court decided it was legal. I read a Supreme Court case about it in school. Justice Breyer said the Establishment Clause does not demand that the government purge from the public sphere everything religious."

"Okay, Karley, enough lecturing."

"I wouldn't call a clarifying statement a lecture," said Karley in her own defense."

"I doubt anyone would want to see a granite monument with the Ten Commandments," said Abby. "Why don't we do what the group wants?"

Karley snatched the stack of bills and walked into her office where she reviewed the titles on the spines of her old law books. She pulled the one on constitutional law and sat down in front of her computer. Rehnquist got up and followed her into the kitchen where he sat next to her; his brown eyes asked her to rub his ears, which she did.

She heard her sister exhale and imagined her twitching her nose the way she did when she smelled something bad. But Karley continued, expanding her theme of constitutional issues. "You know, I love free speech issues."

"I know that," said Abby, sighing loudly. "So why are you practicing family law?"

"I don't know anymore," admitted Karley. She set aside the heavy book and thumbed through the recent statements from creditors that arrived promptly like Swiss trains. "I used to think I was protecting women and children. But most of them can protect themselves. They just want me to help them get a big settlement. Of course, the work pays well."

"Karley, we've had this discussion before. You complain about practicing divorce law, but you continue to do it."

"I know, but I just don't know what else to do." Karley's posture sank into her ribcage.

"Have you prayed about this?"

"I pray a lot, Abby."

"Yes, but have you asked God to show you the direction He wants you to take?"

"I will," said Karley. "I just think I should be able to figure this out on my own."

"You haven't been able to so far. You just keep talking about it."

"I won't bring it up anymore, okay?" said Karley. "I'll sit down and make a list of pros and cons."

"Why don't you think about your professional future when we're in Texas?" said Abby. "You and Bill could talk about a career change. And the two of you can pray about your future together."

Karley listened but wondered how agreeable her husband would be if she told him she was giving up a job that helped support them. Her sister continued. "But let's make a decision first about attending Cousin Cheryl's wedding. Greg will be back soon with the kids."

"Let me think about it," said Karley, preparing to weigh the pros and cons of attending another wedding in Texas in July.

Since law school, she had become accustomed to considering both sides of the argument but not to making a decision. The same was not true, however, of her religious and moral convictions. She didn't debate her religious beliefs; instead, she believed. The foundation of her faith was solid, at least she thought it was. Or had the strength of her convictions slowly diminished as the courts had ruled in favor of an empty public square and the removal of most Ten Commandments monuments? Gone were concrete reminders of principles undergirding Western civilization. Maybe her own convictions had left with them. Why am I practicing family law? she asked herself, but didn't have an answer.

Karley finally said, "Whatever happened to the marriage covenant and our covenant with God?"

"It's too early in the morning to discuss hot-button issues like religion," said Abby. "Besides, not everyone has the same beliefs as you do. Let's leave it at that before we start arguing."

"You're right," said Karley. "We agreed not to discuss religion and politics, or how much candy a mother should give her children."

"Karley," warned her sister. "Leave it alone. Call me later, and who knows? By then maybe the marriage will be called off or postponed until cooler weather."

That won't happen, thought Karley, as she ended the call and sat down to send payments through the upper regions of space. Maybe I should visit the Ten Commandments monument by myself, she thought, before nine Supreme Court justices blast away the evidence.

She felt Rehnquist's warm tongue licking her hand and knee. "You lick me like I'm an ice cream cone, don't you, Rehnny?" Karley smiled at her faithful friend. He rested his large head on her knees as she organized her bills. She wondered what she would do if it weren't for their bills, but she couldn't even consider changing fields until her school loans were paid off. Or could she . . .

"Rehnny, what do you think I should do with my life?" she asked as she pet her dog's noble head. "Should I continue to help women get divorced, or should I work to keep religion in the public square?"

Rehnquist looked up at Karley and licked her face.

The wedding was on. In July. When Abby insisted on taking her Chevy Traverse and paying for the gas, Karley didn't put up much resistance initially, especially when Abby promised to provide a clean vehicle for the trip. "I'll clean out the van so you won't have to worry about sitting in Cheerios again, or dog hair, or gum."

"What about lollipops?" asked Karley. When Abby added sticky candy to the list, Karley relaxed but insisted they split all the costs. Even though Karley and Bill would be saddled with her school loans for the foreseeable future, at least until she died or the planet exploded, she liked paying her own way. "We could take my SUV, but I don't have a navigational system or movies."

"We've driven down so often," said Abby, "we may not need directions from Lilly."

"Lilly? You named your GPS system Lilly? Is there a story involved?"

"Yes, one already written by Jonathan Swift," said Abby. "You remember *Gulliver's Travels*?"

"Of course, the Lilliputians," said Karley. "The little people."

"The kids saw the movie and started calling the voice Lilly," explained Abby. "At the time that's all Tommy could say, and of course Audrey went along with it. Paul thought the whole thing was stupid."

"I respect children who dismiss technology," said Karley.

"Oh, he likes technology," said Abby. "He just thinks naming inanimate objects is what stupid people do."

"Shouldn't everything have a name? Like weddings in Texas in July, for example?"

"How about 'Weddings Revisited'?" suggested Abby.

"Or 'Texas Revenge at the Altar'?" said Karley. "Are the kids excited about going on a road trip?"

"Yes, but they get happy when we drive to the carwash," said Abby. "Of course, I haven't told them we're going to Texas."

"Why not?"

"Don't you remember the ants on the golf course and the spiders in Cheryl's bathroom?"

"Oh, yes," said Karley. "What are you going to do?"

"Squirt guns with magic powers," said Abby, "and lots of treats."

"Of course. Guns and candy."

"Don't start," said Abby. "We'll pick you up around nine tomorrow if we get an early start. Tell Bill that Greg will meet him at the airport at five on Friday. Greg's actually looking forward to the trip."

"Greg is such an optimist," said Karley. "I've always admired how he sees something good in everything despite the facts on the ground."

"Greg knows how to make the best of every situation," said Abby. "Maybe it's his youthful outlook on life."

Karley knew that was a jab at her husband, Bill, who was twelve years older than Karley and ten years older than Abby and Greg. According to Abby, Bill was a relic from the past. Like the Ten Commandments, thought Karley. Maybe the Court could pick up Bill the next time they hired a moving company to pack up the Ten Commandments. The Court could put the two stones together in a storage locker.

"Do you think we'll like husband number four?" asked Karley.

The two sisters paused. In unison they laughed; then each of them placed a wager on how long this marriage would last.

That was a mere ninety-six hours ago, Karley calculated, as she drove her sister's van toward Austin, Texas, for a field trip with her family. After parking several blocks from the State Capitol building, she checked her iPhone for client messages. Her latest client had left half a dozen. Karley tried to explain to her that she would bill her for each phone conversation they had and for each email she had to write; she wasn't her client's buddy or confidant. The woman didn't believe her or grasp the concept of billable hours, but she would when she received Karley's bills. The woman had already blown through a retainer of five thousand.

Part of the problem with her clients was that they hired an attorney before they consulted a therapist about the problems in the marriage. As the attorneys worked to divide the marital property, the marriage partners sometimes realized a divorce may not be the answer to what really troubled them. Instead of seeking help, however, they filed for divorce. Why was it so hard for people to ask for help?

As she parked, she checked the mirror to make sure she wasn't going over the curb. She caught herself in the mirror and paused. Do I have the same problem my clients have? I still haven't asked God for direction. I say my faith is intact, but I haven't asked God what He wants for my life. I'm no different from my clients, she realized. All I think about is the money.

Her phone vibrated, and she looked down and saw the call was from her latest client. Before leaving town, Karley had met with her new client again. Karley told her to make a list of the marital property and devise a way to divide it. The division of property usually required more effort than a visitation schedule for the children, but not always. When the husband had a girlfriend, like the one in this case, she prepared for a protracted battle. More money for me at the end, she thought, then asked herself if she was only in her profession for the money. Where was her faith in what she did?

Squinting through the stickers that nearly covered both back windows, she slowly backed the SUV into the parking spot. She turned off the ignition and then watched her sister unpack Audrey's stroller and shrug into her backpack filled with juice and water bottles. Since she and Bill had no children, Karley enjoyed spending time with her two nephews and niece. Cheryl, who sat next to her, scrolled through the messages on her phone. Cheryl was two years older than Abby. It wasn't unusual for strangers to assume the three of them were sisters.

"Is the wedding still on?" Karley asked when Cheryl threw the pink-covered phone into her purse.

"Of course," Cheryl responded, pushing back her short blonde hair. "Just more questions from my boss. I'd live on bread and water before I went back to work for the IRS, especially after my friends and neighbors started asking me if I was going after Tea Party groups. Like I had that kind of authority."

Karley nodded. "Doesn't Chapman want you to work after you get married?"

"He doesn't care what I do," said Cheryl, "as long as I'm happy. Today, he's more concerned that we see all seventeen monuments and twenty-one historical markers in the right order."

"Is there an order?" asked Karley, pulling the State Capitol map from her backpack. Her pack was stuffed with saltines, apple slices, and diapers for her niece. She wondered what was inside Cheryl's large purse.

"No, not that one," said Cheryl. "He wants us to use the map he gave me last night." She dug into her purse. "But I can't find the damn thing."

Karley locked the van and watched her cousin pick up Audrey and strap her into the stroller. She wondered if Cheryl's two adult children would be attending the wedding but didn't ask. Cheryl had divorced their dad shortly after the kids entered kindergarten. "That man couldn't keep his hands to himself," she told her two cousins when they were in Austin visiting. "I plan on staying in the house, so I hope none of my female neighbors give birth to his progeny. It would be awkward seeing my kids' little brothers and sisters running through my backyard."

Cheryl's future husband, Chapman, didn't seem to have that problem. His first wife had died, and he liked being married. "Oh, he's not perfect," Cheryl had explained. "Well, he thinks he's perfect, but at least he's not a womanizer."

The night before, Karley and Abby had met Chapman, a man who did not go by a diminutive of the name on his birth certificate. Instead of talking to Abby, the sister most men gravitated to since she was so pretty, Chapman stood talking to her. He suggested taking the kids on a field trip to the State Capitol. He couldn't join them, of course. He told Karley he was stuck looking for a cure for cancer inside an air-conditioned lab with a pop machine loaded with Dr. Pepper. Karley had added the part about the Dr. Pepper. She didn't tell Chapman that she wanted to see the Ten Commandments; she didn't know Chapman's religious affiliations. Perhaps he had none, but why was she afraid to broach the subject?

"I wish I could join you," Chapman told her at a pre-rehearsal dinner for colleagues and friends. Her future brother-in-law, whose salt and pepper hair and mustache appeared perfectly groomed, leaned against the bar as he spoke highly of a trip he had never taken. Karley stood next to him drinking Perrier and checking his suit pockets for test tubes. She watched the tic in his left eye spread to his right. Or maybe the tic was in her own eye. It was hard to tell. In her heels, they were nearly the same height. Absentmindedly, she pulled at the collar of her white blouse.

"My kids love to learn about Texas history," Chapman told her as he paused to drink from a salted margarita glass. "When the boys were young, my wife, Lindsey, always took them to the State Capitol over spring break."

"What's the temperature here in March and April?" asked Karley. She couldn't resist needling him about the wisdom of an outdoor Texas field trip in July—with children.

"Oh, the weather is perfect then," he said, failing to connect the dots of Karley's skepticism. "I never can join them, of course. But Lindsey told me the boys memorized the names of all seventeen monuments and twenty-one historical markers after their first trip." He motioned for another drink. "Cheryl probably told you they're both straight-A students. The older boy, Chapman Jr., just got accepted into Princeton, my alma mater, and the younger boy, Phillip, got a perfect score on the SAT."

Karley saw Abby roll her eyes. She noticed that the bride-to-be drank the rest of her margarita in one gulp.

"I didn't think anyone could get a perfect score on a college entrance exam," said Karley. "Why go to college when you know everything before you start?"

"Oh, he'll finish undergrad in three years and save me some money. Then he'll start medical school," explained the man who would pledge his love to her cousin the next day beside a swimming pool in his backyard where a second living room and kitchen for outdoor activities had been built and furnished. Texans liked their castles big, she decided, and wondered how long his pledge would last before it melted beneath the glaring sun. She also wondered if his lawn had been sprayed for bugs and spiders.

"I read that James Madison finished Princeton in two years," said Karley, watching Chapman's eyes scan the crowd, like he was looking for a redeemer. "And sank into a severe depression after saving his father the expense of two more years in college."

Chapman spotted his treasure, on the other side of the room, and smiled. Before joining them, he said, "Madison had epilepsy, Karley. Chapman Jr., on the other hand, has perfect health."

After politely excusing himself, Chapman left the bar. Karley watched his retreating figure. He would have been a good attorney, she thought. Without hesitation, he had undercut her main argument. He thinks well on his feet, she decided. Either that or Chapman had a stockpile of responses that abruptly ended any conversation.

She watched her opponent thread his way through the guests and stop in front of a middle-aged Indian couple who stood with martinis in their hands. The woman's husband took her drink while she opened her purse and foraged through it like a Hindu believer looking for Vishnu and Shiva. Karley wondered if the woman would find the past she may have traded to fit into American culture.

What did I trade in, Karley considered, to fit into the legal profession? Maybe God can break into my life while I'm here in Texas and guide me to my perfect career. I really need to pray, she thought, but continued to watch the Indian couple interact with Chapman.

Karley leaned against the bar and considered why the woman drank liquor yet still wore a sari. The couple reminded her of the Jews in the Old Testament who worshipped foreign gods and carried idols into their homes. Every time the Jews lived around people with other gods, they intermarried and built Asherah poles. Human nature, she decided. We do anything to fit in with our neighbors, even if it means forgetting our most cherished beliefs.

Karley considered her own situation; being an attorney meant you could argue both sides in a debate. Being a Christian attorney also meant something else: you kept your faith to yourself. Was she losing her faith because believing in God was politically incorrect in the legal profession? If she lived in Texas, she decided, her faith wouldn't become a problem, unless of course she lived in Austin.

"Was Chapman bragging about his children again?" asked Cheryl, pulling Karley back into the present and away from the debate in her head. Karley nodded, and Cheryl continued. "He is so proud of his kids. He tells everyone who will listen about their achievements."

"Does he always flash his progeny's brilliance like a bank statement?" asked Karley.

"Almost always. Sometimes he simply recites the names of all the schools he and the boys have attended and assumes you appreciate who you're talking to," said Cheryl. "Once he's sure you understand who he is, he can't do enough for you. He buys all of my clothes."

"You know, Cheryl," said Karley, "that dress fits you perfectly. It brings out your best features. Is it made of spandex?"

"No, but it does fit nicely, doesn't it?" said Cheryl as she raised her head like Cleopatra. Karley wondered if Egypt was as hot as Texas. She watched Cheryl quickly look around, then step behind Abby to pull at the sides of the hot pink dress wrapping her like the sugar coating on a Tootsie Pop.

Karley heard Abby ask their cousin where she and Chapman met, but Karley lost Cheryl's response in the country music playing in the background. She sang along with the lyrics of a Rascal Flatts refrain about his woman not looking a day older than fast cars and freedom. Karley looked down at what she was wearing. Dressed in a conservative black suit, she felt older than those cars and all the heroes of the Texas history preserved in sunset-red granite, waiting for her tomorrow at the State Capitol. Why did she pack a black suit, she wondered, as she observed the pastel dresses fluttering like butterfly wings around her?

They stood in front of a monument different in shape from all the other monuments and historical markers. While the other monuments spoke through gesture and expression, replicating human activity, this monument was different. Its flat rectangular shape did not look like it represented the original settlers of Texas or those who represented the state in war. This block of granite was different. Surprisingly, the Court upheld its right to remain on the grounds outside the State Capitol and mix in with the other tributes to the state's past. The statues depicted those brave men and women who took a stand for Texas.

"Karley, are there dirty words under this blanket?" demanded her six-year-old nephew Tommy, who sat beside the sunset-red granite on the capitol grounds. Karley smiled at the young boy. "Tell me the truth. Are they bad?"

Tommy stared at her and waited for an answer. He had paused in his pursuit of pulling up the black velvet covering that protected the monument like a cocoon. Karley doubted he could disrobe the stone, but he had surprised her before, like when he pulled up the weeds in a neighbor's yard because they smelled bad. No one had told him the weeds weren't weeds, but plants purposely grown for enjoyable personal consumption. She leaned over and brushed back the damp blond hair clinging to his forehead.

"Aunt Karley," she said, correcting him. "You know I want you to call me Aunt Karley."

Shielding his eyes with his hand, Tommy looked up at her.

"Okay," said Karley quickly. "You can call me Aunt Kay."

"Are there dirty words under this blanket?" Tommy insisted as he sat up to examine the padlock uniting the ends of the stainless steel chain circling the stone. "Aunt Kay," he added, a smile forming on his face.

"Thank you," she said, wondering what was going on inside his head. "Now tell me why you don't like calling me 'aunt.'"

"I don't like ants," he admitted, snickering. Karley watched his eyes grow larger. "When I call you Aunt Kay, I see big black eyes on your face and huge antlers poking out of your head."

Suddenly Tommy exploded with laughter, rolled onto his side, and held his knees. Startled, Karley swatted at her face and hair.

She looked around her, checking for large attack ants, and caught sight of her nine-year-old nephew Paul darting through a crowd of tourists leaving the statue of a Texas Cowboy riding a rearing horse, a monument they had just visited. By an invisible homing device, Paul knew something was up and ran to join the fun.

Skillfully, he pushed his little sister's stroller like a small boat through water, dodging a group of seniors headed in the direction of the Texas Pioneer Woman who held her baby in her arms as she stood proudly beneath the blue sky. They would see that monument next. Paul pulled the stroller up sharply in front of Tommy and looked down at his brother, who was still rolling around, laughing in delight. Abby and Cousin Cheryl followed in Paul's wake.

"What's so funny?" asked Paul, looking first at Tommy and then at Karley.

"Aunt . . . Aunt Kay," Tommy said, but his laughter eclipsed his attempts to explain. "She looks like a big ant with big eyes and—"

"Oh, yeah," said Paul, who faced Karley and smiled. "He hates ants. Sometimes he has nightmares about them."

"I do not," said Tommy. "I just don't like them."

"What's under the blanket, Aunt Karley?" asked Paul, getting down on his hands and knees to examine the black velvet cocoon and the words it attempted to hide on the red granite monument. Karley wondered if the Ten Commandments began as larvae inside the mind of God, until Tommy's voice reclaimed her attention.

"Dirty words," said Tommy, who sat up and grabbed the padlock and chain circling the monument. "The park covered them up."

"Maybe the park covered the monument on purpose," surmised Paul, "to protect little kids like Audrey from seeing the bad words."

"They're not dirty words," said Karley. "But I'm not sure why this monument is covered and chained." She looked around for other shrouded monuments but saw none.

"But they're covered up," repeated Tommy, looking at his older brother, "like Daddy's naked lady magazines." Karley felt their eyes on her, waiting for a response. She stood very still.

"The pictures of big boobs and butts," said Paul as he stole a glance at his smiling brother. "Dad hides the magazines, Aunt Karley, but we always find them." The boys laughed, stood up, and started chasing each other around the monument.

"Boobies," said a little voice. Karley's three-year-old niece, Audrey, watched her brothers chase each other. "Big boobies," she repeated. Paul and Tommy stopped and looked at their sister. When the little girl saw her brothers' eyes lighting up like fireworks, she continued loudly, "Big butts and big boobies, butts and boobies."

Shrieking in laughter, the boys fell to the ground and rolled back and forth, their faces pink and sweaty. Audrey kept repeating the funny words. Karley smiled. She couldn't hide her amusement from the kids and joined in with their laughter. When their gaiety faded, she could hear chanting and the pounding of drums. She saw a sea of demonstrators trailing Abby and Cheryl.

Feeling encouraged, Audrey continued. "Poopie, wee-wee," she squealed, "and butts. Big butts and big boobies."

"Audrey!" her mother exclaimed as she hurried forward. "What are you doing? Those are bathroom words." Abby pressed her forefinger to her own lips.

Audrey stopped. She looked up at her mother. "I did pee-pee in my pants," she said, hesitating between more laughter and sudden tears.

"Paul, Tommy," warned their mother. "Don't say another word." Abby reached for Audrey, but both mother and daughter froze in a tableau of confusion as young men and women marched toward them. Their voices chanted, drums pounded, and someone played a high-pitched flute.

"Hail, Satan!" the young voices shouted. "Hail, Satan!" The devil's young minions lifted their faces and strained to appear as fierce as their words. Except for the epithet emblazoned on their red T-shirts, Karley thought the young demonstrators could pass for young patriots who protested against the British soldiers outside the customs house in Boston. Instead of rocks and chunks of ice, these believers in Satan carried a banner stating "Religious Parity: A Satanic Monument."

"Abby, do you think these young men and women in their identical shirts and black shorts could fight and die for their cause?" Karley asked.

"Like the young Patriots in their ragtag farm clothes?" asked Abby. "I don't think they could lift a rifle or a musket, let alone fire it."

"I wonder if these clean young people know anything about the history of their freedom to protest today," said Karley.

Abby shook her head, then turned to pour water into Audrey's sippy cup. Interrupting Karley's musings, a short teenager with dyed red hair and green eyeshadow stopped in front of the Ten Commandments monument, covered by someone, like the girl, who took offense to its presence. The girl stepped in front of Audrey's stroller, opened her mouth wide, and wagged her metal-studded tongue at the little girl. Audrey started to cry, but fascination soaked up her tears.

"Nails," Audrey cried, "she's got nails in her tongue!" Audrey opened her mouth, stuck out her tongue, and wiggled it. She wiggled it some more and giggled.

Paul and Tommy dropped the chain and padlock they had been examining and looked up at the young marcher.

"Yuck," said Paul, grabbing his mother's arm to get her attention. "She's got a metal thing in her tongue! That's disgusting!"

"Yucky!" echoed Audrey and Tommy.

As a distraction, Cousin Cheryl pulled three large bags of Skittles from her purse. "Here, kids," she called. "Eat some candy."

The boys stepped forward to receive the gift. "Thank you," they said like mechanical toys and ripped the bags open. But before they could enjoy the sweets, the satanic leader appeared. Karley watched her nephews and niece stare at the tall, broad-shouldered man who wore a huge goat head with horns over of his head.

The mask perched on the man like a red comb on a rooster's head. His black robe dragged along the ground. When he turned, Karley saw wings jutting out below the goat's head, paralyzed wings that could not lift the man or his followers off the ground and into heaven. The gray headgear appeared to be slipping. Tilting to the leader's left shoulder, the goat's head threatened to slide off the satanic hero like a big scoop of ice cream from a sugar cone. Pausing, the man adjusted his headgear. Two small children, one on either side, walked solemnly beside the tall, black-robed man. When their leader stopped, the young children mimicked his movements and stood motionless beside the monument bearing the Ten Commandments. Covered, it provided no guidance.

"Hail, Satan!" their leader said, pausing before the monument. "The forces of darkness will overcome the words on that stone. Don't touch that cover, boys."

Paul and Tommy looked back and forth between the goat man and their Aunt Karley, who had stepped in front of both boys to stand opposite the man who barked commands at the children. Between the opposing camps, the disputed monument stood, its words invisible, its covenant between God and His children in limbo.

"Excuse me," Karley said firmly. "But this monument is legal. What is not legal is the black material covering the Ten Commandments."

"No, ma'am," the man exclaimed, and Karley watched as long, muscular arms shot from beneath the robe's folds to remove the headgear. Standing so close, Karley thought the headpiece looked like it was made of papier-mache, and the leader more of a college student than a grown man.

He looked down at her from the perch of his superiority and continued. "The monument chiseled with the Ten Commandments is illegal until the Satanists have an equal monument beside it. In the name of religious parity, we march and will continue to march for a monument of equal size, outlining our belief in the powers of darkness."

"You're wrong, Mr. Goat Man. You're so wrong," said Karley. "In 2005 the Supreme Court upheld the state's right to display the Ten Commandments here, on the Texas State Capitol grounds. The monument is legal!"

"This monument is an abomination! We march for equality for all, and our group will shut this monument down until the state engraves our laws on a commensurate stone," the man asserted, his low opinion of the commandments tied around him like a belt.

"The issue has already been litigated, Goat Man, and the Ten Commandments remain!" Karley stood, her hands on her hips.

The goat-headed man turned to walk back to his group of marchers. As he did, a small piece of his black robe appeared to snag on the padlock and chain, which lay on the ground beside the Texas red granite. One of the Goat Man's minions reached down, picked up the torn material, and handed it to the leader, who made a business of folding and refolding the piece of material before shoving it into the pocket of his costume.

Karley stood with her family and watched the Satanists walk toward the Capitol. She doubted that Goat Man would ever surrender his power.

"How did Goat Man's robe tear?" asked Karley. She looked at the silent faces around her. "Come on. Which one of you has a pocket knife and just cut off a piece of the man's robe?"

"Paul did it," said Audrey, pointing at her older brother.

"I did not," said Paul. "I left my knife at home, but Tommy has his."

"Tommy did it," said Audrey, pointing her finger at her other brother, the second miscreant capable of naughty business. "It's Tommy. He's bad."

"I just cut a little," admitted Tommy. "His robe was too long. He was going to trip."

Karley quickly covered her face with the map of the State Capitol before Tommy could see her shoulders shake. Instead of snorting, she coughed her laughter away. Behind her, Karley heard Abby snort. "Eat your candy," said Abby, "and don't do it again." Karley and Abby exchanged smiles.

Saved by the call to eat sweets, the boys stood quietly munching their treats. Audrey held up the big bag toward her mother and shook her head. Her mother took the large bag of candy and handed it to Karley, who put it in Audrey's stroller, along with the map.

"Audrey," Karley asked, "do you like kisses or hugs best?"

"Huggings," said Audrey. "I like huggings." The little girl reached up, and Karley took the child, wet pants and all, into her arms.

"I wet," said Audrey.

"That's okay," said Karley. "I can't feel anything it's so hot. I think I know how the oven felt to Shadrach, Meshach, and Abednego."

"It's not that hot," said Cheryl, defending her homeland with the fierceness of the Texas heat. "You folks from the North fold like cheap suits down here. You're all wimps."

Abby unzipped her backpack and took out a chilled water bottle. She handed the cold bottle, dripping with condensation, to Cousin Cheryl. "Here, Dixie Chick," Abby said. "Drink it and zip your lips. Just remember, you were defeated at the Alamo."

At least they took a stand for their convictions, thought Karley. Against tremendous odds, they fought and died for what they believed. She doubted she could ever do the same.

"A fight," said Audrey, her eyes hopping back and forth between her mother and Cousin Cheryl.

"Well, I am folding," said Karley, but she stopped at the sight of another group of demonstrators. "Now what?"

"I forgot to tell you how popular these grounds are with protestors," said Cheryl. "Some group is always railing against something or other. We've been here less than an hour, and we've seen three groups."

When Karley heard the sound of a group of voices singing "Amazing Grace," she looked up expectantly. Passing before her, she saw a second group of men and women of all ages walking toward the Capitol building. These demonstrators wore blue T-shirts and different-colored shorts and pants. The words stamped across their T-shirts identified their pro-life cause. Two older women carried a large banner that read: "End Late-Term Abortions."

Behind the pro-life group Karley watched abortion supporters, trolling the first group like the exhaust behind a city bus, alerting everyone nearby of their presence. The pro-abortion group shouted, "Freedom to choose!"

"Not this again," said Cheryl. "I swear, every time I come here, these two groups are marching. If abortion were a state issue, states could choose which way they wanted to go and people could vote for their beliefs. The Supreme Court should have left the issue with the states."

"I agree," said Karley. Before she could weigh in further on the subject, Karley felt a little hand pulling at her shorts. She looked down at her youngest nephew. Tommy grabbed the lock and spun it around. "Do you know how to open locks, Tommy?" she asked, holding her breath.

"No, but Paul does," he said and motioned to his older brother, who sat next to him. Both boys stopped watching the demonstrators and studied the lock. Karley knelt beside them and turned her attention to the action on the ground.

When Paul pulled the lock apart, she was afraid to ask him where he learned how to pick locks. Would Paul acquire a record of arrests, she wondered, before he earned a college degree? She didn't have the energy to lecture him. Instead, she watched silently as her two nephews removed the black velvet cocoon from the ten rules that had guided mankind's conduct for thousands of years.

In the heat of a Texas morning in July, Karley imagined flames shooting into the sky and black clouds descending from on high, shrouding the city in darkness. She imagined the Lord speaking from the fire as He did in the book of Deuteronomy when He proclaimed His covenant with the Jewish people in these Ten Commandments. Karley looked into the cloud, hoping to discover the Lord's plan for her life, but saw and heard nothing. She hoped the Lord would again break into human history, her history, and guide her to her true purpose. She didn't think guiding women through a divorce was it.

"Karley, what are you looking for?" said Abby. "Are you okay?"

"I don't know," said Karley. "I guess it's the heat."

"Here, drink some juice," said her sister.

Karley accepted the cool carton of grape juice and drank its contents. "Thanks," she said. "I needed that."

"Are you still thinking about your career?" asked Abby.

Karley nodded.

"Have you prayed about it yet?"

Before Karley could respond, their cousin Cheryl called for their attention.

"Hey, look over at the Heroes of the Alamo statue," said Cousin Cheryl. "Isn't that the Goat Man?" The visitors looked beyond the monuments to a tall figure walking toward them.

"The return of Satan," said Abby, "but where are his followers?"

"Passed out under the bushes," said Karley.

"He's pulling a wagon," said Paul, "with brown bags inside."

"What do you think are in the bags?" asked Cousin Cheryl.

"Skittles," said Karley as she looked at her cousin and smiled.

Karley stood and observed the satanic leader as he approached, pulling a little red wagon behind him. He stopped in front of the uncovered monument, liberated from darkness by a child. The satanic defender removed the papier-mache goat head with horns and wings from his shoulders and placed the headgear next to the monument. He unzipped the black robe, eased his arms out of it, and laid it across the papier-mache head piece. Karley felt her forehead wrinkle with concern. He doesn't look good, she thought. Too much sun, she assumed.

"His face looks really red," said Karley. "I think he needs something to drink."

"Why do you care about him, Karley?" asked Cheryl. "He hates all of your beliefs."

"He's a fellow human being," Karley said as she took out a carton of juice, a bottle of water, and a package of saltine crackers from Abby's backpack.

"He's a cunning fox, getting ready to attack the henhouse," said Cheryl, who stood protectively near the children.

Karley and her sister approached the young man, who had collapsed against the rectangular stone. The red wagon stood innocently nearby.

"Hi," said Karley as she observed that the wilted young man was really a boy, a boy with his little red wagon. "This heat is really something, isn't it?"

"You aren't from Texas, are you?" asked Abby.

The defender of darkness shook his head.

"You look like you could use some water, or juice," said Karley, offering to share what they had. "We have both. And saltines."

The tired young man reached out and accepted what Karley offered. As he drank, Karley sat on the ground and motioned to her cousin to bring the kids, but Cousin Cheryl shook her head. "My name is Karley and this is my sister, Abby.

"You may be dehydrated," Abby said. "Where are you from?"

"Seattle," he said, without introducing himself. "This heat is a scorcher."

"Don't let our cousin hear you complain about the heat," said Abby, "or she'll accuse you of being a Northern wimp." She poured some water on a clean diaper and handed it to the man. "Put this against your forehead. By the way, I'm a nurse practitioner."

"Thanks," he said quietly. "I came here from Oklahoma, so I thought I was used to the heat."

"What's going on in Oklahoma?" asked Karley as she glanced at the wagon and wondered if the satanic leader was as innocent as his little red wagon.

"The ACLU is suing the state to remove their Ten Commandments statue," he explained as he looked around the State Capitol grounds. "I led the march in Tulsa."

"Where is your group?" asked Karley, noticing that his leg bounced nervously up and down on the ground like a native drum warning others of potential danger.

"On the bus headed back home," he said. "I'm sticking around until Monday."

"What's in the little red wagon?"

"Just some pamphlets we usually pass around to the crowd." He looked sideways at the woman who questioned him.

"Could I see one?" asked Karley, trying to remember if she had seen anyone in his group handing out pamphlets. After walking around the 22-acre Capitol grounds, she couldn't remember seeing any pamphlets littering the ground. Something didn't feel right.

"Sorry," the young Satanist said. "We passed them all out."

"We need to leave now," Abby whispered to her sister. "Let's go. Now."

Abby gathered her family members like a mother hen gathering her chicks. Cousin Cheryl sidled up to her. "It's about time you figured him out," said Cheryl. "He's got tools in those bags, and I bet he's going to use them on that monument. I saw two young men peeking from behind trees. They must be waiting for his signal."

Karley stopped to turn around, but Cousin Cheryl urged her forward toward the street. "We're going to keep walking," Cheryl said. "Do not look back. Forget about the Goat Man and his dehydration."

Karley was nearly convinced by the urgency in Cheryl's voice, but curiosity got the best of her and, like Lot's wife, she turned around. Instead of seeing a conflagration like the one in Sodom and Gomorrah, however, she saw three men standing in front of the monument, hammers poised in the air above the stone. Karley held her breath as God's covenant swayed in the balance.

She heard a baby cry, and then a dull, high-pitched ringing pierced the air. Metal hammers struck the fragile, glasslike surface of polished granite. The ringing reverberated in her head. She watched as words, hewn on the stone, spit from its smooth surface and shot out like bullets from a gun. Defaced by the opposition, the red Texas granite could not speak to passersby in words that had upheld and encouraged the early pioneers since they settled the Lone Star state.

"Oh, my God!" gasped Karley. "They're destroying the Ten Commandments!"

"They're defacing a piece of stone, Karley," said Cheryl, "not the commandments. Moses threw the first stone tablets on the ground. Remember? And God used His finger to make another copy. A professional stonecutter will do the same."

Stunned visitors hurried in every direction. Karley and her family hurried with them.

"Did you see what those monsters just did?" said Abby. "They destroyed the Ten Commandments!"

"Like I said before," said Cheryl, as she put an arm around both of her cousins. "You Northerners are wimps. The world is not coming to an end."

"Look!" said Abby. "The Capitol police are already cuffing them. That was fast!"

"Maybe they were expecting that something was going to happen," said Karley, looking at Cousin Cheryl. "Or maybe someone called them."

"Yes, and the police came," said Cheryl. "Look at everyone scatter, like chickens in a henhouse when the wolf breaks in."

Karley watched blue and white T-shirts scatter. Other protesters ran toward buses parked around the Capitol building. She felt a little hand in hers and looked down at Tommy. She gave his hand a squeeze. "Everything is under control," she said. "Cousin Cheryl called the police."

Cousin Cheryl lifted Audrey from her stroller so she could walk freely and held her small hand firmly in her own. Paul ran to steer the stroller to safety.

"Now I expect both of you to cheer up," Cheryl said to her cousins. "I'm getting married tomorrow!"

Karley looked at her favorite cousin. "For keeps?"

"For keeps," said Cheryl. "What's the matter, Karley? Where's your spunk?"

"I'm just hot," said Karley.

"No, there's more to it," said Cousin Cheryl. "Abby said you weren't happy helping women get divorced."

"No, I'm not," said Karley. "But I don't know what to do instead."

"Have you prayed about it?" asked Cheryl. "God does answer prayer. For years I've been praying for a man who honors his commitments. And look what He sent me?"

"Congratulations, Cheryl," said Karley. "You know we are all happy for you."

"Karley," insisted Cheryl. "What are you waiting for?"

"I'll figure it out," said Karley, biting her lip.

Karley decided she liked this new husband. He had invited them into his home, canceled their hotel reservations, and treated them like family. And so far, Karley and Abby's kids had not seen one spider or ant anywhere. Tomorrow was the wedding. But tonight the stars shone in the vast Texas sky, and the water in the pool felt refreshing. She toweled off, then sat in one of the chaise lounges around the pool. She watched Audrey walking toward her with toys in her hands and bulging pockets. Karley thought the kids wanted to play. The glitter in Audrey's Little Mermaid dress sparkled in the outdoor lights. Tommy followed behind with little toys of his own.

The children stopped in front of her, but instead of asking her to play, they quietly performed a ritual. Audrey placed the toys in her hands beside Karley. From her pockets, her niece removed a little toy and placed it carefully on Karley's shoulder. "Don't move," she told her aunt. "I decorate you."

Karley did as she was told, but stole little glances at this princess, who bent over and pulled up a handful of grass. Audrey slowly lifted her hands above Karley's head, and Karley felt the soft grass drizzle on her face like a light rain. She watched Audrey pull a blue rubber whale from her pocket and wondered what she would do next.

Softly, the little girl's hand placed the small toy on her right shoulder. On her other shoulder, Audrey dropped her favorite Beanie Baby. She left Karley's side and walked behind her. Karley wondered what her niece was doing when she felt a little finger poke her lightly in different places around her back. Was Audrey trying to plug her into a power source only a child could see?

After a few moments, Audrey returned and stood beside her aunt.

"No lights," said her niece.

"How come no lights?" asked Karley.

"Your spirit's gone," said Audrey. "I fix. I fix." As Karley watched the little girl walk around her a second time, she wondered how this child knew. A few moments later she felt the little hand turning in her back like Audrey was adjusting a knob.

Audrey reappeared. She wiggled her fingers above her aunt's head, and Karley imagined fairy dust falling on her.

"Better," said Audrey, clapping her hands together. "Much better. You happy now?"

"Much better," said Karley. "I think I'm better. Thank you."

How is a child able to sense my sadness, she asked herself, when I have tried so hard to cover it up?

Karley saw her husband walking toward her. In the moonlight his hair looked completely black as it had when they first met. "Did Audrey recharge your battery, Karley?" he asked.

Karley nodded, took his hand, and pulled him down beside her on the chaise lounge.

"How was your workout today?" she asked.

"Fine," Bill said and kissed her. "But do you really want to talk about my time at Chapman's club?"

Karley shook her head. "Is it that obvious?"

"To someone who knows you, yes," said Bill. "You are like a young plant trying to establish roots in rocky soil."

Karley nodded her head and tried to hold back her emotions. She wondered if the star constellations in Texas were the same as those in the Midwest. And then when she could find no other questions with which to divert her attention, she felt tears slip from her eyes.

"Is it time to make a change?" asked Bill.

Karley exhaled sharply. "Maybe it is. I wonder if I should be doing something else, but I don't know what to do instead."

Bill continued to listen.

"This morning I watched three men chip away the words of God's covenant. They destroyed the Ten Commandments monument at the State Capitol," said Karley. "I watched but did nothing."

"What did you want to do?"

"I don't know. I love first amendment issues," said Karley. "I hate it when our rights as Christians are violated. But I didn't call the police, Bill. Cheryl did. I just watched."

"You felt helpless."

"Yes, just like I feel every time I get a new client and hear her story," Karley said. "I listen, but I'm too late to help. I just file her papers, meet her at the courthouse, and pick up a big check."

"What kind of law would you like to practice?" asked Bill.

"I don't know. I keep making lists of the pros and cons of other fields."

"Have you prayed about it?"

"No, not yet. I should be able to figure this out on my own."

"After you weigh the pros and cons, you mean?" asked Bill.

"Well, yes," said Karley.

"After you consider both sides of the argument, will you make a decision?"

"I guess so. I just need to take some time to figure it all out."

Karley felt Bill's comforting hand in hers.

"Chapman told us that Cheryl was leaving her job," said Bill. "A new husband and a new career." Bill lifted her up from the chaise lounge and guided her toward the dinner table where Chapman was proposing a toast.

"To new beginnings," Chapman said as he lifted his glass. The groom held close the woman he loved and would marry at sunrise the next day. "Thank you all for being here with us to celebrate."

Karley thought about new beginnings. She wondered if Cheryl had really asked God to send her a faithful husband.

Following Chapman's words, a chorus of champagne glasses lifted in unison. Karley held her glass close to her waist and looked up at the sky. A film of white clouds passed over the moon like a veil placed over a bride's expectant face.

She would figure it all out, she told herself, and set her champagne-filled glass, brimming with bubbles, on the edge of the table. Soon she would be celebrating, but not tonight.

Almost Redemption

Hosea 14:8

Turn to me while there is still time.

Joel 3:14

Thousands upon thousands are waiting in the valley of decision.

P rofessor Endimes had taught a general survey course of legal history nearly every term since joining the faculty at a state law school on his thirtieth birthday a decade ago. In addition to a law degree, he had attained a doctorate in history with an emphasis on ancient cultures. His dissertation surveyed the social fabric of the Roman Empire before and after Christianity had become the dominant religion, after Constantine had accepted Christ. Creating and refining the class syllabus had taken nearly a year but had been a stimulating experience.

His efforts had paid off. If student feedback on class evaluations were a reliable metric of student learning and proficiency, and many in his profession believed they were not, the students reported that they had learned a lot. His classes were always fairly full, and as he glanced around the lecture hall as he taught, he observed that the students actually listened and did not use class time for Internet shopping or reading sports stories. At least he didn't think they did.

Although students commented that he was arrogant, he chose to ignore their criticisms. After all, a thin line existed between confidence and arrogance. In addition, he believed that students who did well in the class, the ones who consistently attended and prepared beforehand, could distinguish between the pride he took in his work and the arrogance he was accused of by his detractors. Thus, he ignored these criticisms. After a decade of teaching, he had not found any arguments, worth considering, against his conclusion.

A tall man, he had run track in school and still worked out regularly. He ate salads and stayed away from pizza and beer. He quit smoking when he finished his education and rarely drank more than a couple of glasses of wine on the weekends. Every morning he examined his hair before the mirror and was relieved that he had not found any gray strands or thinning spots. He wore his hair rather long, and because it was thick and wavy, this style hid the slight protrusion at the top of his forehead. When he was a kid, neighbor boys called him the fourth beast, because he lived in the fourth house from the corner, and teased him about the "horn" on his forehead. But that was long ago; still, he continued to wear his hair longer than other members of the faculty.

A year ago, when he observed that his male students rarely wore mustaches, he shaved his off at the end of the term. For several months, he had considered wearing a diamond stud in his left ear, but earrings seemed to have become passé instead of an indication of sexual prowess. His teeth were square and, thanks to the whitening treatments, white. White, shiny teeth brought out the color of his blue eyes. He had never worn makeup, except when he was being photographed.

Women found him attractive; younger ones often assumed he was in his thirties. While he enjoyed women, it would be more honest to say he enjoyed sex. He had never married. Why commit when so many women now preferred casual relationships? Friendships with privileges they were called. A relationship with no strings attached was easy and did not interfere with one's life. If problems arose, women simply took care of things and made no demands. As far as he was concerned, life was far more refined now compared to when he was in school and nearly got caught. He liked women but not messy passion or commitments.

He focused most of his time and energy on the law. He still used the same syllabus and slides he had prepared nearly a decade ago, but since they were still topical, why change them? He wrote articles for law review publications, and some were even published. Well, occasionally.

Since he had graduated, law school had changed. All of his Ivy League professors had used the Socratic method in all first year classes. He and his classmates were expected to stand when called upon and had to remain standing until the professor uncovered something the student did not understand. Sometimes they just enjoyed humiliating their charges. He found this method stimulating and looked forward to every challenge.

Later in the law school program, after the messy relationship, he just wanted to complete law school, take the Bar, and move on with his life. He did move. He left California, alone, and found a job in a good law school in the Midwest. He felt proud of himself for moving on and never looking back, at least until recently when he had to admit he thought about little else. Yes, he had moved on with his life, but the messiness and broken promises flagged his efforts to achieve greater recognition. Lately, he seemed to think of nothing else. It didn't make any sense. Why should one relationship, one that occurred so many years ago, still color the present?

For many years, any feelings of guilt he may have had did not unduly encumber him. He didn't even know what happened to the young woman after he demanded that she leave. Threats had helped as well. Plus, he had been very convincing and led her to the truth about the impossibility of a future together.

A new future had opened up to him; it was just different from the one he had imagined. At the Midwestern law school where he now taught, students could miss up to six classes. He could not understand why they would pay nearly $50,000 each year to stay home or show up to class to search the Internet. But this was a different generation, and in this school many of the students came from wealthy families, or at least more wealthy than he and his family. These students rarely read for class the way he did. They focused only on class notes and memorized prepared outlines. In contrast, he had wanted to learn it all and had attended every lecture and tutorial. The library became his home.

Students who made appointments with him were satisfied to know just enough to get a decent grade. They focused on the Bar exam and during the summers worked at the law firms of family friends and relatives where they would likely receive a job. These students rarely had to work while they attended classes and yet lived quite well in new apartments with all the conveniences. Money from parents, no doubt. Nearly all of them drove new cars.

In contrast, students who had his background, the firstborn children from first-generation families, strove for academic honors and high grade point averages. Everyone like him worked several jobs to finance their lengthy stay in school. Academic studies of first-generation children confirmed this theory. He had worked all through undergrad and graduate school and during law school as well. When had he not worked? But in the end, it had been worth it because he had become part of the American dream. If he had taken time out for a family, his present success would have been in jeopardy.

He loved working and being published. Soon he would start receiving awards for his work; he was sure of it. The display case at home, the one he had spent so much time and effort building, waited to be filled. Sometimes he wondered how long he would be able to continue teaching young students. A decade was a long time to teach the same subject over and over again. But the perks were sometimes well worth the effort. The majority of students these days were no longer male but female, many of them quite attractive and more than willing to step outside the conventional boundaries between professor and student. Life was good, so he was puzzled when he found himself spending more and more time reflecting on his past instead of his future.

Rumors rose like miniature dust storms in the faculty lounge. His colleagues discussed the nationwide drop in law school applications, and while the talk centered on the causes for this recent phenomenon, he was sure everyone wondered when the decline in applicants would impact their school and, more to the point, their jobs. He had heard rumors. While he hadn't talked directly with his colleagues, he had overheard their conversations, and of course he read the newspapers. He knew what was going on but felt confident about his relationship with the department head. They had a solid relationship; it was set in stone.

Just last week, the department head had requested a meeting with him in his office. When they met, the conversation was usually about general topics. Professor Endimes arrived promptly for the meeting, scheduled an hour and a half before his Thursday night class. Standing outside the department head's office, he could have felt like a schoolboy miscreant, but he didn't. After lightly tapping the glass pane in the center of the door, he stood motionless as he waited for permission to enter. Papers rustled from within the light-filled interior, and he could hear the department head talking with someone. Finally, after waiting ten minutes, the department chair told his caller he would call him later.

Suddenly the door opened. "Come in! Come in, Professor," the chairman said. "Don't stand out there in the drafty hallway." He motioned for Professor Endimes to enter.

"Didn't you speak to my secretary? She didn't notify me you were here." He continued asking unanswered questions until he saw the professor sink into the chair in front of his desk.

"Good of you to come early. I won't keep you long because I know you teach an evening class." He cleared his throat. "As you know, applications and enrollment are down," he began. Professor Endimes dropped his head and wondered if any adjuncts would be cut or their teaching assignments reduced. He doubted tenured staff would be touched. He swallowed, then held his breath.

"While we are not going to lay off any of our teaching staff, the administration must make certain adjustments. Instead of teaching two classes per term, some faculty will have their teaching load reduced to just one class; their pay will be adjusted accordingly." The department head cleared his throat again and sat back in his plush leather chair. "Professor Endimes, you have always done an admirable job teaching The History of Law, but the administration must eliminate this course. When enrollments pick up, we will reconsider the curriculum."

The phone rang. The department chair told his secretary to hold his calls and to contact someone Professor Endimes had never heard of. "Yes, set up an interview with her for Monday, sometime in the morning." The smile disappeared from the chairman's face when he turned back to face Professor Endimes.

"Yes, I was saying that instead of teaching this class, you will pick up one section of Torts and work in the administration office and help with student applications and graduation. We are all aware of your experience with and knowledge of computers . . ."

The department chair droned on until he startled Professor Endimes with a personal question. "What do you think of your new schedule? Will you be able to make the adjustment?"

With composure and unearthly stillness, Professor Endimes responded, echoing the words of the famous scrivener. He hoped he could live up to the scrivener's decisive response. "I would prefer not to," he said.

Assessing the man before him, the dean altered his tack. "Change is not easy, but it sometimes stimulates growth. What do you think?"

"I would prefer not to," said Professor Endimes.

"Well, we must make adjustments to these changing times, even when it is an inconvenience."

"I would prefer not to."

"Yes, I heard that the first time. I know you have a class in an hour, so I won't keep you further. If this change is one to which you won't be able to adjust, or one to which you refuse to comply, inform the dean in writing by the fifteenth. That is all," said the department chair.

Professor Endimes sat. He appeared to be ruminating. Then his head jerked like it did when a driver behind him honked his horn because the light had turned green just as he was about to formulate the exact time and reason his life had veered off course.

The department chair stood. "You may leave now," he said firmly and waited for the recalcitrant man to respond.

"Yes, of course," the professor muttered and closed the door without understanding how he had ended up on the other side.

Inside his own office he sat down slowly behind his walnut desk. He stroked its smooth surface, then spun around in his chair to review the framed degrees behind him. He had asked the custodian to place them there to remind students that although he didn't come from money as they did, he was very well educated. The school would manage the downturn in applications, and while it may not become a first-tier law school next year, maybe a year or two later after the downturn in enrollments. They would need him then—in the classroom.

His large and impressive desk faced an unadorned wall, its uninterrupted emptiness broken by a rectangular window. He stared at the brick wall approximately three feet away. After three quarters of an hour of silence, a bell sounded from his smartphone to announce the beginning of his pre-class preparation. He couldn't remember any of his thoughts prior to the bell toll.

He opened the folder on his desk, briefly reviewed his notes, and chose the appropriate PowerPoint disk for this evening's lecture. From the middle desk drawer, he removed his travel kit and walked down the quiet hall to the faculty bathroom where he freshened up for the evening lecture. Next year, he wondered, would he teach on Tuesday or Thursday evening? Certainly they would find something for him to teach other than negligence, joint tort-feasors, and proximate cause. He would have to pull out his old books, outlines, and notes.

Back in his office, as he realized that his sabbatical would be ruined, he heard a knock at his door. He rose from his large desk but then sat down again and called out, "You can enter." A young male student entered like they all did, with energy, purpose, and confidence.

"Professor Endimes, excuse me," he said quickly, "I won't be in class tonight. My wife's water broke, and I have to get home. She's a week early." He wondered why the student's face was flushed but beaming.

"Yes, of course. Good of you to stop by. Good luck. The lecture will be podcast."

"Thank you, sir. See you next week." The young man hurried down the hallway. To avoid looking at the smiling young man, who looked very much like he did many years ago, he looked down at the unopened journal on his desk.

His wife is a week early, he thought. Marianna was five weeks early, right in the middle of my comprehensive exams. He looked down at his empty hands and unadorned fingers.

In tonight's lecture he would discuss family life in pagan Rome before Emperor Constantine converted to Christianity. He locked the door to his office and pushed an app on his mobile device. Instantly the dissonant refrains of Prokofiev flooded his ear plugs, keeping him company until the empty elevator descended to the sixth floor.

Part Two

At precisely 6:55, he entered the lecture hall. Students sitting in the front rows stared into their computer screens like new converts searching for the keys to the kingdom. He handed the tech assistant his PowerPoint disk and scanned the room for the older student. She was there; she was always there, dressed in gray or black, both colors repeated in her short hair. He was uncertain of her age, but it was obvious that she was much older than those who sat around her. He wondered why she was in law school at her age and why she asked so many questions. The first picture and caption flooded the screen.

He began, the lecture so clearly outlined in his mind that at night he sometimes recited it to fall asleep. "Good evening. Tonight I will lecture on the laws governing private life in pagan Rome detailed by Phillipe Aries in his book by the same title and Russ Versteeg's book *Law in the Ancient World.*

"Ancient Roman law recognized two legal types of marriage: the first was marriage with power and the second was marriage without power. In marriage with power the wife lived under her husband's power. He was her paterfamilias, and she was subordinate to him." He observed the young female students fidgeting in their seats.

"If her husband's father was still living, her husband was under the authority of his paterfamilias, and she was under the power of that superior paterfamilias. In both cases, she was legally her husband's daughter in terms of her rights. Her husband took legal ownership of any property she may have had before her marriage, as well as any property in the dowry she brought to the marriage."

Across the class, female students shared disgusted looks. Didn't they understand, the professor reflected, that a man was designed to rule? If they didn't now, they soon would.

He continued. "Between 451 and 450 BC, Roman law was codified and became known as the Twelve Tables. Prior to the Twelve Tables no one knew what the law was except for the priests. If a Roman citizen broke the law, the priest could fine the errant man any amount he determined to be just." He paused, allowing time for parallels to be drawn between the church and the male dominance they professed to hate.

"Moving on, a marriage could be formed in three ways: the first was a religious ceremony with a priest and a cake; the second was exclusively for the aristocrats and was a mock sale of the bride by the paterfamilias to the groom; and the third was created when a man and woman lived together for a year." He looked up when the sound of fingers clicking against keys faded and then stopped altogether.

He cleared his throat and continued. "During that year, the woman could not stay away from the man's home for more than three nights. If she decided not to go through with the marriage, she would leave the man's home for more than three nights and return to her former home; thus the marriage was avoided."

The corners of his mouth lifted as he remembered when Marianna finally left after he explained to her that their marriage could not take place because she had returned to her country. She had believed him.

"This third form of marriage was eventually abolished. In the second type of marriage, the bride had no power because she was still under the power of her own paterfamilias, her father or grandfather. Marriage without power was the most common civil marriage."

A male student dressed in a school sweatshirt and sitting in the third row raised his hand. He closed the copy of *Black's Law Dictionary* he held in his hand and asked, "What was the age of majority for males and females?"

"A girl had to be twelve and a boy had to be fourteen."

A female student sitting in the back raised her hand and asked, "Could a girl refuse to marry at the age of twelve?"

Professor Endimes's brows pulled together. "Why would she refuse? Women did not work, except as prostitutes. In marriage she was protected and taken care of by her paterfamilias." He watched as she frowned and whispered to the female student next to her.

Another female student's hand broke the steady pace of his carefully timed lecture. He nodded to her. "What kind of laws governed divorce? Were women allowed to divorce?"

"During the earliest period of Roman law, between 753 and 509 BC, a husband could divorce his wife for one of three reasons: first, if she committed adultery; second, if she 'tampered with the household keys,' which meant she altered the keys to the house so her lover could enter; and three, if she poisoned a child."

"Why would a wife poison her own child?" interrupted a woman in the front without raising her hand.

Patiently, he explained, "If there were no children at the time of her husband's death, the wife was entitled to all of his property." The professor paused and stared at the questioning student, as if to determine her motive for asking the question; was she disingenuous or simply naive? She must have studied wills by now.

He cleared his throat and continued. "Neither a wife nor her father was entitled to the return of her dowry if she was at fault. If a husband divorced his wife for any other reason, he had to return half of the dowry. If, however, the husband was entirely at fault for the marriage ending, he had to return the entire dowry to the wife or her father. So, yes, a woman, with the help of her paterfamilias, could divorce her husband. But the emperor Constantine did not approve of divorce except under extreme situations. Under Justinian, a woman who divorced for any reason other than those he outlined was banished to a nunnery. In contrast, her husband paid only a fine."

Perhaps he was being too melodramatic, the professor thought to himself, but half the room appeared more than ready for a break.

Professor Endimes closed his notebook and said, "After a ten-minute break, we will discuss the subject of children." Without looking at the students in front of him or waiting for them to approach the podium with questions, he abruptly turned and left the room.

Facing a mirror in the faculty restroom, he checked his face for telltale signs of stress or worry. Appearances were everything, in a court of law or a law school lecture hall. He raised his forehead, then pushed it down again. He repeated this stretching exercise to erase worry lines and smooth out the furrow in his brow. He exercised his facial muscles, smiling and frowning in counts of five. He rolled his shoulders and pulled his arms in front of him. He counted to seven as he inhaled and then again to seven as he exhaled. He rolled his head like a boxer getting ready to enter the ring and left for his podium after locking the door.

Only an hour remained. At least the untraditional student had not boxed him into a corner with another impossible question. Not yet anyway.

The class quieted when he took up his position in front of the podium, and he continued after checking the time on his iPad. "A citizen of Rome did not 'have' a child. Rather he 'took' a child. When a woman gave birth to a child, the husband, as the head of the family, decided whether or not that child entered society."

"Say what?" complained a female student of indeterminate origin. He stopped talking and stared in her direction before continuing.

"A father who decided not to raise a child had the legal right to expose the child to the elements and let it die." Professor Endimes paused, took a handkerchief from his pocket, and wiped his brow. He drank from his designer water bottle and continued.

"He could take the child outside the house and expose it. He could leave it in a public place or at a crossroads, and those who passed by the child could take it up or not. He could put it on top of a mound of garbage." He felt sweat slide down his sides but continued, standing upright.

"Even if his wife wanted to keep her child, she did what her paterfamilias told her to do. The father could order his wife to expose the child, and she had no legal recourse to protect or save it. If she died, the baby could be cut out of her uterus."

A student in the back uttered, "Oh, yuck."

The professor stumbled on. "If a husband suspected his wife had cheated on him, he could expose the newborn child. More female children were exposed than male children. A malformed child could either be drowned or exposed." Briefly, the professor rubbed his hands together like Lady MacBeth when she walked the floors of the castle at night. He felt a chill as he observed the serious faces before him.

"Seneca, a philosopher and writer of tragedies, said: 'What is good is set apart from what is good for nothing.' Children of daughters who went astray were also exposed." He heard a computer slap shut.

The professor faced his inquisitors in time to see a familiar hand go up. Tonight she wore a red knit top that contrasted nicely with her dark hair and tanned skin tone. She waited patiently, probably accustomed to life moving more slowly than her thoughts. He wanted to continue speaking and ignore her hand; he wondered again why her husband had allowed her to return to school at her age anyway. Was he wealthy enough to throw thousands of dollars away on a law school education for someone without a legal future? But she sat toward the middle of the lecture hall, so he couldn't ignore her. He considered that possibly she would enflame the younger students with her traditional ideas, and while she would become the object of their youthful wrath, he would become their savior.

"Yes, Ms. Marshall, what is on your mind tonight?" he said gallantly, hoping he could charm her into forgetting what she wanted to say or at least make her blush. He noticed that she did neither.

She looked at him askance and stated, "The law regarding abortion changed in 1992 in *Planned Parenthood of Pennsylvania v. Casey* to include late-term abortion."

Where is this going? he wondered.

"In this law a male-dominated court provides a woman with the choice to govern her own body. While the law in ancient Rome gave total authority to the husband, aren't these two laws more alike than they are different?" Hearing a challenge to their freedom, the younger female students swiveled in their seats to face her. One young woman sitting closest to her placed her arms across her chest. Others leaned forward, ready to defend the new liberty rights Justices O'Connor, Kennedy, and Souter discovered in the Constitution.

"In what way could these two laws be similar?" asked Professor Endimes. "In Roman law a man governed a woman's body and her child, whereas in the twentieth century ruling the Court stated that a woman governs her body and that of the unborn child. I don't understand your comparison."

"The genders do-si-do like in a square dance, and while seeming to exchange places, or power, nothing has changed. Both genders engage in a grab for power, but the focus of their power struggle is forgotten in the battle. The child drops to the dance floor and both of them stomp on it. How is *Casey* any different from pagan Rome? One gender loses all rights while the other gender gains total control. The object of this battle is not liberty but power. The child, forgotten by everyone, loses its life regardless of the historical time period. *Casey* changes nothing, only the gender of the person who has the power."

The professor's ears echoed with groans and professions of outrage. "While your argument certainly examines the existential question, if not the spiritual, of liberty rights, the study of ancient legal systems does not address the issue of liberty or of a child's rights." He stopped short of telling her what he really thought of her and her right to steer the class into the mists of right-wing extremism.

He then watched as a young woman dressed like Joan of Arc in a business suit swiveled in her chair and addressed the older woman instead of the lectern where he stood.

Before he could regain control, she said, "To answer your question, the late-term abortion ruling defended a woman's liberty and, to quote the words of the justices, 'a woman's right to define her own concept of existence, of meaning, of the universe, and of the mystery of human life.'"

While the nontraditional student smiled after the young speaker recited the litany of existential possibilities, the professor winced as her voice rose with each concept.

The young student thundered, "Those are the words of the case!"

Professor Endimes watched as she gathered her shoulders together and inhaled the sweet aroma of truth. He saw her look around the room at her classmates.

Then, just as he was ready to assert control, he heard the older student respond. "Do you believe that truth and justice have been attained because the Court's decision now revolves around female genitalia and not male organs?" He looked around the room, all eyes riveted to the challenger of female power over life and death. "Does the Court consider the life of the baby created or the genitals of those creating? The Court claims the Constitution provides women the right to abort their babies. Does this liberty come from the same source that grants us life, liberty, and the pursuit of happiness?" She paused. "Isn't that source God?"

He listened. Cries of protest broke out, uniting like a Greek chorus. While maintaining the appearance of objectivity, he secretly enjoyed watching the younger students attack the older woman and tried not to smile as they glared at her in anger and disbelief. He felt inflated by the strength of their youthful convictions.

Transformed into an object of ridicule and scorn, she had become the scapegoat of contemporary mores. After her words of opposition, he imagined the younger women thrusting the older student over the hilltop of religious tradition into the waters of progressive oblivion. But instead of discomfort, he watched the nontraditional student look around her and shake her head. She shook off their denunciation like dust from her sandals.

Professor Endimes continued to watch her. The nontraditional student sat patiently, as if she had expected to ignite a firestorm of protest. Perhaps she had planned it and was fulfilling her mission as a crusader for the church. He wondered if she actually believed that these young female warriors, who held their liberties like dead prey in their mouths, would actually drop them to consider the implications of their hard-fought liberty rights. He knew they would never let go of their prize and questioned the older woman's connection to reality.

Abortion, like exposure of the newborn, was a right once belonging only to the paterfamilias but now available to all, like a new product on the shelf of possibility. Before he could look away, she caught him staring at her. Their eyes held for what seemed like ages, and he wondered if judgment day would be a public event. Was she judging him? Their eyes held, and he found himself wanting something from her. Forgiveness or redemption perhaps; he didn't know what. In that extended moment he felt trapped. She must know my secret, he concluded.

He looked away from the older student and glanced around the room, remembering that microphones could pick up nearly every word spoken throughout the lecture hall. He spoke into the microphone, carefully choosing his words. "I trust this exchange of ideas will stimulate thought. See you next week."

He departed for his office where he locked the door and sat in the dark while his heartbeat slowed. How did she know? Why did she say both sexes stomped on the unborn? He wondered how she had figured out that he had stomped on Marianna's desire to keep the child they created. She seemed to know his secret, a secret so carefully protected that he had avoided close relationships with women and colleagues just to protect it.

He rose from his desk to open the window, but it didn't budge. But did she also realize that the final action of his ancient affair was legally justified and not merely a choice that modern men and women made when a child was an inconvenience? He had not been legally married; she had left his home to visit her family for an entire week, not just three nights. She had left on her own free will. Supporting his conclusion was codified law: *Cassie v. Pennsylvania*. He had followed the law, yet he felt overwhelmed by resounding guilt.

At the time, he was living in California where he attended the best graduate school in the state. Perhaps this older student had worked in the admissions office at the school or in financial aid. She could have attended his graduate school or lived next door, a nosy neighbor perhaps. He did not understand how she knew the truth about him and what he had buried inside a dumpster over a decade ago. At present, he could not unearth the reasons for her knowledge of his past. But she knew the truth.

"It isn't possible," he asserted to the empty room. "I'm not thinking clearly." He turned on his desk lamp. "But she might know," he whispered into the shadows around his desk. She seemed ubiquitous. Someone like her could have seen him that night.

He was always so careful and hoped he had not strayed from his usual pattern by leaving evidence of his past at the podium. How did she know he had been the paterfamilias to Marianna, a girl who had gotten pregnant because she didn't understand how to protect herself? How did he know his pregnant lover would want to keep her child? Didn't she know he had had other plans and dreams for his future, and they did not include marriage to an underage, illegal girl who could barely speak English.

How could the nontraditional student know about what he did late one night after Marianna had fallen asleep? Did she smell his fear when she stood next to him at his podium to ask a question? Could she hear the pride in his voice when he discussed the right of a paterfamilias to expose his child?

He needed to calm himself down. He grabbed a bottle of water out of the small refrigerator next to his desk and opened the cap. In one easy swallow, he gulped the water and several tablets of the Xanax he kept in the desk drawer next to his shaving kit. Like a priest who never missed mass, he religiously restocked his pharmaceuticals. They weren't really drugs, at least not street drugs, the kind he had given Marianna. He sat back in his leather chair. He could feel the effects of the drug enter his system. In less than five minutes, his breathing slowed and he stopped sweating. He stood up, removed his damp shirt, and replaced it with a clean one.

No one could possibly know that he had been a modern-day paterfamilias who had exposed his child, despite his lover's protest. Drugs were easy to obtain then. You could put them into anything, even brownies. And no one checked the dumpsters, not even street people. They didn't need to scour the dumpsters for food back then because they could panhandle enough money for food and drugs from those who thought a handout was religious compassion.

His phone revealed the time. It was not too late. He could call her, a young colleague who was eager for his approval and highly suggestible. She picked up after the second ring. When she agreed, he ended the conversation, gathered up his briefcase, and took the elevator to the parking garage where his black BMW sparkled in a parking space reserved for faculty. Surely he would still have parking privileges and his reserved space next term.

The parking lot was empty. Only a few students lingered outside the building. They were probably waiting for friends or a ride home. The majority always left quickly, finding their cars and heading for home or the campus pubs. He looked into the darkened lot and knew what pleasure awaited him, pleasure that expunged all pain and regret.

He saw her enter the parking lot and pretend not to know he was waiting for her. She always parked away from the building entrance and security cameras like he had told her. She did not have a reserved parking spot like he did. She leaned over to unlock the trunk of her car and carefully stow away her laptop, accordion files, and briefcase. Her short skirt rode up to the bottom of her panties, which were always black and lacey. He wondered if she was moving slowly to tantalize him further. Had she recognized the hunger in his voice? Before he could decide, his sex responded furiously and pushed against his trousers as he watched how she separated her legs, squatted, and thrust the last of her accordion files into the mouth of her trunk. He knew exactly what would happen next. Craving freedom from constant guilt and shame, he advanced, his dark form piercing the night.

He never knew if he satisfied her. It didn't really matter because she didn't have tenure; in fact, she was fresh out of law school herself. She would certainly lose her position before he completely lost his own. He smiled at his daring, some might say his recklessness.

Twenty minutes later, she drove off without looking back at him. He had convinced her that it was important to preserve their anonymity, so they never talked in the hall or elevator. Before falling asleep that night, he began reciting his lecture for the following week.

"Every paterfamilias determined the number of children he would take. The birth of another son meant that the seal of a previously written will had to be broken. To avoid breaking the will, middle-class families gave male offspring away to friends after they had enough children. Often, a middle-class family chose to concentrate their efforts and resources on a few children rather than a large number of them. If more children were born, the husband could either expose the child or give it away. Greeks and Romans exposed unwanted children and thought it odd that Germans, Jews, and Egyptians raised all of their offspring."

Surely someone in his family was of Roman heritage, he said to himself. With the assurance of probabilities, he slept.

Part Three

All faculty members were expected to attend the dinner when the school president addressed the faculty. Alumni, state legislators, and US congressmen as well attended the yearly event. Awards were presented to faculty members who had published or been recognized during the past year. He was looking forward to going home with a trophy of smooth chiseled wood. His colleagues joked with him, asking him if the wooden trophies didn't remind him of Babylonian idols. He knew they were kidding when they bowed down in front of him. He decided they were simply envious of the recognition he might receive; he didn't tell them he had built a walnut cabinet for their display in his study and that he prayed each night to receive not just one but several trophies for his personal enjoyment.

Everyone sat at round tables, assigned according to departments, and though some tables were positioned closer to the president's table than others, they all drank wine from golden goblets. The school's position on the list of the top twenty law schools had risen in nearly every major magazine. It was a great feast.

As a congressman, who was also an alumnus, spoke, Professor Endimes looked around the room. He was surprised to see the woman he frequently met in the deserted parking lot sitting at a table beside him. But before he could speculate on why she was there or what her presence might mean for her future, his attention was drawn to the wall behind the woman's table. He could have sworn it had been blank when he first walked into the dining room. But letters he could barely discern appeared on the wall's surface as if written magically by invisible fingers. He wondered if a divine presence was trying to contact him. Because the writing was in Aramaic, he could not make out the words. He looked at his colleagues seated around the table for signs of their recognition of a divine presence. But they continued to talk, too engrossed in their desserts, each other, and themselves to notice what was happening in their midst. Apparently his colleagues did not want to see the fingers moving on the wall.

He scarcely noticed the dessert in front of him or his colleague's wife as she approached his table, the one who had slipped into the bathroom with him last year and onto his waiting lap. He had tasted of the pleasure hidden in darkness though he was surrounded by light. When he realized that tonight she stalked him like a dreaded disease, he narrowed his eyes and shook his head. She pivoted and without looking back walked away from his table. He looked again, past her gently swaying hips, to the wall beyond and continued to watch as the letters grew larger. Then he remembered that the words formed a message for the king. He held his breath as the message grew larger and more threatening. In bold black letters the message text changed from Aramaic to English. It read, "Your days are numbered." He paled, pulled back his chair as if the table were on fire, and bolted for the exit. With every frantic step, the accolades and applause he heard others receive that evening receded in his ears.

Outside he hurried to his car, searching the sky for signs of the moon, the eternal moon that David had described in a psalm as his faithful witness in the sky. In its place, thick sluggish clouds moved slowly across the sky. All week clouds appeared stationed across the sky, like celestial sentries forbidding movement inside the city. No rain fell. Like the land, he was dry and needed renewal.

As he looked around the parking lot, he felt afraid, an emotion he had refused to feel since the morning he had watched the dumpster being emptied into the garbage truck, their unborn child—their secret—pushed into the detritus of civilized living. He charged into his car and sped off to his favorite bar but changed direction and headed for home instead. If the message were a window into his future, he wondered how many days he had left. If the message did not pertain to his life, was the moving finger warning him that his days at the prestigious law school would end soon?

In the past he had refused to consider that what he had done beneath the sunny skies of California had been a mistake. Standing on the side of the law, he had done what was deemed legal, even responsible. Disposing of unwanted pregnancies was legal and had been since 1992 when the Court determined that abortion, during all three trimesters of a woman's pregnancy, was a woman's right, a liberty guaranteed by the Constitution. To judge otherwise was an undue burden for a woman.

When he turned forty, however, he had started to question his actions as well as the principles upon which they were based. New liberty rights found by the justices had torn an unborn child away from its mother's womb, and at the same time those rights had also torn a man and woman away from their foundation. Had he loved Marianna? He wasn't sure, but he knew he hadn't come close to loving anyone since he told her to leave. He had chosen to accept the decision made by those who wore black robes and took an oath to protect the Constitution—had they forgotten to protect his soul?

Stopping for a red light at an intersection, he saw the open doors of St. Casimir. Light from inside the church shone in the surrounding darkness, and he shivered inside his climate-controlled car. Despite the fact that he was Catholic and the church was close to his apartment, he had never been inside. As he waited for the light to turn, he watched a woman walk quickly down the street in the direction of the church. When the light turned green, he remained at the corner wondering where he had seen her before.

Of course. She was the older student in his class. She must belong to this parish, he decided, and her presence tonight explained her outburst in class last week. She was a Catholic who defended her faith and the Church's teachings. He followed her movements, and as she neared the intersection she saw him sitting in his car staring at her. He thought he saw light coming out of her mouth like a sword and swallowing the demons inside him. Was she coming to judge and condemn him or to offer him salvation?

He sat motionless, unable to think of what to say to her. After all, they were no longer in the classroom where he had the power. Outside, in front of the church, she did. She paused, and after recognizing him she smiled and started walking toward his car. Instead of speeding off, he hit the button to roll down the window and waited for her to speak. "Good evening, Professor. Are you looking for a place to park?"

He hesitated. Yes, he wanted to park the car. He also wanted to park his memories as well in the safety of a brightly lit parking lot next to a place of worship, a place that promised deliverance from sin. He questioned whether their God could deliver his sins or relieve their weight on his soul. He doubted it, but he wanted to believe the words he read in the Bible. He wanted to trust that these words did contain the forgiveness he needed. He felt the demons of his past pounding in his head, and he could not answer her question directly, not yet.

"Do you attend St. Casimir's?" he asked, deflecting her question about parking lots and a desire to find a place to park.

"Yes, my husband and I have been members for several years, since we moved here. I always meet him inside. Why don't you join us?"

He hesitated. "Do you always attend mass on Saturday?" he asked, hoping to expand their conversation and the time he had to decide what to do with his life.

She looked at him before answering. "We'll look for you inside," she said and left him hesitating between heaven and hell.

The light turned green. He didn't proceed through the intersection, and the driver behind him honked. When the light turned green a second time and he didn't press on the accelerator, the next car behind him swerved around him.

The light turned red, and he waited. Closing his eyes, he saw Marianna lying in their bed holding a small baby covered in blood and mucus. He had not called for an ambulance.

He sat motionless inside the car. After half a minute, the light turned green again. Instead of moving forward, however, he continued to sit, staring at the church door. Was there a prescribed circle of hell for those who committed sins against the newly born? Into which circle of the Inferno would Dante assign him?

Another driver behind him honked, then charged around his inert car. He could not move forward; he could not park the car in the church lot and walk through the door. He could not scan the pews for a familiar face and slip into grace before her expectant eyes. Not yet; he wasn't ready.

In the distance he heard thunder. Lightning flashed like camera lights, then darkness displaced brief snapshots of the grounds surrounding the church. He had noticed a statue of the Virgin Mary beside a small pond, her outstretched hands an invitation for forgiveness. But the events of his past snapped at him like a tethered dog, restraining his movement toward grace. Lightning flashed again, and the Virgin Mary's arms begged him to step into her embrace. If only he could.

He looked out the car window at the stragglers holding umbrellas and racing to get inside. He lifted his foot from the brake and slid through the intersection.

His smartphone rang. He looked at it but didn't answer. He knew who it was and what she wanted. Instead of answering and returning to his past, he observed how the tree branches bent before the wind's force. For nearly twenty years he had resisted his faith like a child who refused to be born.

He continued driving in the direction of his apartment, proceeding cautiously down the deserted streets. Slowing the car completely, he pulled up beside the curb and stopped. He sat midway between his apartment and his parish church. After pushing the CD button, the dissonant sounds of Prokofiev, the master of unharmonious sounds, surrounded him, and he pulled his arms into the sides of his chest like a swimmer slowly immersing himself in cold water. As he listened, he craved harmony. He desired completion. But not yet; he wasn't ready.

It was dark. He turned down the music and lowered his window. Nothing in his surroundings looked familiar. Had he missed his turn? In the distance, he heard the shrill scream of an ambulance like a baby's cry in an empty room.

Where was the directive he could follow to put his life back together, the kind of firm command issued by Sister Antonia telling him what to do and when to do it. The kind of rule he could do nothing but obey. The night responded with silence.

He reached for the volume control and, turning it higher, attempted to repress the agony in his soul.

ABOUT THE AUTHOR

Vicky Wall had the privilege of teaching for sixteen years in Chicago: on the south side, the west side, and the north side. She then had the privilege of teaching for seventeen years in Evanston, Illinois. She received a BA from the University of Illinois, an MA from Northwestern University, and a JD from Thomas M. Cooley Law School.

A free eBook edition is available with the purchase of this book.

To claim your free eBook edition:

1. Download the Shelfie app.
2. Write your name in upper case in the box.
3. Use the Shelfie app to submit a photo.
4. Download your eBook to any device.

Shelfie

A **free** eBook edition is available with the purchase of this print book.

CLEARLY PRINT YOUR NAME ABOVE IN UPPER CASE

Instructions to claim your free eBook edition:
1. Download the Shelfie app for Android or iOS
2. Write your name in **UPPER CASE** above
3. Use the Shelfie app to submit a photo
4. Download your eBook to any device

Print & Digital Together Forever.

Snap a photo   Free eBook   Read anywhere

The Morgan James Speakers Group

www.TheMorganJamesSpeakersGroup.com

We connect Morgan James published authors with live and online events and audiences whom will benefit from their expertise.

Morgan James makes all of our titles available
through the Library for All Charity Organizations.

www.LibraryForAll.org